T0154189

Charles Lambert is the author of several novels, short stories, and the memoir *With a Zero at its Heart*, which was voted one of The Guardian readers' Ten Best Books of the Year in 2014. In 2007, he won an O. Henry Award for his short story *The Scent of Cinnamon*. His first novel, *Little Monsters*, was longlisted for the 2010 International IMPAC Dublin Literary Award. Born in England, Charles Lambert has lived in central Italy since 1980.

Praise for Charles Lambert:

'Charles Lambert is a terrific, devious storyteller.' – Owen King

'Charles Lambert writes as if his life depends on it. He takes risks at every turn.' – Hannah Tinti

'Charles Lambert is a writer who could one day attain classic status.' – Maggie Gee

'A writer who never ceases to surprise.' – Jenny Offill

'A seriously good writer.' – Beryl Bainbridge

The Bone Flower

Charles Lambert

Also by Charles Lambert:

The Children's Home
Two Dark Tales: Jack Squat and the Niche
Prodigal
Little Monsters
The Scent of Cinnamon and Other Stories
Any Human Face
The View from the Tower
With a Zero at its Heart

The Bone Flower

Charles Lambert

Gallic Books
London

A Gallic Book

Copyright © Charles Lambert, 2022

Charles Lambert has asserted his moral right to be identified
as the author of the work.

First published in Great Britain in 2022 by

Gallic Books, 12 Eccleston Street, London, SW1W 9LT

This book is copyright under the Berne Convention

No reproduction without permission

All rights reserved

A CIP record for this book is available from the British Library

Typeset on Fournier MT by Gallic Books

ISBN 978-1-913547-27-1

Printed in the UK by CPI (CR0 4YY)

2 4 6 8 10 9 7 5 3 1

Part One

Chapter One

One cold November evening in 188– six men were sitting around a cheerfully blazing fire in a club in the centre of London, a stone's throw from Piccadilly. The room, its walls lined with portraits of earlier club members, the severity of its hardwood floor softened by the deep and elaborate weave of a Persian carpet, was a shade too warm, and smelt of cigar smoke, a cloud of which had gathered above the heads of the seated men. They were of various ages and professions, or of good enough family to have no profession, and were united less by common interests than by their common standing, of which club membership was a guarantee. They were drinking brandy and talking, in a desultory way, about life after death. The oldest among them, a portly man with an off-white beard that reached the second button of his waistcoat, was making the case for reincarnation. He had a dog, he told them, who was the spit and image of his nurse, a dour woman with a whiskery mole on her cheek in exactly the same place – he repeated this with considerable emphasis, beating his free fist on the arm of his Chesterfield – as a liverish spot on the jowl of the dog. An ill-tempered beast, he added, as further proof. The company was amused, with the exception of a bald man, in his forties and bony as death itself, who was sitting in an armchair as far from the heat of the fire as could be achieved without leaving the circle. His name was Arthur Poynter.

'There are excellent reasons,' he said in his quiet, dry way, 'for believing in the principle of reincarnation.' He leant forward. 'The number of souls is finite, according to an early heresy, which, assuming this to be the case, would render reincarnation not only plausible, but of an absolute necessity. Waste not, want not.'

'Those of the Hebrew persuasion believe in a tree that furnishes souls willy-nilly,' said another. 'It is situated in the Garden of Eden.'

'I have known Congolese bearers with the souls of English gentlewomen,' said a man whose face was burnt ochre by the sun, dressed in the khaki suit of an explorer.

Arthur Poynter nodded. 'That only confirms my belief,' he said. 'The right to possess a soul should resemble the right to vote before it was so sadly extended. The possession of a soul should be restricted to gentlemen with a decent income.'

This was greeted by grunts of approval and a burst of laughter, abruptly stifled, from the youngest man in the room. His name was Edward Monteith and he was twenty-three years old, recently down from Cambridge and wondering what he might do with his life. His more than decent income made doing nothing an option, and he was tempted by that although he would deny this if asked. He had looked at the explorer several times and tried to imagine himself in a similar outfit, on his feet a pair of highly polished boots that were oddly reminiscent of hooves, his skin like leather fresh from the tannery. The fog had been so dense this evening, and the cold so biting, he had felt a sort of winter in his soul. Yes, there it was, his soul. His soul had craved the company even of these men, as old or older than his father, world-wise, world-weary. He had eaten with them, the usual club fare, and followed them into this room, where every painted face looked down on him, and had taken a stool near the fireplace. A manservant furnished the coal that was required, but Edward had seized control of the poker, and the blaze was his.

'It's a well-established fact that working-class women have no soul,' said a tall man seated next to the bearded fellow with the reincarnated nanny. Edward knew the man by name, which was Frederick Bell, and by reputation, which was bad, but had never spoken to him before this evening. He was some years older than Edward. Born in Scotland, he had qualified as a doctor in Edinburgh but, to Edward's knowledge, had never practised, having no need. 'Imagine if that were not the case,' he added, relighting his cigar. 'How complicated life would be.' He looked at Edward and smiled, a complicit smile that both intrigued and unnerved the younger man.

'But if the number of souls is finite,' said the other occupant of the Chesterfield, who had appeared to be asleep during the discussion, 'what on earth will happen on the Day of Judgement? Bodies will resurrect and find their souls already taken. They will be like shells without a snail to reside in them. They will be empty boxes.'

This was met by silence, as though the subject had finally been exhausted. Poynter called the manservant over to replace the empty decanter of brandy and refill their glasses. Edward's eyes drifted towards Bell and were apprehended by the doctor, who smiled again and gave an almost imperceptible nod, as if of recognition. Edward turned away, discomfited. When all the men had brandy in their glasses, Poynter raised his. 'To our eternal selves,' he said. The other men, without exception, lifted their glasses and toasted their eternal selves before falling once again into a companionable silence.

After some minutes had passed, the silence was broken by the explorer, whose name was Rickman. 'I must say though,' he said, 'I have seen certain manifestations that make me, how shall I put this, a little apprehensive about the possibility of life after death.'

'On your travels, I imagine?' said Bell. 'In Africa.'

Rickman assented to this with a nod.

'Perhaps you would like to enlighten us?'

'I'm not sure that enlighten is quite the word,' Rickman said. 'I fear that my story will induce more gloom than light.' He shifted in his chair until his face could be seen by the other men. His eyes were sapphire blue in the tanned skin. He drew on his cigar and examined the burning tip for a moment before continuing. 'I had been there for some months,' he said, 'with the same small group of men, who had become as friends to me, comrades one might say, despite their origins. We were equals, gentlemen, as we are equals here. We had crossed deserts and hacked our way through jungles. Waterfalls that would dwarf St Paul's twice over had marked our path, animals whose paw prints would fill that tray' – he indicated the tray on which the brandy decanter stood – 'had crossed it, and left us whole. We had a language in common that we had fought to achieve and part of its vocabulary was fear. Make no mistake, gentlemen, the continent of Africa is grand and terrible, more grand and terrible than you can imagine.'

'And the manifestations of which you spoke?' said Poynter, with the slightest trace of impatience.

'Forgive me,' said Rickman. 'I was told this by my closest companion, a young man I called Joshua, his own name being unpronounceable to me. Joshua was my guide and friend, and he would amuse me as we walked by telling me tales from his childhood. One of these has remained with me, for reasons that will, I hope, become clear as I speak. His grandfather had a house at the edge of their village. He lived alone, his own wife having died some years before and his children having constructed their own houses in other parts of the village. I use the word house to describe the simplest of structures, a central pole, a weaving of local grasses, fragile and easily moved. One night, he was woken by a presence in his house, a shaking, a trembling, Joshua said, caused by no earthly wind. The spirit of an ancestor, known in that part of the world as *obambo*, had come to visit and the purpose of his visit was that Joshua's grandfather should build him a house for his return. Normally, such a desire would have been met and would have provided an occasion for celebration in the tribe. But the old man knew this ancestor as someone evil, as someone who had brought the tribe and his own people into disrepute, and refused. The *obambo* began to dance and wail, beating his fists against the pole until the whole house shook and neighbours arrived, including Joshua and his father. Joshua was no more than a child at the time but he has never forgotten what he saw.'

Rickman paused.

'Which was?' said Poynter.

'A spectral being, more bones than flesh, the skin stretched over the bones but ripped and incomplete so that tangled plants could be seen inside the ribcage, the head a skull but with sharpened teeth that could rip the arm off a man, the white hair tangled with sticks and vines. Its eyes were bright as stars, he told me, and when the *obambo* looked his way he began to cry, which made the creature cackle and dance with even greater fervour. But the worst thing was the stench of decaying matter, of leaves and roots and human flesh, so strong the people in the house began to fall to their knees and retch. And the *obambo* laughed even more and shook the central pole until the whole house collapsed in a rain of dust and rat droppings and dried grass onto their heads.'

Rickman paused once more.

'And you believe this?' Bell said, with a slightly mocking laugh. 'You believe your young friend Joshua?'

'I would not have believed it,' Rickman said slowly, 'if I had not seen an *obambo* with my own eyes.'

Bell laughed again.

'It was in our last camp, no more than a month ago. The first sign of its presence was the stench, which seemed to come from all around, rising from the very earth. The men began to look at one another, terrified, because they knew, as I did not. At first I thought we had pitched camp on some kind of malodorous sinkhole, if such a thing can exist, emanating its rottenness from the centre of the earth. But then I saw Joshua blench. *Obambo*, he said. He was facing me but his eyes were fixed on someone, on *something*, behind me. I turned and saw it. It was crouched and gibbering, a tangle of bones and putrefaction, but with a mouth and teeth, as Joshua had described them to me, and eyes.' Rickman shuddered. 'Such eyes,' he said. 'I shall never forget those eyes.' He sighed and raised a hand. 'It lifted a fleshless finger,' he said, and mimed the action, 'and pointed to a spot between our huts. I knew what he wanted without being told.'

'What did you do?' said Edward, who had listened to Rickman's account enthralled.

'What could we do?' said Rickman. 'We built the *obambo* his house.'

Bell burst out laughing, slapping his thigh repeatedly. But he found himself alone in his mirth. The other men looked at one another with a mixture of expressions that ranged from curious to distressed. As if to ward off an unexpected chill in the air, Edward beckoned the manservant over to add some coal to the fire.

'To each his own,' said Poynter, when no else had spoken for some moments. 'This would seem to apply to the spirits of the dead as it does to everything else. Our home-grown variety of spectre is, I would hope, a little more refined.'

'We could always find out,' said a voice that had not previously been heard that evening, a voice with an American accent that belonged to a man in his thirties, of vigorous build, sitting some distance from the fire. He nodded to the other men, as though he had just arrived, and introduced himself as Daniel Giles. 'I'm new in town,' he said, 'and a guest of our friend here.' He nodded towards Poynter, in acknowledgement. 'I arrived from Boston three days ago. My best wishes to you all.' He raised his glass.

'We could find out?' said Rickman.

'A compatriot of mine, although from the opposite coast, is performing in one of your music halls next week. He's well known at home for his abilities.'

'Which are?' said Poynter.

'He speaks to the dead,' said Daniel Giles. 'And the dead speak back.'

Outside the club a small group formed as cabs were summoned. The fog was thick and the waiting men blew into their gloved hands. Rickman, unsuitably dressed for a London November, had already left. Cabs arrived and soon only Daniel Giles, Frederick Bell and Arthur Poynter remained, along with Edward, who preferred to walk, to clear his head of the brandy and overheated air of the club. His house was half an hour away in Holborn. He would pass through Covent Garden, already at work for the following day, and Lincoln's Inn, where a light might still be burning at this late hour.

'An informative evening,' said Poynter.

'Informative?' said Bell. 'Rickman has been dining out on that story since he left his young African catamite and returned to London.'

'Isn't that rather harsh?'

'Believe me, I have nothing against catamites, African or otherwise. But I don't like being made a fool of.'

Giles wrapped his scarf tighter around his neck. 'You won't be joining us then?'

'Did I say that? On the contrary, why should I not take advantage of an opportunity to have my scepticism confirmed? Besides, young Monteith will be in our company, I believe.' He smiled at Edward, who flushed and nodded. 'Excellent. Because a serious man such as myself needs a challenge and I have every intention of corrupting him. The kind of innocence he still possesses, against all odds in this infernal city, is an affront to any pleasure-loving man. You see my point, Poynter?'

Poynter gave an assessing glance at Edward, who felt himself blush. 'Seeing a point and sharing it are very different things, Bell,' said Poynter as his cab approached.

'So we have a date?' said Giles.

'We do indeed.'

Chapter Two

Edward Monteith wondered if Bell was right about his innocence. He had a rather tenuous wisp of blond moustache, but the mouth and chin beneath it were strong and his eyes, though grey, were deep. He suspected that he was attractive, and wished he knew what to do with that suspicion. He had had opportunities at Cambridge but a sense of his own discomfort, and of his worth, had drawn him back from a brink his friends had been prepared to pass beyond. His mother had died when he was a child, and his father was distant but proud of him, or professed to be, although Edward saw that pride as the product of absence; he had simply done nothing of which his father might need to be ashamed, and that made it seem a rather wretched achievement, and the pride that his father claimed to feel seem both false and demeaning. He had listened to Rickman talk about Africa and, despite Bell's scorn and insinuations, imagined himself in the explorer's place, surrounded by wildness, his emotions reduced to their essence, tested by a continent in its entirety. He wondered if that was what he was here for – to find new worlds. His first nanny had taught him to be obedient, but also to question, and she had responded to his curiosity with a willingness that had led to her dismissal. He had never quite forgiven his parents for that. He still remembered her name, which was Miss Josephine, and the smell of her hands, of carbolic soap and violets.

Now, alone in his house in John Street, apart from his valet, George, and housekeeper, Mrs Rokes, idling his days away in rereading the classics he had been obliged to read at Emmanuel, he was wondering if he should consider a profession, despite his father's resolve that he live the life of a leisured gentleman, as his father had not been able to do, disfigured as he was by the stain of commercial activity in his earlier years that he had not been able to erase. Burmese oil sticks to the skin, he once told Edward, with a sad laugh. You can never quite get rid of it. These days, Edward woke from troubled sleep long after the light had entered his room, he wore the clothes that had been laid out for him by George, drank coffee prepared by Mrs Rokes and walked around the gardens of Gray's Inn, half envying the profitable lives of those within. He lunched with old friends from college in various eating houses around the City although their friendship seemed to rely on a routine he no longer had, ate little, drank too much though not enough to lose control. He had always had a great fear of losing control. Abandoning his books, he would play a few sets of lawn tennis when the weather was fine and he could find an opponent, rugby football but without commitment, billiards at his club, where he spent more time with each month that passed. He went there most evenings, at first because his father insisted and then because he felt lonely and because the cooking was reasonable. His role as post-dinner tender of the fire had become habitual. The poker was his, the height and depth of the flame his only apparent concern. He listened rather than spoke, observed but was not observed. Or so he had thought, until Frederick Bell had decided that he was innocent and needed to be corrupted. The notion intrigued, amused and frightened him in equal measure. Bell had a reputation he would rather not find attached to himself, but a little of its surface gleam might rub off and maybe Edward would not find that so distressing; maybe a scattering of libertine glitter would provide him with the excitement his life sorely needed. But he thought of Rickman and wished he had been noticed, not by Bell, whose adventures rarely took him beyond Canning Town, but by the other explorer, noticed as someone whose life cried out to be resolved into something larger and more complex than it was. He wanted to be useful, and brave, and at risk, but had no idea how that might be done nor who to ask. He dreamed of Africa, of its dark heart.

The music hall was in a side road off the Strand. Edward arrived first, walking there as was his custom, as much to kill time as to take exercise. A crowd had already gathered outside in a loose queue, with a certain amount of jostling, good-hearted and otherwise. Some young women, unaccompanied, stood at a little distance from the crowd, alert to every gaze. One of them caught Edward's eye, lifted her skirt an inch or so from her ankle and gave him a broad wink. Startled, he stepped back and the young woman laughed and murmured something to her colleagues. He turned away, abashed. Some feet away from them, a stocky man in a tattered top hat and with a ragged scarf around his neck stood behind a small brazier roasting chestnuts. Walking across, Edward warmed his hands and was about to buy a half-dozen when a dark-skinned man in a voluminous cloak edged up to him, raised one corner of his cloak and displayed three puppies, bull terriers. 'Good fighting dogs,' he said to Edward, a leer on his face. 'You look like a sporting gentleman.' Edward shook his head and moved off, leaving the chestnut seller to angrily defend his pitch as a chorus of yaps broke out and was stifled by the weight of the cloak. He looked around and saw a solitary girl some distance away at the far end of the queue, selling nosegays of flowers from a tray, and he wished he had a companion to whom such a small thing might give pleasure. She caught his eye as the other young woman had done and returned his gaze without shame, but this time there was no wink, no lifted skirt. She looked back at him, unblinking, her face impassive but for an air of evaluation. He might have said that she was trying to stare him down, but that would have been wrong. There was no antagonism in her gaze, and only the slightest suggestion of challenge. She had made him catch his breath, that was all. He was about to walk over to her when a hand fell on his shoulder and he turned. Frederick Bell was standing behind him.

'The early bird, I see,' he said.

'I'm sorry?' said Edward.

Bell nodded towards the flower seller. 'You appear to have attracted the young lady's attention.'

'I imagine she is trying to sell her wares,' said Edward.

'Indeed,' said Bell. He looked at Edward appraisingly. 'You're a rather pleasing young man, you know. But of course you do. I'm sure I can't be the first person to tell you. Box, do you?'

Edward, embarrassed, shook his head. 'I used to,' he said. 'Before I came down.'

'Oxford?'

'Cambridge.'

'Trinity?'

'Emmanuel.'

Bell nodded. 'Harvard's alma mater. So I find myself up against the good old Puritan tradition. Now I understand that I will have my work cut out with you. No wine, no women, and very little song. But you mark my words, my lad. You will find that Puritanism lays a cold table at which to sup and provides a cold bed in which to sleep.'

'I really can't imagine why you wish to see me in that light,' protested Edward, deciding to be amused and even flattered by the older man's almost flirtatious attention. 'I'm not the slightest bit puritanical.' He was about to continue when he heard Bell's name being called.

The other two men had arrived together and were waiting outside the theatre, standing apart from the crowd. Entering the foyer, they were greeted almost instantly by the manager, who grovelled to Bell for a moment or two, briefly touching the sleeve of his coat as though it might possess some thaumaturgic power. 'It is always an honour to have you with us, Doctor,' he said. He regarded the other three in a judicious and then unctuous manner before beckoning them to follow him with a wave of his fat hand. 'I think you will find your evening of great interest,' he said, leading them to their box and closing the door behind him.

When they were all seated, Poynter turned to Edward. 'I'm glad to see you here, young man. I think you will be amused and possibly surprised by what we are about to witness. Our American friend, Mr Giles, has been telling me a little more about the spectacle we have in store. This may be a place of common entertainment,' he said, looking across the theatre at the other box, still empty, and below, at the stalls, where the crowd of people from outside had noisily begun to settle, hot faces turned towards the curtain and the box in which the four men sat, then down at the orchestra pit, which was slowly being filled by a handful of musicians in black, 'but tonight's performance will, I beg to hope, be anything but common.'

'I hope you won't be disappointed,' said Giles. 'I've only hearsay to report, I'm afraid.'

'I have no intention of being disappointed,' said Poynter.

The curtains opened to reveal a lit stage, empty apart from a small table and the portly figure of the manager. He raised both hands and the lights within the theatre were dimmed, one by one, until the audience sat in darkness. Edward turned to look at Bell but the only sign of the doctor's presence was the bright tip of his cigar. He felt a hand on his shoulder and was reassured, although his thoughts were far away from the performance he was about to witness, and were on the flower girl, on the nonchalant way she had examined him. The manager coughed, a sonorous cough that had the desired effect of calming the restless crowd and imposing silence.

'We are here tonight,' he said, 'for what may be the most unforgettable night of our lives, a night that will remain with us until the day of our deaths and beyond. I repeat, beyond. Beyond the very wall of death that separates us from our loved ones, our dearest departed. How dark it is, how drear. And yet, ladies and gentlemen, I say to you now that despite that darkness, and despite that drearness, there is light, there is a brilliant light, and our loved ones are waiting to be heard.' At the words 'brilliant light', a burst of what looked like orange flame illuminated the back of the stage. There was a murmur from the crowd, of disbelief and anticipation, and a hint of stifled laughter, as two men rushed out of the wings with cloths to douse it. The manager continued. 'Our guest this evening, ladies and gentlemen, is not an entertainer but the doorman to a portal. He will open a breach for us in the wall of death. He will reunite us with those we have lost.' He paused, then raised his left arm and made a brief beckoning gesture. 'My lords and ladies, gentlewomen and gentlemen, I ask you to welcome from the Golden State of California, Thaddeus McEnroe.'

'This all sounds very familiar,' said Poynter in a low voice to Edward.

'You've been to this sort of thing before?' said Edward.

'I make it my business to expose fraud in the hope that I will one day be convinced that no fraud has been committed. To this day, I have been disappointed, but I continue to be both optimistic and sceptical. I fear that this evening I shall have my scepticism confirmed.'

Accompanied by a few bars of music from the band, the manager left the stage and was replaced by a tall, robust man in a white tie and tailcoat, with a Stetson on his head and some ornately decorated leather boots on his feet.

'A chimera,' murmured Poynter. 'Arisen from the depths of the Atlantic to haunt our shores.'

The man waited for silence, observing the crowd beneath his feet, glancing up towards the box and nodding as though he recognised someone there. Giles will have told him of our presence, Edward thought, and his initial scepticism was reinforced, accompanied by the first faint twinge of boredom. For a moment, he contemplated leaving the music hall. Maybe the flower girl would still be there; maybe she would be waiting for him. He shifted in his chair and was about to rise when McEnroe began to speak. His deep American brogue filled the hall.

'Many people here have lost a loved one,' he said. He raised both hands and held them out to the audience. 'But we are mistaken to think of them as lost. They are not lost so long as they can be heard. And I hear them. I hear them clamour from behind the wall we think of as death, a wall of illusion and pain. I hear them call out names, the names of people they have left behind. Mary. George. Hermione.' His eyes skimmed the crowd. 'They are eager to be heard.' A rustle of skirts and coats, a nervous cough, and then quiet once more. 'I hear a lady.' He looked down into the crowd. 'A lady who has recently departed this life and passed across. She wishes to speak to someone here in this room.' He lowered one arm and pointed with his other hand, slowly moving his index finger across the raised heads beneath him, before finally coming to a halt.

'You, madam,' he said.

A woman a few yards from the orchestra pit touched her chest in alarm. 'Are you meaning me, sir?' she said.

'I am indeed, madam. I see that you have suffered a bereavement.'

'I have, sir,' the woman said.

'Your mother,' McEnroe said.

'Is dead, sir, as you say.'

'And when did she make her journey beyond the wall?' he said.

'It must be seven months ago now,' the woman said.

McEnroe nodded. 'I thought so. Recently, you confirm this,' he said. He paused a moment for applause, which failed to arrive. 'She was a stout woman, of a certain age, a hard worker, a good mother. I see health problems. Her heart.'

'That's true,' the woman said, in a marvelling tone. 'All of it.'

McEnroe sniffed. 'She had something to do with flowers. I smell flowers.'

The woman burst into tears. 'She loved flowers, she did. She would have killed for a garden of her own.'

McEnroe tilted his head, as if to listen. 'She loved you very much,' he said. He lowered his voice to a resonant whisper. 'She misses you.'

A voice shouted from the back of the hall, a man's voice. 'So what's her old ma's name then? You tell us her name, Yankee.'

McEnroe peered into the gloom, then beckoned with his right hand. 'Come closer, sir,' he said. The crowd parted and a small poorly dressed man was pushed towards the stage. 'Now I see you, sir. And I am not alone.' He paused and when he spoke again his voice had dropped into a cavernous travesty of itself. 'There is someone here who wishes to speak to you. He wants to speak to a Mr Grainger. That is your name, is it not?'

'How do you know that?' the man said, defiant, looking around at those nearest to him in the crowd.

'Because I have an old acquaintance of yours with me here.'

'And who would that be?' the man said, apparently determined to brazen it out.

'Someone you have some unfinished business with, business that he would like to see concluded, Mr Grainger. He tells me that he will not rest until he has justice. His name is Henry. Henry Stiles. The chains are heavy, he says.'

'I don't know what you're talking about,' the man said, his voice more feeble, the fight gone out of him. He edged back into the crowd as McEnroe turned his attention once again to the rest of the audience. He put his hand to his ear. 'I hear you,' he said, his eyes lifted up to the ceiling. He nodded twice, then raised both hands for silence. 'The voice is faint,' he said, 'but audible. I hear a presence whose daughter is about to be married.'

'That will be my poor dead wife,' said a voice from below the box. 'My Betty is due to be wed next week.' Edward craned over the edge, curious to see who spoke, but was restrained by Poynter.

'I think we've seen more than enough,' he said. 'The man who challenged him is clearly an accomplice. It's an old ploy and no more than this crowd deserves but I have no intention of wasting any more time here.'

Leaving the theatre, Edward saw the flower girl on the pavement opposite. On an impulse, he left his friends and crossed the road. She watched him approach and he had the impression, an impression he immediately dismissed, that she had been waiting. The dog seller and the chestnut man were nowhere to be seen. He came to a halt in front of her, abruptly lost for words. Smiling, she picked out a nosegay from her tray and offered it to him.

'Here you are, sir,' she said. Her voice was soft, with a hint of something foreign that he couldn't place. 'This will help to protect you from the poisoned air of the city.'

He took the nosegay, surprised, unexpectedly touched. 'Thank you,' he said. He started to reach for his wallet but she caught his arm.

'It is a gift, sir,' she said.

'I cannot accept a gift,' he said.

'Why not? Do I not have as much right as anyone else to make a gift? You offend me, sir.' She smiled, slowly removing her hand from his sleeve.

He lifted the nosegay to his face, tentatively sniffed. His heart was beating fast in his chest. Although her hand was no longer on his arm, he could feel the weight of it.

'It has a beautiful scent,' he said.

She nodded. 'The commonest flowers are often the sweetest-scented,' she said.

He was speechless. Her head was bonnetless and her hair, gathered into a loose knot behind her neck, was the blue-black of a raven's plumage, and as glossy, and her eyes were unfathomably dark and her lips were full, but not too full, and her skin was a dusky rose. She held herself straight and there was a neatness about her, or rather, a completeness. Nothing about her could be bettered, he thought. He was about to say something, anything, the first words that came to mind, when he heard Bell call his name.

'I have to go,' he said.

She lowered her eyes. 'Remember me,' she said. 'I am always here.'

'I have seen that young woman before,' said Poynter, when Edward returned to the group.

'You surprise me,' said Bell.

Poynter ignored this. 'Of course,' he said, after a moment's thought. 'I noticed her at a séance I attended some weeks ago. She assisted the medium, a woman of the Romani people, or a Gypsy as they are more commonly known.' He paused. 'She was not entirely a charlatan, I believe. I should like to visit her again.' He looked at Edward. 'Perhaps you would like to accompany me?'

'I should like that very much,' said Edward.

Chapter Three

A few days later, Daniel Giles and Edward met in a chophouse in the City, where Giles had business. Giles was already seated at a table when Edward arrived. He stood up as Edward approached and held out his hand.

'I'm glad of this opportunity,' he said. 'I know very few people here in London, other than those with whom I have to do business, and, believe me, their company is not always the most pleasant.'

'Really?' said Edward, amused.

'People who have money on their minds twelve hours a day rarely have room for much else, I've found.'

'I wouldn't know, I'm afraid.'

'You have enough money not to need to know, I imagine.'

Edward was startled by the American's forthrightness. 'Well, yes, I suppose I do.'

The idea to meet had been Edward's. He was curious about the business that had brought Giles to London, wondering if some opportunity might be found for him. He saw the United States as a place where things might happen. He had imagined himself standing on the banks of the Hudson with the flower girl beside him, her hand in his, teetering on the edge of a new life, and been physically excited by the vision and had then pushed it to one side, as absurd, and even shameful.

'You need not feel ashamed,' said Giles, as though he had read

Edward's mind. 'I am here on my father's business, not my own.'

'Your father is a wealthy man.'

'My father is a philanthropist, and philanthropists require wealth in order to exist. They dirty their hands for the good of others.'

'A philanthropist, Mr Giles?'

'I beg you, Edward, call me Daniel. I hope we may soon become friends.'

'I hope so too. Your father knows Poynter?'

'Yes, they have interests in common. My father is a disciple of Henry David Thoreau and has corresponded with Poynter about transcendentalism, among other things.'

'Such as communicating with the dead?'

'That too.' Daniel laughed. 'Rather a fiasco, wasn't it? Our evening at the theatre.'

'Yes,' said Edward. 'I really don't know what to believe about the whole business. I think that there must be something in it, in life after death, but what? Do we really go on forever, do you suppose? And if we do, do we really have nothing more useful to do than answer foolish questions or pester the living? Like Rickman's ghost.'

'The *obambo*,' said Daniel. He paused, then took a long sip of ale. 'It isn't the first time I've heard about spirits of that sort.'

'Really?'

'My father is a long-standing abolitionist. I was brought up in a house in which all men were brothers, masters and freemen alike. My father took in people who needed to be protected, set them on their feet, gave them the chance they had been denied by the cruelty of fate and other men. My childhood companions were people who had been bought and sold as chattels. They told me stories that I have never forgotten.'

'About their time as slaves?'

'Yes, and that was the greatest horror of them all. But they also told me stories they had learned from their parents, if they were lucky, or the older people they found around them, stories that had travelled across the Atlantic years before in the vile inferno of the holds. Dark stories, about death and ghosts and vengeance. These were the stories they needed to survive, you see.'

'Of course.'

'I remember one, about a place where someone was murdered, a river bed that used to be visited at night by creatures like Rickman's *obambo*, unearthly creatures, who groaned and writhed in the swampy ground. Whoever approached them was seized and dragged down into the swamp until they were dead. I used to wonder if the swamp was in Africa or closer to home. That part of my country is filled with swamps. I think they took old tales and changed them to suit their new purposes, to make sense of what they had suffered because sometimes the stories talked explicitly of their lives as slaves. There was one of them I remember, about the ghost of a man who was whipped to death who returned to haunt the plantation where he died. The skin hung in shreds off the ghost's back and his face was flayed. Heal me, he would cry. Make me whole again. In another, a black woman beaten to death by two white men, her owner and his son, by both of whom she had been used, came back to haunt their sleep with her screams. They would feel her hands on their bodies, as cold as ice, and her tongue forcing its way into their mouths. Both men died, suffocated in their beds.' He stopped, and shivered. 'I'm sorry,' he said. 'I lose all sense of myself when I think of these things. My father says that I must learn to forgive or I shall never be free. But there are some things it is difficult, if not impossible, to forgive.' He looked hard and long into Edward's eyes, until Edward would have turned his head away if he had had the courage. 'Perhaps we have no right to be free,' Daniel said.

'I have every intention of being free,' Edward said, determinedly. 'Whether I have the right to it or not.'

Daniel smiled. 'Forgive me.' He called the waiter across. 'I think it's time we ordered.'

When they had eaten and talked of other matters, Daniel asked Edward if he had been back to the music hall.

'Why would I do that?' said Edward.

'To buy a nosegay,' said Daniel.

Edward blushed. 'I was that obvious?'

'I'm afraid so.' Daniel laughed. 'But there's no need to explain or justify yourself. She was a perfect jewel, in a setting quite unworthy of her. I would have returned myself if she had shown the slightest indication that my presence might have given her pleasure. But she didn't notice me, I'm afraid. She had eyes for you alone.'

Edward might have said nothing; that was his first instinct. But he overrode his instinct, to demonstrate his trust in his new friend and because he had to speak to someone. 'I have been back every night, but she is never there. I asked the chestnut seller if he knew where she might be but he swore to me that he had never seen her before that night. I would think I had dreamt her if I didn't have you and Poynter and Bell as witnesses. But she was real. She was there that evening and she was real, and I don't understand.' He paused. 'I think that she has bewitched me, that that was her purpose there outside the music hall that night, and I think that such a thought is a sign of madness in me, because how could that be?'

'I think you are in love,' said Daniel.

The séance was to be held in one of the upstairs rooms of the Rochester Castle, a public house in Stoke Newington, not far from the cemetery of Abney Park. The four men met in the saloon bar. When the moment arrived, Poynter led the way to a small room, barely furnished and poorly lit, with a round table in the middle. There were five chairs at the table. Poynter sat down and indicated to his companions that they should follow suit. As soon as all four of them were seated, a door opened and a woman came out, accompanied by two younger women, all three wearing complicated robes of velvet and satin, with small lace caps on their heads. Edward's eyes picked out the flower girl immediately and he felt his heart leap, and would have fallen on his knees and kissed Poynter's hand, such was his gratitude. She looked straight ahead, but in a way that persuaded him that he had been seen as profoundly as she had been seen, and that her wonder was as strong, and as heart-shaking, as his desire. Silently, like the handmaidens of an antique queen, she and the other girl followed the older woman to the table, standing behind her as she took the remaining chair.

'Good evening, gentlemen,' the woman said in a country accent. 'My name is Madame Arlette and I am your spirit guide for this evening. Welcome.'

'Good evening,' they said, in unison.

'You are here in good faith,' she said, and they understood that this was not a question, but a requirement. When no one spoke, she smiled and laid both hands on the table. They were unadorned, apart from a large gold ring on her left middle finger. Her skin was darkened by the sun, roughened by work. 'Good. Because without your faith, I shall not be visited.' She looked at Poynter. 'You, sir, have a face I recognise. You have been here before, I think. You have already made the acquaintance of my spirit child.'

Poynter nodded. 'Cassy,' he said.

Madame Arlette acknowledged this. 'Your hands, gentlemen. You must place your hands on the table as I have done. I shall require silence. Cassy is but a child and not of this country; she is timid as she was in life, and may prefer not to speak at all if she senses danger. Silence and faith, gentlemen, are what is needed. Have I made myself clear?'

The four men placed their hands on the table as she had done.

Edward's eyes were on the girl, whose name he still did not know, but both she and her companion were staring into the middle distance in what appeared to be a state of trance. In what amounted to a state of trance himself, blinded to all else, he studied her every feature in the dim light of the room until he became aware that Madame Arlette had turned her gaze towards him. Abashed, he glanced down at the table, at the ten hands splayed against the white cloth. If it were not for her, he thought, he would rather be anywhere in the world than here, in this dark cold room with this overdressed charlatan.

'Close your eyes, gentlemen.' Madame Arlette waited for some moments and then made a low groan. Edward opened one eye a little and saw the woman throw her head back, baring her throat. She groaned again, before shaking her head violently from side to side. She must know we'll be watching, he thought, or this would have no sense. He looked at the girl and this time, to his surprise, he had his look returned, followed by an admonishing glance at the woman. Immediately, he closed his eyes again.

'Speak to us, Cassy. Have no fear,' Madame Arlette said in a voice both tremulous and profound. She paused, then said once more, in the same tone, 'Speak to us, my dear. Come to us from your place of obscurity, my little dark baby, my child. Come to your spirit mother.'

The table rocked beneath their hands. This time, Edward resisted the temptation to open his eyes, but he felt the hand nearest his, that of Frederick Bell, start and make contact with his own. He was about to ease his hand away when he heard a new voice in the room, a mewling voice that seemed to belong to no one and said no words that he could understand. His blood chilled.

'My love, my little dear,' said the woman in the same deep, shaking tone as before. 'Do you wish to speak to someone here?'

A wittering noise, barely human, came from the corner of the room.

'I hear you, Cassy, my little darling. I hear you.'

A whistle, as of air escaping from a valve. And then, a single word, high-pitched, drawn out until it was almost without meaning. 'Edward.'

'You wish to speak to Edward?'

Edward, at the mention of his name, half opened an eye and turned his head to the corner from which the voice seemed to originate. He saw something move as if dragged across the wooden boards of the floor, some small black creature that might have been a child, or an adult doubled over, some malformed creature draped in darkness. A horrible half-giggle came from it. 'Yes,' said the thing. 'But I am shy. And he is looking. He is looking at me. Make him stop.'

Immediately, Edward closed his eyes.

'Then speak to me, my little dear, my little Cassy.' The woman's tone was soft now, maternal, coaxing. 'Ignore him for the moment, and then I shall pass your message on.'

There was silence in the room, apart from a rustling, as of paper that seemed to cross the floor, until Madame Arlette began to speak. Her voice had the hollow depth of an echo.

'You are in danger, Edward.'

'Danger?' said Edward. 'What do you mean?'

'She sees an earth floor, cold and hard, tamped down by uncaring feet. And fruit; there is the smell of fruit gone bad. There is something rotten, something that only love can heal. Heal me, someone says. Free me. She says you are lonely now, but you will know love and you must cherish it above all else. If you don't, it will be the worse for you.'

'What else does she say?' said Edward.

After another long moment of silence, during which Edward heard only the beat of his heart and the same slight rustling noise, of something soft and light being dragged across the wooden boards of the floor beneath their feet, of dried leaves or petals being moved by an absent wind, the woman uttered a sharp cry. 'No,' she cried. 'No.' She took a deep breath, stifled what sounded like a sob. 'She says there will be blood, much blood, but blood can also cleanse a wound, if it be allowed to flow.'

'Whose blood?' said Edward, his eyes still closed out of fear, the sound of his voice not his, strange to him.

'Cassy knows no more,' said the woman. 'Or can say no more.' She paused once again, and when she finally spoke her voice had returned to normal. 'She is only a child.'

'I think she has already said enough,' said Poynter. He stood up. 'I thank you, madam, for your efforts.' The spell was broken. Edward opened his eyes and saw that the corner of the room, though poorly lit, was clearly empty. There was no child any longer, so that what he had thought he had seen was unclear to him. He looked at the floor and saw nothing, no leaves, no flowers, only bare wooden boards. Daniel and Bell were also rising from the table, pushing their chairs back with sighs of relief, as the two girls left the room and returned with lamps. Madame Arlette was bathed in sweat. Poynter looked shaken. He glanced at Edward with an expression of apology and shame. Bell leant over and squeezed Edward's arm. 'Don't worry, old fellow, it was all for show,' he said. 'I know how these people work.' He looked at Poynter. 'I wouldn't put it past him to have set this up.' Edward nodded, willing himself to believe this, remaining unconvinced. All the time Madame Arlette had been speaking he had felt a coldness in the air and the presence of the spirit child in the room; despite all reason, he had picked up a scent of rottenness. He stood, moved away from the table, looked towards the girl, who was hanging an oil lamp from a hook beside the door and had her back to him. You have no part in this, he thought.

'It's time we went,' said Poynter. He walked to the door, with

Madame Arlette beside him, speaking to her in a voice too low to be overheard. Passing the girl, he glanced back at Edward, a meaningful glance, but whether it expressed encouragement or warning was impossible to tell. The other two men followed him. Now Edward found himself alone in the room with the two girls.

'Please,' he said.

The flower girl turned towards her companion, indicated that she should leave with a brief nod of her head. As soon as the girl was gone they were alone and everything that had taken place in the room before that moment was forgotten, was of no importance.

'I searched for you,' he said.

'I know.'

'How do you know?'

'You shouldn't ask questions like that,' she said. She moved towards him. 'You should only ask questions that can be answered.'

'But how do I know which they are?' he said. She lifted a hand and placed a finger across his lips, to seal them.

'You know,' she said.

'I want to see you again.'

'You see,' she said. 'That wasn't a question.'

'Tell me where and when,' he said. 'I shall be there.'

'Do you know this part of London?'

He shook his head, but carefully, so as not to dislodge her finger.

'There is a cemetery near here, called Abney Park. I shall be there tomorrow, at three o'clock.'

'Where? In which part of the cemetery? Cemeteries are like mazes. How will I know where to look?'

'If you want to find me you will find me,' she said.

'I will find you,' he said.

They were leaving the room when she caught his arm. 'There is one thing.'

'Anything.'

'You must never ask me about what happened this evening. Do you promise? Never.'

'I promise.'

He left his friends summoning cabs, turning down their offers to take him home. He walked the empty streets from Stoke Newington to Holborn in a haze; his only thoughts were thoughts of her. It wasn't until the following morning that he realised he had forgotten to ask her name.

Chapter Four

Edward was there at half past two. He passed between the tall Egyptian-style columns and walked up the main avenue, lined by trees of varying species, their bare branches offering little shade to the jumble of tombs beneath, and then along a road that skirted the southern boundary of the cemetery. By and by, he found himself at the entrance once again. There was still no sign of her, but no more than fifteen or twenty minutes had passed since his arrival. He would have pulled out his watch but the thought that she might witness his state of anxiety, and of impatience, dissuaded him. He stared up into the sky, grey with the promise of snow, and shivered, pulling his greatcoat about him. His heart was pounding with apprehension. Part of him wished that he had never come.

He had been called on that morning, without warning, by Arthur Poynter, a visit that had left him shaken and confused. Poynter had begun by offering an apology.

'I had no idea,' he said, sitting in an armchair beside the fire, 'that Madame Arlette would go to such lengths to provide our entertainment.'

'You saw it as entertainment?'

'I use the term advisedly.' He sighed. 'I have been her guest on several occasions before and I believe that she possesses a genuine gift. This does not mean that she is averse to, how shall I put this, embellishing her gift. Gilding the lily, one might say.'

'Did you see the creature she refers to as Cassy?'

'You saw something?' Poynter was startled.

'Yes.' It was Edward's turn to be surprised. 'You surely don't mean to tell me that you kept your eyes closed throughout the entire performance?'

'That was always my intention, although I must admit that I did take a brief glance now and then. But I saw no creature. What kind of creature did you see exactly?'

'Small, a small black child, it seemed to me, wrapped up from head to toe. I thought at first that it might have been a doll, but I'm sure that I saw it move.'

'How curious. You clearly have a gift yourself.'

'You saw nothing, you say? I suppose you heard nothing as well?'

'You mean the infantile noises?' Poynter laughed. 'Ventriloquism, my dear boy. Very common in this sort of show.'

'I'm afraid I don't understand you,' said Edward, exasperated. 'You call it a show, you refer to it as entertainment, and yet you appear to take the whole business seriously at the same time. I don't quite see where you stand.'

Poynter stared into the fire. He seemed to be considering what to say. Finally, he spoke. 'Madame Arlette was deeply shaken last night. She saw and heard phenomena she had never encountered before. Cassy is a child of hers as a parable was the child of our Lord, a work of fiction if you like but conveying a truth. She has always described herself to me as a channel, and everyone knows that whatever a channel carries it also shapes. What passes through does not pass through untouched, unchanged. And yet that is what occurred last night. She heard truths that were stronger than she was, that broke and overflowed the banks of her. She could not contain what she bore, that is the truth of it. She has always said to me, and I have heard others in her profession say the same, that her mouth is opened in power. She cannot explain this, none of them can, and when they do, they fail to convince. They are all of them charlatans at least in part, but that does not mean that they do not *hear*. They are almost always people without culture, and that is also their strength.' He paused, then looked with great intensity at Edward. 'There is power, Edward. Believe me, there *is* power.' He stood up, reached for his hat. 'Be careful, Edward. Heed her words.'

Poynter was leaving the room when something stopped him. He hesitated, then turned and walked back until he was standing in front of Edward. He took both of the younger man's hands in his and stared once more into his eyes. 'That girl,' he said.

Edward resisted the urge to pull his hands away, to take a step back. The presence of Poynter was oppressive. 'What about her?'

'She has power. I felt it. Her mother warned me.'

'Madame Arlette is her mother? You knew that?'

Poynter shook his head.

'That is neither here nor there. The girl has her own power and already you have felt it. She has bewitched you.'

Edward stepped back, freed himself from the hands and eyes of Poynter. He looked out of the window.

'Your cab is waiting,' he said.

She arrived at the entrance to the cemetery at the stroke of three from some distant church bell. She was dressed more modestly than he had seen her, her flower seller's outfit and the velvet robes of the séance discarded in favour of a neat black dress with a lace trim at the collar and sleeves. Her hair was covered for the first time, and he was saddened; it was so much a part of her beauty. But her eyes were the same, and her lips, and he was satisfied. She held out a white-gloved hand, and let him take it.

'Edward,' she said.

'I have no idea how to address you. Miss——?'

'Settie,' she said. 'Call me Settie.'

'Settie,' he repeated, as though the word were an incantation.

'You have been waiting for me,' she said.

He nodded. 'And now you are here,' he said.

She glanced over his shoulder. 'It is a dismal place, in its way, because death is dismal, isn't it? But not entirely so. It has a certain beauty.'

'It is rather beautiful,' he said. She continued to surprise him. She spoke like a lady, he thought, and wondered how this was possible. Unless Poynter was right and I am bewitched, he told himself, so that what I hear is what I wish to hear.

'I suppose it is.'

They were silent, unexpectedly embarrassed, each waiting for the other to speak. Finally, Edward offered her his arm. 'Shall we take a walk?'

Walking together, her arm in his, she began to talk. 'This is a place that is close to my heart. It is open to everyone, you see, regardless of what they believe. It is open to those who do not conform, although once one is dead that may no longer matter very much.'

'Do you have family here?'

She shook her head. 'No, we have our own special places and nowhere else will do. If we are buried elsewhere we cannot rest. We are not even thought of as properly dead until we are safe in our own resting place.' She looked at him. 'We move around a great deal, you see.'

'Where are you now?' he said.

She looked around and then pointed to her right. 'Over there,' she said. 'We have set up camp in the Lea Valley. It is one of the many places we live in. Sometimes we are moved on and sometimes we are left in peace and choose to move on ourselves.'

'How strange it must be,' he said, because that was his first thought. He had dreamed of movement for as long as he could remember.

'You were born here?' she said.

He shook his head. 'No, I was born in Worcestershire. My father lives there still. I moved to London after I came down.'

'Came down?'

'From Cambridge.'

She smiled. 'So you are a man of learning,' she said.

He laughed. 'I am hardly that. Although I should like to be, I suppose. But I feel that I know nothing and have done nothing and have lived nowhere.' He shook his head, abruptly embarrassed. 'I apologise. I am talking nonsense.'

'You are being honest with me,' she said. 'I like that.' She smiled again. 'I saw at once that you were different from the others. From your friends.'

'Let us not talk about my friends,' he said.

'Well then, what shall we talk about?' she said. 'Why don't you tell me some more about yourself?'

'There is nothing much to say, other than what I have already said.' He was ashamed of himself, of the dullness of his life. 'My father made a fortune in Burma before I was born and brought it home in order to live the life of a lord and to make sure that any son of his did the same. And I am that son. And that is what I have done. Except that he is not a lord, and neither am I.'

'And would you like to be?'

'I would like to do something good with my life. I'm not sure that being a lord, even if that were the case, quite fills the bill.'

She squeezed his arm to her side. 'You could be a good lord, I suppose. Some lords are good. Or a bad commoner. There are any number of those.'

'I suppose you're right,' he said, with a laugh.

'You mustn't laugh,' she said, in mock reproof. 'We are in a cemetery.'

'I can't help it,' he said. 'I'm happy. You make me happy.'

'You see, now you *are* talking about yourself.'

'I'm talking about the effect you have on me, Settie.' It was the first time he had said her name in conversation, as though it were natural that he should use it; and it *was* natural, but the naturalness of it scared him as well. He felt that some boundary had been crossed. He was walking, alone, with a woman he barely knew, a humble flower seller, and he was quite aware that this was immoral behaviour and would be frowned on, by his father and by the world, and equally aware that his whole body was alive with the rightness of it. Settie, he said to himself. Settie.

'So you are really talking about me,' she said. 'What a clever young man you are to flatter me in that way.'

They walked until they came to a chapel at the centre of the cemetery. Edward led her towards the door, curious to see what it contained, but she slowed down as they approached, gently restraining his arm until he came to a halt.

'I'd prefer to stay outside,' she said. 'I'm a creature of the open air.'

'As you wish,' he said.

They were leaving the chapel behind them when they heard a howl of pain some distance away to their left. At first, Edward thought it might be a fox, but looking towards the source of the sound they saw a small group of people standing together beneath the canopy of a cedar. A woman detached herself from the group, stumbling as she ran. She was followed by a man, who caught up with her and held her as she wept, uncontrollably. They watched her push him away and then fall once more into his arms. The group gathered around the couple again and moved off. When the mourners were far enough away, Edward and Settie walked over and found a small patch of trodden-down earth and a makeshift marker, a piece of tin with the words *My dearest son Paul, dead at five years old, now with the angels* written on it in an unpractised hand.

'It is the worst thing that can happen,' said Settie. 'To lose a child.'

But all Edward could think of was the prophecy. The cold, hard earth, tamped down by feet.

Before long it was dusk and Edward suggested they leave the cemetery while there remained sufficient light to see the path. 'And before any ghosts arrive,' he said.

'You believe in ghosts?'

'Of course,' he said. 'As do you, surely?'

'You promised me that we would not speak about yesterday evening.' She looked around her, at the tombs and plinths and statues that marked the presence of the dead. 'Certainly, if it is true that ghosts exist, this is the perfect place for them.' She shivered. 'Sometimes I think we may be surrounded by ghosts all the time without our knowing.'

'But we are alive,' he said. 'That is what counts.'

She turned to face him. 'Yes,' she said. 'We are alive.'

Hesitant but determined, he raised a hand and touched her cheek. 'I have to see you again.'

She pressed her face a little against his palm. 'If you wish,' she said.

'But not here.'

She lifted her hand and took hold of his, then led him away from the path, between two ivy-covered tombs, until they were standing together behind a tree, where they could not be seen. The ground was soft with vegetation; the scent of a bruised herb rose from it. She took off her bonnet and shook her hair free, then lifted her face. He stood before her, shocked into stillness. Smiling, she reached up and guided his head down towards hers until their mouths met. He had never kissed a woman like this before; he felt his heart tremble at the shock of it, the heat of her lips, the subtle probing of her tongue. It was a new language, a new world; every sensation it offered was strange and beyond his understanding. He was a migrant, an exile from all he had known; he had been lost and needy, and then, as if some switch had been thrown within him, some points on a line that redirected him, he was found, he was replete. When she gently pulled away, he let out a sigh.

'I shall come to you,' she said, her face barely visible in the dusk. 'If you will let me.'

Chapter Five

He was standing by his bedroom window when she arrived, on foot, dressed in a heavy greatcoat that hid her figure and with her hair tucked inside a bonnet, so disguised in her wintry outfit he only recognised her by her walk, by the lightness of it, as though she were on the point of lifting off into the air. I'm being foolish, he thought, but there was no help for it. He calmed his breathing, looked up into the sky. After a weekend of pallid sun, the weather had turned cold again, the snow that had threatened to fall a few days before still hung in the air. She may need to stay, he thought, if the snow in those clouds begins to fall. He had dismissed his valet, George, for the rest of the day and the night to come, sending him to his family in Southwark with a tip and enough beef to feed a regiment. George, who was not much older than Edward, had intuited the reason for his master's generosity and had agreed that he would not present himself before midday. Mrs Rokes, the housekeeper, had been similarly dismissed. Now, as she climbed the steps, Edward realised that he would have to open the front door himself. He tried to hide his excitement as he hurried down the stairs, arriving seconds after she had rung the bell.

She stood there, waiting for him to stand aside to allow her to enter the hall. He darted forward, took her by the elbow and guided her in, then closed the door behind them. She turned and smiled. Neither of them had spoken. She took off her bonnet, shook her hair loose as she had done at the cemetery, and then looked down, watching his hands as he unbuttoned her coat, not moving as he lifted it from her shoulders and let it fall behind her to the floor. He stepped back to look at her, to take her in, as she did him, as though neither of them quite believed the other was there, and then they kissed. He held her close to him and felt her arms reach around his waist, felt her encircle him as he had done her, no longer hiding, pressing against her, waiting for her to open to him, barely aware of his actions.

After a moment, gently, she pushed him away. 'Edward,' she said, with what sounded like reproof. 'You move too fast. You have misunderstood me.'

'Forgive me,' he said, dismayed. He had lost control, something he hated. He bent down and picked up her coat from the floor, hung it on the coat-rack. 'Let me have your bonnet,' he said and, taking it from her, hung it on the adjacent hook. 'May I offer you something? Tea? Coffee? Hot chocolate perhaps? The weather outside is bitter.' When she didn't answer, he opened the door to his left. 'Come into the sitting room,' he said. 'There is a fire.'

In the sitting room, he repeated his offer, and she chose coffee. He left the room. Five minutes later, he returned with coffee for them both and found her seated on a small stool by the fire, staring into the flames. 'How beautiful fire is,' she said. She had unbuttoned the top of her blouse and her neck was exposed.

'Forgive me,' he said again. 'You are so beautiful and I have thought about nothing but you for three entire endless days. To have you before me, within reach, like that. It was too much for me. I behaved like a beast.'

She laughed. 'And now you're being silly.'

'To have thought about nothing but you?'

She sipped her coffee. 'I have a confession to make. You have also been in my thoughts. Constantly. You may think I have done this sort of thing before, I acquiesced so easily. But that would not be true.' She looked up at him. 'I am as innocent as I believe you are. Am I right to believe in your innocence, Edward?'

He thrilled at his name on her lips. He blushed. Any answer he gave her would also be a confession.

'There is no need for you to speak,' she said. 'I see from your face that I am right.'

He knelt beside her, took the coffee from her hand. 'I have never known anything like this before,' he said. 'You have bewitched me.'

She took her hand away. 'That is not a kind thing to say. It suggests misconduct on my part.'

'No, no,' he protested. 'God forbid. I simply meant——'

She placed a finger on his lips. 'I know what you meant.'

What happened after that was natural and it was only when Edward was alone, hours after she had gone, that he saw that it had also been a sort of miracle. They had discovered each other, slowly, with an attention he had never imagined. It was true that he had been a virgin, unlikely though that was, and so had she; he had the proof of that. But their bodies had known what to do and they had applied that knowledge with a passion, and a gentleness, he would never have thought possible. They had made love, in the strictest sense. They had made it from nothing, from their two hearts, from their hands and lips, from the burning contact of their thighs and arms, from the whole of them, united, made it where before there had been nothing. Love. When it was over, she had stroked his stomach with her hand. 'How white you are,' she had said. 'I have never seen skin so white. You are like milk fresh from the churn.'

'And you are my dew-kissed rose,' he said, touching her breast.

'And your hair is fair as the sun,' she said.

'And yours is dark as deepest night,' he said.

'And yet we have the same blood running in our veins,' she said. She lifted his hand and turned it until they could both see the inside of his wrist. 'But look,' she said, 'you see how yours is blue and mine is dark. Blue blood. Black blood. How can they mix?'

'Why do you say that?'

She laughed. 'Because I'm a fool,' she said. She reached further down, between his legs. 'So soft,' she said, touching him there, 'when before it was so hard.'

'And now, thanks to your gentle hand, it is becoming hard again,' he said, 'and its needs are urgent and must be met.'

The following morning, he opened the drawer in his bedside cabinet and took out a small box, inside which was a ring. It was gold, with two small rubies set in it, a woman's ring.

'It belonged to my mother,' he said. 'She died when I was small. She died while she was giving birth. I heard her crying out but they wouldn't let me go to her. I would have had a sister if they both had lived.' He took her hand and slipped the ring onto her finger. 'I want you to have it.'

'You know what this means?' she said.

'It means that I love you,' he said. 'What more is there to know?'

She touched the ring as though to convince herself of its existence. 'There is nothing more than that,' she said. She moved the ring around on her finger, played with it, began to take it off and then slid it back on. 'Your mother didn't deserve to die.'

'My father has never forgiven me.'

'Why should he blame you?'

Edward shook his head. 'My mother was damaged when she gave birth to me, or that's what I've been told. My own view is that her constitution was weakened by the time she spent in the tropics, before my father brought her home. In either case, she should never have had another child.'

'How can you be blamed for your mother's death? Your father is a cruel man.'

'You will see for yourself how cruel he is,' he said. 'One day.'

She turned away. 'Enough, Edward.'

'What do you mean, enough?'

'You know nothing about me.'

'I know all that I need to know,' he protested.

She shook her head. 'In that case, what little you do know ought to be sufficient.'

'Sufficient?'

'Sufficient to know that I am not suitable. Your father, and not only your father, would never accept me as your wife.'

'That's for me to decide,' said Edward hotly.

'I said, enough.' She took his face in her hands and kissed him. 'I must leave now,' she said.

'You can't leave like this,' he said, grabbing her wrists.

'I must,' she said. 'Your servants will be coming. They mustn't find me here.'

'My servants are of no importance.'

'But you sent them away, Edward, because I was coming.'

'But that was for you, my dearest,' he said, almost crying with frustration. 'To protect your reputation.'

'I have no reputation to protect, Edward. If I had a reputation or you had none, there would be hope for us.'

'I can't bear this,' he said, letting her go and walking over to the window. He wanted to punch the glass, hurt himself, hurt the world that would judge them. He swung round. 'Do you really believe I give a tinker's curse what people think?'

'My grandfather was a tinker,' she said coldly. 'And a respectable man.'

'I didn't mean to offend you,' he said. 'Oh God, Settie, please try to understand.'

She nodded, but didn't speak. 'We are a proud people, Edward. We won't be misused.'

Edward crossed the room and fell to his knees before her. 'You can't give me all that you have given me and then simply take it away as though it counted for nothing.'

She laughed and gave his shoulder a push, hard enough to force him to thrust out an arm to maintain his balance. 'I will take nothing from you, you fool. Can't you see what you have done to me? What you have given to me? What I have given to you? We have given our whole selves to each other, Edward, we are one. Can't you see that? ' She put a hand on his head, as if to bless him. 'Now get up and take me to the door. I have to go.'

He spoke to Daniel Giles that evening, at the club. 'You remember when you told me that I was in love?'

'I do.'

'Well, you were right. I was, and I am even more in love now.'

'With the young lady at the séance? Your lovely flower seller?'

He nodded.

'So you found an opportunity to meet?' He refilled Edward's glass and patted his friend's arm in a gesture of appreciation. 'Congratulations. That was highly enterprising of you.'

'Yes,' said Edward. 'In a cemetery, appropriately enough.'

'I don't follow.'

Edward drained his glass. 'Because I think our love might be stillborn.'

'She doesn't reciprocate your feelings? I find that hard to credit. You're quite the catch, I would have thought.'

'No, it isn't that.' Edward sighed, then shook his head. 'On the contrary, her feelings are as strong as mine.'

'So what is it that stands in your way?'

'My father. My world. My class. If I were American I would

head west and take her with me,' said Edward with sudden fervour. 'I would kill buffalo and pan for gold. I would turn my back on petty convention, and bigotry. And fear.' He looked at Daniel with longing in his eyes. 'How I wish I'd been born American. You have so much more freedom, you have no idea how much. You have a whole continent to move in. If you only knew how much I envy you.'

Daniel looked sceptical. 'But if she feels for you as you feel for her, surely a way may be found?'

'You don't understand. My father is not like yours,' said Edward. 'Your father is a man of conscience, a man who believes in the rights of others. My father is not like that. He has sacrificed his life, his health, my mother's health, in the pursuit of wealth and now that he has achieved it he can find no satisfaction for himself. He despises the easy life he is expected to lead, the people around him, who look down on him and will always do so because he is that worst of creatures, a self-made man. You can have no idea what that means, Daniel. You come from a land where all men are equal, and your father has helped to make that possible. My father is a bitter man, a man without rank, whose soul is calloused although his hands, by now, are smooth.' Edward sighed, looked down into his own cupped hands as though searching for what to say. When he continued, his voice was low. 'My father dislikes me, you see, whatever he might tell himself, and others. In his heart, he believes that I am good for nothing and he is probably right. But I am also what he has made me, and he knows that, and he resents me for it. And yet he supports me, and supports me richly, because I have one thing that he treasures above all else, and that is my reputation. My reputation is something that I must never lose. It is worth more than his life, or mine, to him. If I lose that, I lose everything I have. And so does he.'

'You have spoken about this to her?'

Edward shook his head a second time. 'I think that is unnecessary. She understands, you see, she understands what my position is and she is trying to protect me, I know that's what it is.' Edward turned beseeching eyes on Daniel. 'It isn't that she doesn't love me. You have no idea. She loves me too much. She is of such purity, of such perfection. She has no fear for herself, none. She is afraid for me.'

'If there is love,' said Daniel, 'all else will follow. I have seen people cross continents for less. Believe me, Edward. Love will find a way.'

'How deeply touching,' said a voice behind them. They turned and saw Frederick Bell, cigar in one hand, brandy glass in the other. 'I thought young Edward here was the innocent one, but I see that he has found his match in our American friend. It comes with the passport, I imagine, a condition of citizenship. To have such faith in the power of love is a colonial attribute, or ex-colonial attribute in this case. You do your country almost too much justice, Giles. You are independent now. If you wish to be taken seriously, you must become cynical or perish.'

Daniel stood up. 'It's time I left,' he said. He looked at Edward. 'We shall speak about this another time.' Picking up his hat, he nodded. 'I bid you both good evening.'

'Do forgive me,' Bell said, taking Daniel's armchair. 'I hope I didn't interrupt you.'

'No,' said Edward.

'You were talking about love in the abstract, I suppose?'

'Precisely.'

'And your pretty young lady of the flowers, if that isn't too blasphemous?'

'I'm sorry? I don't know what you mean.'

'Forgive me,' said Bell. 'I seem to have touched on a delicate matter.'

'Not at all.'

'Because they are two a penny, my dear boy. Girls like that are two a penny. Don't let yourself be charmed by some guttersnipe.'

Edward stood up, irritated by Bell's disparaging tone. 'If I need any advice on these matters, Bell, I shall know who to ask.'

Bell looked briefly contrite, then nodded. 'Forgive me, I have been too direct and I have offended you without intending to do so. However, whatever you may think of me now, my offer still stands. I shall say it again, at the cost of losing your respect. Don't let yourself be charmed into something you may regret.'

'Thank you,' said Edward. 'I shall bear your advice in mind.'

'You are leaving,' said a voice at the door. 'Bell's company has proved too much for you, I fear.' Edward turned and saw Arthur Poynter brushing rain from his hat. Behind him, a manservant held a tray with a decanter and three glasses. 'I have taken the liberty,' said Poynter, 'of ordering a little refreshment for us. It would be a great pity if you had to go so soon, my dear Edward. It is hard enough that I should have missed our young American friend.'

'You saw him?'

'In the hall. He said I should find you here.'

'Sit down, man,' said Bell. 'Don't hover at the door like one of Rickman's restless sprites.'

As soon as Poynter was seated and the brandy poured out, he dismissed the manservant. 'Now,' he said, passing a glass to Edward, who took it with some reluctance, 'I believe I heard you gentlemen talking about a lady of the flowers. Can I assume that you are not referring to the blessed Virgin?'

'Don't encourage him,' said Bell. 'The poor boy has taken a tumble for that girl outside the theatre.' He lifted his glass in mock obeisance to Poynter. 'I hold you responsible.'

'Bell is exaggerating,' said Edward, irritated.

Poynter looked at Edward, holding his gaze until Edward turned away. 'That is Bell's way,' he said, 'but he should not be disregarded too lightly.'

'You surely don't think I would discuss my feelings with Bell, on this or any other matter,' said Edward hotly.

Poynter dismissed this with a brief movement of the hand, as if batting away a fly. 'Her people dabble in sorcery, or the women do, in love philtres and the like. They are a race of great subtlety, Edward, and should not be underestimated. The men are more violent. They are horse dealers by trade, and pugilists. For almost two hundred years, the very fact of being a Gypsy was a hanging offence, and even though no one, I believe, has been hanged since the seventeenth century, that leaves its mark on a people. They learn to defend themselves with whatever lies to hand, whether it be sorcery or brute strength. When I was a boy I was taken by my father to see a prizefight, a vicious business that I have never forgotten, but what I remember most vividly is the stature of the fighter. He was a giant, and so perfectly made that he might have been the model for Praxiteles. He fought like a beast whose power had been unleashed. One man he might have killed, such was his strength, if he had not been pulled away by his own brothers.' He paused. 'They are magnificent people, Edward, but dangerous and not always to be trusted.'

Bell laughed. 'Now, who exaggerates? Sorcerers and Greek heroes! Good God, man. They are cattle poisoners and charlatans.' He glanced at Edward. 'Even the pretty ones. Especially the pretty ones.'

Edward put down his half-full glass. 'It is late,' he said, 'and I have business to attend to.' He stood up. 'I shall leave you gentlemen to your discussion. Good evening.'

He next saw her three days later, early in the morning. He heard the house bell ring and, rising from the breakfast table, hurried to the nearest window, but could see no one. Moments later, George entered the sitting room. 'There is a young lady in the hall,' he said. 'She has no card, but says you know her. She refuses to give me her name.'

'Bring her to me.'

George gave a little bow. 'As you wish, sir.'

She was dressed as she had been at Abney Park. His heart leapt.

'I have looked for you everywhere,' he said.

'I know.'

'I have combed the Lea Valley,' he said.

'Really?' she said. She raised an eyebrow. 'All of it. In so short a time? You have certainly been very industrious.'

'I needed to see you again.' He moved towards her, paused when he saw her hesitate. 'You were there, weren't you? I was sure you were.'

'Will that be all, sir?' said George, at the door.

'Bring us another cup and saucer, George,' he said, taking Settie's hand and leading her across to the table. 'And tell Mrs Rokes to prepare some fresh coffee. The young lady will be staying.'

As soon as George had gone, Edward took her in his arms and kissed her. He stepped back. 'Now take off your bonnet,' he said.

She did as she was told. She sat down at the table and smiled at him, with an air of satisfaction, as he took the chair opposite her. She peeled the glove off her left hand and he saw the glint of a ring.

'I have been seen by your servant,' she said. 'My reputation is ruined.'

'In that case,' he said, 'we have crossed the Rubicon, and we are free.'

She reached across the table and took his hand. When George returned with a place setting for her, she flinched but strengthened her grip.

'I am ready to abandon all I have for you,' she said.

'And I for you,' he said. 'But it need not come to that.'

She brushed this aside with a gesture of irritation. 'I will never leave you, Edward,' she said. 'I will always be by your side. You know that, don't you? You understand what we have done?'

In his whole life, he had never needed anyone as much as he needed her. His desire outweighed everything else, his father, his world. Her world, which to his shame he had not considered before now. Aware that George had paused by the door to listen and that every word they spoke would be repeated, minutes later, to Mrs Rokes in the kitchen, he said, 'I know that you have all my heart, and will always have it. Always.'

Chapter Six

It was true that he had searched for her. He had walked along the banks of the River Lea until he saw smoke in the distance. He had approached the camp, but been warned off by a dark-skinned man with a pair of lurchers, straining on their leashes. When he had asked if Madame Arlette lived there, the man had laughed and told him he was a trespasser. There's no Madame Arlette here, he had said. You'd best be off. He had backed away, but stayed within sight of the camp until the light began to fail. He had returned to the music hall, knowing that she would not be there, but what else could he do? Where else could he go? He had thought of speaking to Poynter again, but that would involve an explanation he was not prepared to provide. The words of Bell had shaken him, he couldn't deny it, although the idea that Settie, *his* Settie, should be a guttersnipe, as he had termed it – although the implication was far worse – was more than he could bear. But how would Poynter see it? As Daniel Giles had done? As an act of love, to be applauded? He doubted that. The second day he had returned to the camp, and watched from the same safe distance as women tended the fires and men the horses, and children played, as children do, and he had wondered what kind of childhood she must have had. She is a lady, he thought, despite all this, the roughness of their lives, the impermanence. How had that come to pass, he wondered; what good hand had guided her? He thought of his childhood home, the great grey solid block of it, the portico, the tended empty gardens, his father rattling around inside the over-furnished rooms, and shuddered. Who has had the worst of it? he asked himself. And then the man had come out with his dogs, accompanied by youths with other dogs, and he had been driven away like a common thief.

He told her this, but she already knew.

'I could see you, standing there, my little sentinel. My lighthouse. They were only trying to protect me, they meant you no harm.'

'I know that now,' he said.

'They have always seen me as different.'

'You are different,' he said. 'You are perfect.'

'And you are ridiculous,' she said, laughing.

'How else are you different?' he said.

'Oh, in many ways,' she said.

'Tell me,' he said.

'When the moment is right,' she said. 'Until then, you will have to be patient. Can you manage that, do you think?'

'I think I can,' he said.

They were lying together in the bedroom of a small cottage some thirty miles east of London when she decided that the moment was right. Edward had built up the fire himself, the curtains were closed although there was still a little daylight left, and the room was lit by candles and an oil lamp on the mantelpiece. They had been in the cottage for almost a month and passed their days walking along the shingle beach they could see from the window of the room, or shopping for food at a local market and then cooking and eating what they bought, or reading, Edward preferring works of exploration and natural history, and Settie novels, or making love. Mostly, they made love, and Edward was astonished at the variety of pleasures their love afforded him. He thought of the changing-room conversations he had overheard after rugby or boxing, and the coarseness of them, but, more than the coarseness, what had struck him was the monotony. He had never imagined there could be such a multiplicity of delights in what, his books confirmed, was simple necessity. He had been reading Darwin, initially curious about the expedition of the *Beagle*, and then finding himself enthralled by the theories the scientist expounded. He looked at Settie as she curled up on the sofa, her legs beneath her, reading her novel, and thought about natural selection and how some force beyond them both had brought them together, had wedded them. Nothing is fixed, he thought. The strong will find each other, as we have done.

He was drowsing when she started to speak. Her voice was low and, at first, he thought she was talking to herself, imagining that he was asleep. He wanted to interrupt her, as though afraid he would hear something she might not want him to hear, but then he felt her move closer to snuggle into his side, and he knew that all he had to do was listen.

'My greatest regret is that you will never know my father,' she said. 'He died some years ago, when my brother and I were still small. But he made me what I am. He was my mother's second husband. Her first was killed in a fight before I was born. He left her with five children, but our people took care of her. We are good people,' she said, stroking his chest. 'People think we are thieves and murderers, that we steal their animals and their children, but it isn't true. We are no worse than others, and often we are better. My father is proof of that.'

'Tell me about him,' Edward said.

'He was born in Virginia, into slavery. He was taken away from his mother when he was a child and sold to someone else. He told me that his master wanted to be rid of him because he was half white, and his master's son, and a constant reproach, and I believe him. He was not much darker than I am, although Bartley, my brother, is darker than he was. Blood does what it wishes, my father said. When he was a young man, younger than we are now, a good woman helped him to escape. It took him over six months, moving from one city to the next, sometimes by boat, sometimes by coach, most often on foot. The people who helped him were heroes, he said. They were white men and women, and they risked their lives. Many slaves went to Canada but he had a dream that he would return to Africa, and when he arrived in New England he found a ship that would take him on. He worked his passage to Liverpool, where he met some of our people. He could pass as one of us, and he did. He was taken in and made welcome. He had been trained as a smith, and that was how he met my mother. I told you that my grandfather was a tinker, do you remember? No, don't be embarrassed, I forgave you long ago. She was older than him but not by much. She had her first child when she was fifteen. She was twenty-four when she met him and twenty-seven when I was born. Anyway, they fell in love and he abandoned his dream of returning to Africa and here I am.'

Edward said nothing.

'Are you scandalised?' she said.

He sat up. 'I love you,' he said. 'Why should I be scandalised? You had a father who loved you.'

She nodded. 'He wanted me to better myself,' she said. 'He taught himself to read in secret, as a child, and he made sure that I learned to read as well. My family said that he was ruining me, that he was trying to turn me into something I could never be, and sometimes I wonder if they were right.'

'You are doubly ruined, in that case.'

She kissed him on the nose. 'I think he would have liked you,' she said. 'My dear sweet Teddy.'

He loved it when she called him Teddy. 'I have a friend whose father helped slaves escape. An American. You know him; he was with us at the séance. He would like you, I know. I think you should meet.'

She pulled away. 'Everything in its own good time,' she said.

She was quiet and distant after this conversation, and Edward was anxious that it might have been his fault. Had he failed her in some way? he wondered. Perhaps he had let her down. The story of her father had touched him deeply, had even made him envious. It was true that discovering her origin had shaken him at first, but as something unforeseen, astonishing even, another facet of Settie he had never imagined. The more he thought about it, the more he saw it as a sort of distinction, as something that marked her out in a positive way. He saw her mixed heritage as a badge of honour. It wasn't as though the situation were any worse than it had been before, as far as the world was concerned. To take a Gypsy girl as one's wife was already beyond the pale. Living together in the cottage, they had pushed this truth to one side with a single will. He had lived without staff for the first time in his life, and the challenge had become a game and then a habit. He made coffee, laid the fire, he stretched taut his side of the sheet as Settie stretched and tucked in hers. He felt whole in a way that he had never felt before, and the thought of returning to London made him uneasy, as though he would be leaving something of importance behind him, some essential part of himself that could not be retrieved. And not only because he could not return to the house in John Street without Settie. Even if he went alone, and the idea of that was inconceivable, he could not go back to his old life. That life was gone.

In the end, he asked her what was wrong. 'You're unhappy,' he said. 'Do you think I don't know you well enough to see that?' She turned her back to him and sighed. For a moment he thought that she was about to cry and he fought back the urge to seize her by the shoulders, whether to comfort her or force her to speak he wasn't sure. It was obvious to him that she was considering what to say, considering whether to deny that she was unhappy or share the reason for it, and that upset him too. He had a moment's dread, and wished he had said nothing. Eventually, she shook her head and then looked back at him. Her eyes were moist. 'Come here,' she said, motioning him over to the table. When they were both seated, she took his hand.

'We can't continue like this,' she said, 'like two children playing house.'

'What do you suggest we do?'

'It will be Christmas in two weeks' time. Why don't you take me to your home and present me to your father?'

'I haven't spent Christmas with my father since I was seventeen,' he protested.

'You understand what I'm asking?' she said.

'My home is with you.'

'We can't hide away from the world forever, Teddy.'

'Are you sure that's what you want?' he said, his heart sinking despite himself.

'It's what we have to do,' she said.

'You will have to put up your hair,' he said, trying to make light of it. 'Your beautiful hair.' He stood up and, still with his hand in hers, led her across to the armchair beside the stove. He sat down and pulled her onto his lap. He fumbled at the buttons of her blouse, humming a song they had heard a child sing on the beach some days before, a sort of lullaby that had charmed them both. He nuzzled his face into her neck. 'Your beautiful skin,' he said.

'And you will have to behave,' she said, but playfully, which gave him hope.

*

Later, she said: 'Cassy was my father's idea. Really, the whole business of holding séances was my father's idea. He knew that my mother had the gift because he also had the gift. He said he had brought it with him from Africa although he had never been there. It was in his blood, he said. My father saw ghosts himself, but never spoke with them. When he found out that Mamma was a seventh child, he once told me, he loved her more than ever.'

'Seventh child?'

'Seventh children have powers that other people don't have.'

Edward thought for a moment. 'But you have six siblings, you told me.'

'That's right,' she said. 'That's where my name comes from. Settie is short for Settimia. I'm the seventh child of a seventh child, which multiplies the power. You're scared now, I can see. This is why I never wanted to talk to you about that evening.'

'You tell me now that what I saw was real? Cassy was real?'

'Oh yes,' she said. 'As real as I am.'

'And your mother's prophecies?'

'I've no idea,' she said, with an impertinent smile. 'We shall have to wait and see.'

'Should I be scared?' he said.

She nodded. 'Oh yes,' she said.

Another month passed, Christmas was behind them. They had stayed in the cottage and Settie had made a travesty of a plum pudding. They had laughed and loved each other and drunk a little too much champagne. No further mention had been made of visiting Edward's family home. He had sensed that Settie was waiting for him to speak, and he had failed to do so, partly out of shame, because he knew that she was right, and partly out of fear, because he knew all too well what his father would say, and do. Edward had received a brief note from him a few days after

Christmas, wishing him well for the new year. His reply had been similarly curt. He was leaving the cottage to post it when Settie called out to him to wait.

They walked down to the beach together. 'You needed some fresh air,' she said, as an icy wind blew in from the north-east and threatened to carry away her bonnet. Before she could secure it Edward had halted them both, untied the ribbon and lifted it off her head. She turned towards the sea and let the wind blow her loose hair back from her face. The cold took her breath away. He stood in front of her, between where she stood and the edge of the beach, to shelter her a little. The shingle shifted beneath their feet. Behind her head rose the twin towers of an abandoned church, fallen into decay. They had walked up there only days before and stood together at the heart of the ruin, hand in hand. She had laughed about their being married there, in a church without walls or roof or altar, about how it would be the ideal place for them, and he had laughed with her, not sure what she meant.

'I have to post a letter,' he said. 'To my father.'

She slipped her arm through his. 'I think we have had sufficient fresh air by now,' she said. 'And I have something I want to tell you.'

They had almost reached the path leading up to the church when they saw a flock of seagulls, a dozen or so, fighting over something further down the beach. As one bird rose above the scrum, another swooped down. Their cries, like those of maddened children, could be heard through the whistling of the wind and the pounding of waves on the shingle. Edward turned back. Settie restrained him. 'No,' she said. 'Don't go. It's an omen.' But already he had pulled away from her and was striding towards the scene. Lifting her skirts, she followed at a run.

When he was only yards away he shouted and flapped his arms to scare the gulls off, but was ignored. He picked up a handful of small stones from the beach and flung them at the birds, out-screaming them to make himself heard. Eventually, three or four birds took flight and wheeled around his head. Settie had almost reached him at this point, and waved her bonnet in the air to repel them, her hair blowing wildly in the wind. Edward hurled another handful of shingle, and three more gulls abandoned whatever had attracted them, which still could not be seen, and rose into the sky. One bird plunged to within inches of his face, its beak wide open, as if to pluck out an eye. He flinched, his fist swung out and up in a crazy punch, and the bird flew off with a screech. The last few birds he drove away with kicks.

As the gulls scattered Settie reached his side. Together, they looked down to see what the flock had found. At their feet lay what was left of a small animal, a cat or a lapdog perhaps, now half devoured, its front portion, where the head and shoulders had once been, fleshless by now, stripped to the bone, the rest of the body a tangle of matted, bloodstained fur. Strands of seaweed had somehow become entangled with the exposed part of the skeleton. Of the four legs, three were still attached, picked white and clean. The fourth lay at a short distance, the paw still perceptible, a ring of seaweed wound round it like some ghastly ornament. Edward touched it with his foot. 'A dog,' he said. 'It was a dog.'

She touched his elbow, then pointed towards the sky. The gulls were riding the wind above their heads. 'We need to go,' she said.

Later that day, he found her crying in the second, unused bedroom of the cottage. He took her in his arms and held her. He asked her what was wrong. Had he done something to hurt her? He would die before he knowingly did that, he murmured, his voice trembling. She nodded and let him kiss her tears away and stroke her cheek until she was calm. She asked him if he loved her and would always love her, whatever might happen to them both. He swore that he did, and that he would, and it was only then that she told him that he was about to become a father.

Chapter Seven

'A pretty mess you find yourself in,' said Bell. He was sitting with Edward and Daniel Giles at the club. It was the first time Edward had left Settie alone in the house since their return to London the week before. She had insisted they abandon the cottage the morning after she had told him about her state. He hadn't believed her at first and then, when she had convinced him of the truth of it, he had been euphoric, drunk with elation, unable to understand the reason for her tears. He had held her, examined her with an almost surgical intensity, opening her dress and undergarments and pressing his ear to her stomach, stroking the subtle roundness of it until she had pushed his hands away with an irritated laugh. 'But how do you know?' he had insisted, and she insisted that she did, her body did, he had to trust her. She *knew*. They went to bed and made love with a different kind of passion, cautious, more attentive, as though some bridge of intimacy had been crossed, against all the odds, and they had arrived safely on the other shore. The following morning, when he woke, he found her dressed and with her bags packed. 'We need to go home,' she said flatly. 'We can't hide away here like fugitives any longer.' She touched her stomach. 'Not now.' He saw at once that her mind would not be changed. Two hours later they were on the train for London.

*

The three men had eaten together and were now drinking brandy in a small private room, the door closed, the servant dismissed. Edward hadn't sought the other two out; on the contrary, their presence had initially been unwelcome. He had needed to be alone, that was all, and out of the house. But they had spotted him first, and come over to his table, and he had felt obliged to ask them to join him. They had talked about nothing of importance until the first bottle of claret was finished, at which point Bell asked him where he had been these past two months, and he had said Kent, in a small cottage near the coast. Giles had guessed at once, and asked him outright, as Americans tend to do, and he had said, yes, he had been with the flower seller, and, to Giles's second question, he had answered once again, yes, he was still in love with her, now perhaps more than ever, a response that had provoked a raised eyebrow on Bell's part.

It had taken another bottle of claret for Bell to squeeze out of Edward the confession that had elicited his comment. 'A pretty mess,' he repeated, lighting his cigar.

'I couldn't be happier,' said Edward, defensively.

'And neither could she, I imagine,' said Bell.

'She is thrilled, as I am,' said Edward. 'She is a natural mother.'

'Certainly, she is thrilled. She has you, my dear boy. She has you exactly where she wants you. Never say I failed to warn you.'

'I don't know what you mean,' said Edward.

'He means that you have allowed yourself to be trapped,' said Daniel.

'It's the oldest trick in the world,' said Bell.

'She is no more responsible for what has happened than I am,' said Edward. 'Less, if the truth be told.'

'Bell is a cynic,' said Daniel. 'It is only to be expected that he should think like that. He has spent his whole life avoiding traps of this type, I imagine.'

'Or venturing into them and then escaping, which is far more fun,' said Bell, with a smile.

'I don't see what has happened as a trap,' insisted Edward.

'You will, my dear boy,' said Bell, equably. 'You will.'

Daniel spoke before Edward had a chance to respond. 'So you will be a father,' he said. 'I offer you my congratulations.'

'And talking of fathers,' said Bell, 'I imagine your own pater is delighted that he will soon have a Gypsy's brat for an heir.'

'You have no right to talk about her like that,' said Edward. He was about to rise from his chair, but Daniel caught his arm.

'No, don't leave like that. I think you are doing a rather splendid thing.'

Edward sank back into his armchair, unappeased.

'So?' said Bell.

'So what?' said Edward warily.

'So what does your father have to say about this?'

'My father's opinion is of no importance,' said Edward. But the fight had gone out of him. He had had this argument, or one very like it, with Settie only hours before; it was precisely her insistence that he speak to his father that had driven him from the house to seek refuge at his club. She had threatened to do it herself if he did not, and he believed that she would. The mere idea of it horrified him. How strange, he thought, that he should feel attacked on the same flank by such different assailants as Settie and Bell. What unlikely allies they were. The only ally he could find to help him to defend his position was Daniel Giles; a position, he had begun to sense, that was indefensible.

'From which I gather that you haven't told him,' said Bell.

'I shall tell him when the time is right,' said Edward. 'And that is for me to decide, and no one else. You seem to have forgotten that the child is mine, not his.'

'You know as well as I do, Edward, that the time will never be right,' said Bell, trimming and lighting a cigar. 'I know men like your father. He will have your guts for garters, my boy, you can be sure of that.'

'Perhaps if you were married?' said Daniel.

'Good grief, man,' said Bell, inspecting the tip of his cigar. 'Do you really imagine that a hasty marriage would encourage the man to accept a bastard, conceived out of wedlock with a Gypsy girl, whatever – how shall I put this? – remedial action might be taken later?'

'Hard men have been known to change,' said Daniel.

'And pigs have been known to fly,' said Bell with a laugh, 'but I have never seen a hog in flight, and I'd wager that neither have you.'

'She is a lady,' said Edward, an edge of despair in his voice. 'I have no reason to suppose my father would not welcome her once he knew her. I could take her anywhere.'

'Although you haven't, have you? Apart from a cottage in Kent,' said Bell. 'You begin to sound like Rickman talking about his African conquests.'

'She is better than any lady I have ever met.'

'Well, to appear to be a lady is not much but it is a start, I suppose. She has a certain natural elegance, I seem to remember. I suppose she might pass as a lady if required to and if she had the proper schooling. To be honest, I've never been exactly sure what constitutes a lady, other than a certain unavailability, and even that cannot be guaranteed.'

'So we agree that she might be considered a lady,' said Edward. 'I thank you for that.' He glanced at Daniel, for support, but Daniel was staring into his half-empty glass and seemed lost in thought.

'We agree on that, yes. I believe your father could be brought round to accepting her, however unwise that might be. Blood will out, young man. You remember the story our good friend Poynter told us, about the violent nature of her people. Who knows what it would take for that to rise to the surface? But even if he acquiesces to the marriage, there is that other matter.'

'You're saying that the child is the problem?' said Edward.

'Of course he isn't,' said Daniel, looking up sharply.

'Yes,' said Bell, ignoring Daniel. 'That is exactly what I'm saying.' He put down his glass with an air of satisfaction, as though the conversation had come to its rightful conclusion. 'And it is a problem that can be solved, and without great difficulty, if that is what you choose. You only have to ask and I shall be happy to help.' He stood up, brushed some cigar ash from his waistcoat. 'And now, gentlemen, I shall take my leave of you to pursue less cerebral pleasures. Good evening.'

As soon as he had gone, Daniel poured them both another brandy.

'You shouldn't listen to him, you know. His kind of cynicism is brutal and dangerous. It stifles love, hope, value. It leaves a desert behind it. He is the devil himself.'

Edward drank some brandy. His head was already aching. 'Settie's father was an escaped slave,' he said. 'He might have passed through your father's hands. Who knows?'

'She is of African descent?'

'One quarter of her is. Another quarter is a slave owner in Virginia, and the final half is Gypsy. She is what your people call a cocktail, I believe. A cocktail of blood. And our child will be—' He paused, shaking his head in an attempt to clear his thoughts. 'Well, you can do the calculation, I'm sure.' He stared at his friend in a kind of confused rage. 'We are fractions, Daniel, fractions of fractions. Not one of us is whole. There is no end to us.'

'I think you've had enough alcohol for one night,' Daniel said. 'Let me see you home.' He helped Edward to his feet. 'Fresh air will do you good.'

'Why does everyone always think I need fresh air?' said Edward.

*

Outside the club, Edward told Daniel to take a hansom; he would find his own way home, but Daniel insisted. It was much later than Edward had realised; he had lost all track of time. They began to walk along empty streets, barely lit, the silence broken only by the occasional click of horseshoes on cobbles, the muffled sound of the wheels against stone, when a late cab passed them. A ghost town, thought Edward. As the frigid air drove its way into his throat and nostrils, he realised that he had drunk too much and was grateful for Daniel's arm. Neither of them spoke, and Edward was also grateful for that. They walked as quickly as they could, Edward stumbling a little, leaning on Daniel for support, until they reached Covent Garden. The streets leading into the square were already congested with wagons bringing in produce from the surrounding countryside for the market the following day. Children prowled like rats among the parked wagons, fighting for anything that fell, scampering off with their spoils. Around the edge of the market, skulking in doorways or, more brazenly, strolling arm in arm in pairs, were streetwalkers, not much older than the rat-like gaunt-faced children. One of them came up with a tray of half-dead flowers, and blocked their path.

'See anything you fancy, my dears?' she said.

Edward thought he was going to be sick. For the briefest moment, he had imagined Settie standing before him and the thought that this might have been her, that she might have led this life, was more than he could bear. Without me, without our love, she would sooner or later end up here, he thought, her flowers wilted, the scent of decay on her. He saw his child, scavenging for broken cabbages beneath the wheels of a stinking cart. How many of these poor girls had been dragged down by their children, he wondered. The wave of nausea passed, to be replaced by an awful foreboding. He started to sob without restraint, clutching Daniel's sleeve. 'Take me away from here,' he said.

A woman some yards away called out, 'They've got each other, Bessie, they don't need you.' She came up to them and gave Daniel an unhelpful push. 'There's a molly-house down there,' she said, pointing towards an alley. 'That's for your sort.'

Daniel led Edward away.

'Bothering decent working girls,' she shouted after them. 'That's it, off you go.'

Sunlight woke Edward the following morning, when George drew back the curtains of the sitting room. For a troubled moment, he had no notion of where he was. 'Good morning, sir,' he heard as if from a great distance. He was slumped in an armchair, still dressed, although someone had loosened the laces of his boots and opened his collar. He felt nauseous, his temples throbbed, his left leg had lost all sensation, he had a crick in his neck. He thought he would rather die than live like this. George crossed the room and picked up his master's greatcoat from the floor. 'Feeling rather the worse for wear, are we, sir?' he said.

Edward nodded, wincing at the pain this provoked.

'I'll bring you some coffee immediately, sir, and then I shall prepare you a warm bath. I find that always helps in cases like these.'

'Thank you, George. I don't know what I'd do without you.'

George smiled and was about to leave the room when he stopped and turned. 'And sir, the mistress has gone out. She told me to tell you that she will be back this afternoon.'

Settie had always refused to leave the house before this, either alone or in his company. She insisted that she had everything she needed and saw no reason to walk the streets alone, but he was convinced that this was only half the truth. She was keeping something from him, some secret fear that had made her distant at times, at other times affectionate in an oddly clinging way, as if afraid that he might abandon her, or that she might be torn from him by others. He would never do that, he wanted to tell her, nor allow that to happen. He struggled to his feet when George returned with a pot of coffee, and gulped the coffee down, burning his lips and tongue, then carefully undressed and sank into the warm bath that had been run for him while George laid out fresh clothes. But the conversation he had had with Bell the previous evening began to come back to him, in snatches at first and then more completely, and with that completeness came an anxiety he could not quell. Had he said that his father would accept Settie as his daughter-in-law? Did he believe that to be true? He wished he knew.

He dressed and crossed to the window, looked down into the street below. The weather was even worse than it had been the day before; the bare branches of the trees that lined the opposite side of the road were swaying in a bitter northeasterly wind. He wondered if winter would ever end, and then realised how foolish a thought that was. All winters end, he told himself. He looked to the left, towards the park at the end of the road, and then to the right, to the end of the long street, hoping against hope that he would see her, wondering what impulse had taken her out in such dismal conditions. Perhaps she was angry with him, he thought. She had never seen him drunk, and the previous evening he had been extremely drunk. Had he mentioned something that would have been better not voiced? Had he told her what Bell had said? Had he put into words what he had thought, or half thought, those awful doubts that were still within him, insistent, unrelenting? Had she even seen him? Maybe Daniel had accompanied him to the door, into the house. Had Daniel loosened his collar and shoelaces, or Settie? Had George helped him off with his greatcoat? But George would have taken it away and brushed it, not left it on the floor. He wondered if he still had his hat. Before he realised what he was doing, he had lifted his hand to his head, then laughed, a humourless, self-accusing laugh. So much to understand, he thought, so much that seemed beyond his control. He closed his eyes but all he could see was the market, the girl selling flowers and the urchins darting between the massive wheels of carts, risking their lives for a scrap of food. And he had seen Settie and their child, that was the truth of it, as if they had really been there and were destined to be nowhere else. Now, his eyes still firmly closed, he saw his father smiling and taking a bunch of flowers from the market girl and following her into some dark corner and lifting her skirts, still smiling, and turning to nod at Edward as though it would be his turn next, and the thought disgusted him to his very core. And the greatest disgust was directed towards himself because the thought had been his.

She came when he had almost given up hope. She rang the bell because she had never wanted a key; she had never considered it necessary. Edward had watched her walk along the street towards him, his heart leaping, and had run down the stairs, two at a time, in order to head off George or Mrs Rokes. He wanted to make sure that no one else would open the door for her. There she was, standing on the step, umbrella furled, her coat buttoned up to the neck, her cheeks glowing with the cold, her eyes alive with love. His Settie. He pulled her into the hall, hugging her to him.

'I've missed you so badly,' he said. 'Where on earth have you been?'

She eased herself away from him without speaking, then turned and looked behind her, across the road to where two men were standing, with dogs.

'We need to talk,' she said.

Chapter Eight

Frederick Bell suggested they meet in a tavern behind their club, where they would not be interrupted. Edward arrived first, and waited outside. He was on the point of leaving when Bell climbed down from a cab. He took Edward's arm and led him into a small room at the back of the tavern. Clearly, he knew the place well. Neither of them spoke until they had been served. Bell sipped his ale and sat back, patient, an amused smile on his lips, waiting for Edward to say something. Eventually, Edward did.

'I've been thinking about what you said.' His voice was low, as though anxious that he might be overheard although there was no one in the tavern who might know them. It was the kind of place only Bell would use.

Bell's smile became condescending. 'I'm gratified.'

Edward paused, unsure where to start. Already he wished that he had not come.

'So,' said Bell. 'How can I help you?'

'Supposing I agree to your suggestion—'

'Yes?'

Edward's face was set. 'I would need your assurance that no harm will come to her.'

Bell shook his head. 'It is a simple procedure. She will feel a little pain, I shall not deny that, but nothing that cannot be borne.'

'And she will suspect nothing?'

'Nothing. She will assume that what happens is entirely natural, the body obeying its own mysterious laws. You can trust me. I am, after all, a doctor, although I feel no pressing need to practise.' Bell paused. 'Might I ask you what made you change your mind?'

Edward sighed. 'She has said that she will leave me if I don't acknowledge her and the child. I have thought about what you said when you spoke of my father. I thought it would be enough to stand up to him – if you remember, I was rather under the influence of claret and brandy that evening – but I'm no longer sure that this is the case. I think it more likely that he would disinherit me, and I would find myself with a wife and child and no income to support them. I have no idea what I would do. I have no skills. I know nothing of any practical use. I suppose I could teach but who would employ me, an outcast with a Gypsy wife and child? We would be paupers. But if I present myself to my father with Settie alone, I believe that together we can make him understand, and accept, my choice. Does that sound like cowardice, Bell?'

Bell shook his head once more. 'It sounds like simple common sense.'

'I wish I were as sure of this as you are. My father is a difficult man and has long since ceased to love me, if he ever did. You shake your head, but what I say is true. He resents me, he blames me for his own unhappiness. I should never forgive myself if I felt the same for my child, if I thought that he had ruined my life as my father thinks I have ruined his. I would end up hating him as deeply as my father hates me. It *is* cowardice, of a sort, and I'm ashamed of it, but it is how I feel.' He gave a bitter laugh. 'How absurd that I should be saying this to you, of all people.'

Bell was clearly shocked by Edward's candour. 'I am not the monster you take me for,' he said.

'Forgive me,' said Edward.

'I think you judge your father – and yourself – too harshly.'

77

'Perhaps I do,' said Edward. He paused, as if considering how much to say. Finally, with a deep sigh, he continued: 'But my father is not my only fear. My other fear, my greatest fear, concerns the woman I love. Because I do love her, you see, and I would do anything, anything at all, to protect her.' He looked into Bell's eyes. 'You think I'm a romantic fool, I know that, and perhaps I am. But if I thought that she would be safer, or happier, without me, I think I would accept even that. If I could be certain of her future, and of the future of my child, a child I would never see, I would let her leave me and return to her people. But what would that mean? How would they treat her? What do they do in such cases? How can I possibly be sure, if she leaves me to have the child, as she has threatened, that she will not finish on the streets? A single woman with a child. The thought of it makes me sick with fear. Who would support her? Who would care for her? She would be disgraced. I could not bear that. I love her too much for that. With me, with the two of us united, she will be safe. I will make sure of that. My father will accept us, I shall make sure of it.'

Neither man spoke for a few moments. Edward noticed for the first time the noise from the tavern behind them, a rowdiness that startled him. He had forgotten where they were. When someone began to sing a bawdy song, the words of the song could be heard through the closed door.

The captain's daughter Charlotte was born and bred a harlot
Her thighs at night were lily-white, by morning they were scarlet.

The dreadful vision he had had, of his father and Settie together, the carnality of it, came back to him, as real as the wall of the sordid room in which they were seated, as solid as the ale-stained table before him. He closed his eyes in an attempt to banish it. Eventually Bell reached across and touched his sleeve, as if to wake him.

'You are doing this for her,' said Bell. 'Remember that.'

Edward looked at him, his eyes filled with doubt. 'Is that how you see it?' He moved his arm away from Bell's hand. 'You do see that she mustn't leave me?'

'Of course, my dear boy,' said Bell, with a trace of impatience.

'So you will help me?'

'I have said that I will.' Bell grinned suddenly. 'I am a man of my word.'

'And what will you ask for in return?'

He laughed. 'Who do you take me for? The Prince of Darkness? You do me too much honour, Edward. Everything you do will be done of your own accord, I want you to remember that.'

Edward nodded. He was sweating, a cold sweat. Settie had no idea where he was. He had told her he needed to walk after their conversation and she had looked at him, an imploring look he thought now, but had not answered him. In the street, he had stopped and found that he was short of breath with tension. She will leave me, he thought, and I shall lose everything I have.

'What do I have to do?' he said.

Bell gave Edward a phial containing a pale-green tincture. 'You will give her some of this in a glass of red wine,' he said. 'It is entirely herbal,' he added when Edward examined it with misgiving. 'Which doesn't mean that it lacks potency. As little as a few drops have been known to trigger a miscarriage on their own, although we cannot hope for that,' he said. 'At the very least, it will cause a stomach ache and an overwhelming feeling of nausea.'

'And then what shall I do?'

'You will tell her that she must be taken to a doctor, that her life and the life of the child are at risk. She will be scared and you must comfort her. She has no reason not to trust you. You will send someone to find a cab. I shall be waiting outside the house.'

Edward flinched at Bell's use of the word trust. *She has no reason not to trust you.* She might never trust me again, he thought, and she

79

would be right not to do so. 'We shall be duping her,' he said. 'Is that what you're saying?'

'Don't be ingenuous,' said Bell. 'Would she do what is required of her own accord?'

'No.'

'If she had to choose between you and the child she is carrying, who do you think she would choose?'

'I think she would choose me.'

'You think, or you know?' Bell's tone was persuasive, even wheedling.

'I know she would choose me,' he said, more firmly, hopeless now but determined to see it through.

'In that case, you are duping her, as you put it, to follow her heart and nothing more. That is hardly deceit, Edward. There are times when people lack courage or understanding of themselves, when they have to be helped to do what is needed.'

Edward had had enough of Bell's philosophising. 'And when we are in the cab? What happens then?'

'We shall take her to a certain Dr Hancock, a colleague of mine, with a surgery in Whitechapel and he will do whatever is required to see that she is comfortable and that the inconvenience is resolved as rapidly and as painlessly as possible. The man is entirely trustworthy and has worked for me in the past, when I have found myself in similar difficulties. The costs, such as they are, will be met by me, to be settled between us at a later date.'

'You make it seem so simple.'

'It is simple,' Bell said. He rested his hand once more on Edward's sleeve. If he had left it a moment longer, Edward would have brushed it off, such was his disgust.

'You must always remember that you are not doing this for yourself, but for her and for your future life together,' Bell said.

Edward nodded. 'I shall remember,' he said.

*

He told himself later, when he could bear himself no longer, that it was her fault, that if Settie had not threatened to take her child to her own people he would never have considered it. It is your decision, Edward, she had said. I have spoken to my mother and they will have me as I am. They will forgive me, and they will welcome me back. It is up to you to decide. Either I am yours and you own up to me, to us, and I become your wife and not some creature hidden away from public view, however much we love each other, or I shall leave you, Edward, and return to my people, and take the child with me. I cannot be half a wife, half a mother. I can be all or nothing. If you do not want me, tell me now and I shall go, we shall go, and it will break my heart, and you will never see us again, and I will never forgive you. If you want me, want me fully, tell me now and we shall never be separated again. Whatever happens, whatever you decide, she said, taking both his hands in hers and staring into his eyes until tears sprang up in them, I shall always be with you, my dear heart. We both shall.

The tincture took no more than fifteen minutes to work. Settie clutched her stomach, her face creased with pain. Edward, already regretting what he had set in motion but ignorant as to how it might be stopped, sent George to fetch the cab that had been waiting a hundred yards further down the road and helped her into it. He had expected to see Bell there, and had wondered how he would explain the doctor's presence, apparently so fortuitous, but the cab was empty, apart from a visiting card on the seat, with the name Dr Graham Hancock, and an address, Thomas Street. She gripped his arm, her face beaded with sweat, as he sat beside her. He comforted her as best he could, with words that sounded like lies to his ears, and were lies, and kisses, but the kisses were rejected. At one point, with a half-stifled cry of pain, she pushed him away and said that she was about to die and that she would always love him, and he began to weep, because he had done what he had done and it was too late now for him to change his mind as the cab drew up outside the address he had been given and a man in a white smock opened the door and helped Settie over the threshold. He told Edward to wait in a cold bare room with two hard chairs against the wall but Edward refused to leave her. His mind went back to Abney Park, to the grave of the boy, to Settie and to what she had said there, as the parents moved away, the mother weeping, the father comforting her, the patch of trodden-down earth. *It is the worst thing that can happen. To lose a child.* If she had been stronger, he would have carried her away at that moment, but she clutched her stomach and cried out with the agony she felt. 'Make it stop,' she said. He nodded, held her close. 'I'm here beside you,' he said.

The room they entered was equally bare, apart from a bed in the centre and a sideboard with medical instruments arranged on it. The man in the smock took a kettle from the fire and filled a bowl with boiling water, which he placed on the sideboard beside the instruments. He helped Settie onto the bed, lifted her skirts and told her to raise and part her knees. Edward watched horror-struck as the man began to work. Settie turned her head, straining to see him where he stood. She raised a hand and he took it and held it as hard as he could without hurting her, so that she would know he was there. At one point, she sucked in her breath with pain and he felt her hand go limp and then stiffen as though she had been administered a shock. He asked the man what he was doing, but there was no answer. It could only have been a matter of minutes. And then Settie sighed, the longest sigh he had ever heard, all the air in her body slowly escaping, as though fleeing from her, and it was her life breath that had escaped he realised later, when it was too late and she was dead.

*

He didn't understand at first and, when he did, it made no sense. He watched the man extract from beneath her skirt a bloodied form the size of a skinned rabbit and wrap it hastily in some cloths. He wiped his hands on his white coat, pulled Settie's skirt back into place as if to protect her modesty and threw the bundle into a bucket beneath the bed she had died on. Edward watched all this in horror. 'What has happened?' he asked. 'What have you done to her?' The man gave a shrug and said that nothing could have been done, she was made all wrong down there; the child would have been born dead in any case, he said, and more than likely she would have died herself. 'She is dead,' Edward said, and it was both a question and a statement. The man said he had done what he could and Bell would see to it, there would be no need for him to worry, and Edward understood that he was talking about the cost. He looked at Settie, her eyes open, her beautiful hair in tangles against the sweat on her neck and throat, her face as perfect as it had ever been, but lifeless already, as if it had never lived. The man lifted her arms and crossed them on her breast, like some statue on a tomb, and Edward saw his mother's ring on her finger, the rubies glinting in the lamplight. This is how my mother died, he thought, with a child inside her, and then, with a shudder, *I have sullied my mother's memory*, and that must have been behind the instinct that made him decide to remove the ring. But however hard he tugged it would not come free. 'You leave that to me now,' said the man, moving Edward to one side. He picked up a scalpel and cut the finger free, shaking the now-bloodied ring into his hand and offering it to Edward, dropping the severed finger into the bucket. Without thinking, Edward took the ring and then, as if bewitched by the horror of what he had seen and done, and with a spasm that shook his whole body, he vomited on the floor. 'I say,' protested the man, 'there's no need for that,' and Edward struck him as hard as he had ever struck anyone, wishing him dead, and then collapsed.

When he came to, the room was empty. The body of Settie had disappeared, the bed had been cleaned, the bucket taken away and its contents disposed of. He called out, but no answer came. He searched the house from top to bottom, throwing open doors, tearing at curtains, looking twice in the same room, but there was no sign of the man. The house seemed uninhabited, hardly furnished, bare rooms with beds and washbasins, an empty kitchen, a scullery, and little else. He stood in the room where she had died and cried until he could cry no more, and then walked out of the house, alone.

Part Two

Chapter Nine

'The trees have arrived!' He heard her clap her hands with delight. 'Edward, the trees have finally arrived!' Walking into the hall, he looked up the stairwell to see her leaning over the bannister of the second floor, her dark hair falling over her face, the brightness from the skylight above her head transforming her into a silhouette. 'They're here, my dear Edward!' she cried. 'My orange trees are here!' She rushed downstairs, falling breathlessly into his outstretched arms. Laughing, he lifted her feet from the floor and swung her around until she begged him to stop and to put her down, at which point she took his hand and pulled him towards the front door.

A large wagon drawn by four horses was waiting at the side entrance to the garden. On the back of the wagon, their root balls wrapped in moistened sacking, were eight trees, all in leaf, each tree the height of a tall man. She was about to clamber up the side of the wagon, one foot already on the nearest wheel, to reach them, but Edward caught her arm. 'Calm down, my sweetheart, all in good time.'

'But I've waited so long,' she said, wriggling playfully in his grasp as the two men on the wagon climbed down from their seats. 'They've come all the way from home, all this time at sea. And then the docks, and now this wagon. What a journey they've made, my poor trees, they'll be so tired.'

'We had to prepare a home for them, my love,' said Edward. He led the two men to a greenhouse constructed against the far wall of the garden, a structure of stone and glass and iron the height and size of a cottage, with a terraced area before it. 'This is the orangery,' he said. 'The trees will be housed here in winter.'

The men nodded, returned to the wagon and began to carry the trees to the orangery while Edward's wife danced around them like an excited child, clapping her hands together, stroking and kissing the leaves, until one of the men looked plaintively at Edward. He held her back until all eight trees had been moved into the orangery. 'Now we will decide where to put them,' he told her and she looked up at him with such delight it was all he could do not to embrace her in front of the men, who stood before them, caps in hand, waiting for further orders.

'I am so happy,' she said, to no one, as Edward paid the men. 'It is as though I have my home here with me.' She spun round, her skirts sweeping the loose stones of the path. 'You are my home as well, Edward, of course,' she said, reaching out for him as he came back to her, taking his hands in hers and pulling him into a clumsy dance. 'You are all my home. My family.' Her eyes filled with tears, but she blinked them back. 'They have taken so long to arrive, I'd almost given up hope. I looked at the beautiful pots we brought here for them and it made my heart weep. But they are here now, and they are alive and that is all I ask.' She hugged him. 'You have made me very happy.'

'As you have done me,' he said. 'You have saved my life, Marisol.'

They had been in the house for almost two months when the trees arrived, in late October. Edward had instructed his agent to find somewhere large, surrounded by a walled garden, near but not *in* London, with air that could be breathed and space, above all space. The agent had done his job, found them this Georgian villa in

Highgate, with views of the Heath from the uppermost floors and a garden that could house the orange trees without which Marisol had decided she could not live. Edward had bought the house before seeing it, acting on impulse as he had done so often these past eighteen months, as though he could not be held responsible for something that had been done without premeditation. His relief when Marisol fell in love with the house as soon as she saw it was immense. 'This is how I have always imagined homes in England to be,' she had said, with that faint tinge of an accent that was part of the reason he loved her, and he had smiled to himself. How little she knew, he thought.

They had met in Palermo just over a year before, at a ball held to celebrate Marisol's eighteenth birthday. Among the letters of introduction Edward had brought with him was one to Marisol's father, a Sicilian prince, who had immediately invited the young traveller to his *palazzo* in Via Maqueda and, by extension, to his daughter's ball. 'She will practise her English on you,' he told Edward. 'Be warned.' Edward had been expecting a child. He had not been prepared for a young woman of great beauty and an almost overwhelming enthusiasm for life and, as they became acquainted with each other, for Edward. At the ball they had danced together and he realised as he slipped his arm around her waist and felt her hand on his shoulder that she was the first woman he had touched since Settie's death. The realisation left him shaken and confused. In the days following the ball, as he dined with the family and she acted as interpreter and guide for him, her passion for life overriding all notions of etiquette, the confusion gave way to fascination, and then to love. He had thought he could never love another woman after Settie but he discovered, to his shame, that he had been wrong. What he felt for Marisol was different from what he had felt for Settie, but in degree not kind. She touched the same place in his heart, it seemed to him, and if his heart had been free of guilt and self-accusation, as it would never be, Marisol would have filled it as completely as Settie had done. This realisation caused him both great pain and great joy, and he could share the former with no one, except perhaps George, his valet.

George had been the only person whose presence he could tolerate in the months following Settie's death. The fact that he knew, or had intuited, that Settie was dead, in some way at his master's hand, might have made his presence intolerable, and there were days when even the sight of the valet as he laid the table or poured coffee into the single cup distressed Edward so deeply, so powerful was the memory evoked, that he would have dismissed him on the spot, as he had dismissed his housekeeper. But common sense, or what was left of it, and affection, and the feeling that George was the only bond he had left with the life he had lived before, with *her*, dissuaded him.

George seemed to understand this, and his attention to Edward's needs was infused with care and a touching barely concealed anxiety that filled, and even helped to heal a little, his master's heart. It was George who had first said that Edward should try to leave the house, George who suggested he respond to those friends of his who had called and left their cards and been sent away unsatisfied. It was George who had talked about travel and the benefits of travel. 'A change of scenery,' he had said, and Edward, against his strongest instinct, which was for self-flagellation, had begun to wonder if the young man might be right. The alternative, he told himself, was to end it here, and it was true that he had given that alternative much thought. Some mornings he woke after hours of fitful sleep with the image of Settie so powerfully in his head that he was afraid to open his eyes, afraid that he would find her there before him. Other days her presence jerked him from sleep, his face wet with tears, crying out that he was sorry, begging her forgiveness, and George would be there at the door, and would rush over and put a hand on his shoulder to calm him. At times like these his only hope was to end it all. It had become a sort of beacon for him, offering a glimpse of light when all else was dark. One thought, however, had always stopped him. The thought that he had not yet suffered enough. He had not earned the right to die.

But the seed George had planted slowly began to germinate as the days, and then weeks, went by and Edward was still alive. He thought of Africa, of Rickman's tales of adventure, of the dark continent and how it might swallow him up. He thought of the new world that Daniel Giles had left behind him, and what it offered, the romance of the West, the lure of gold. He thought of Greece and Plato, of Italy and Catullus. He had dreamed of Italy as a boy, of the Colosseum and the temples in the south, of Aeneas and the she-wolf nurturing the abandoned twins, of leaning towers and smoking volcanoes. 'Would you like to accompany me to Italy, George?' he had said one evening. 'I certainly would, sir,' George had said, and the decision had been made.

It had taken them three months to reach Sicily, and Palermo. They had travelled through France and Switzerland and northern and central Italy by train, and boat, and coach. They had crossed the Alps on horseback and camped in the shadow of the Matterhorn, and seen the monuments Edward had dreamed of, and other sites he had never imagined. They had eaten new dishes, and drunk new wines. They had become friends in a way that would have been inconceivable in London, so that people who met them as they travelled sometimes mistook George for the master and Edward for the servant, which amused them both. 'We are like Achilles and Patroclus,' Edward had said, 'or Alexander and Hephaestion,' and George had nodded, not understanding but clearly gratified. One evening in Verona, after a fit of weeping that arrived as unexpectedly as a summer storm, Edward had recounted the night of Settie's death, and George had listened without speaking until

Edward had finished, and then said it was time they both had some rest, and had lain down beside Edward until he was asleep. No further mention was made of it, neither the following day nor later, but it comforted Edward to know that his secret had finally been shared. His load had been lightened. As they continued their journey south, the days grew longer and the sunlight more intense, and he felt the first stirring in his heart of hope.

The courtship of Marisol had been swift, conducted with the approval of her father, a fervent Anglophile whose vineyards produced Marsala for export to England and whose daughter, after the death of her mother, had been brought up by Concetta, her wet nurse, and a series of English governesses. 'We are island people,' he said more than once to Edward and Edward had concurred.

Marisol had been equally keen. 'You are my door to the world,' she told him. 'Without you, I shall live and die here. I shall become a *zitella* – do you like that word? It means old maid.'

He took her hand. 'You will never be a *zitella*,' he said, 'I won't allow it,' and she laughed at his pronunciation of the word.

'I see that I shall have to be a very severe teacher with you,' she said, 'if you are to learn Italian.'

'I promise you that I shall be the most attentive and obedient of pupils,' he had said, and she had rapped his knuckles gently with her fan to remind him of his place.

They had been married in the family's private chapel and Edward had learned the words that were necessary, and had kissed her on the lips for the first time. Their first night they spent in her father's *palazzo*, their second on the steamship that carried them to Marseille. Three days later, they were on the train for Paris. Marisol's trousseau, packed into a number of substantial wooden crates, travelled separately. She was accompanied by her maid Rosaria, a girl her age, the daughter of a tenant on her father's land, who had grown up with her and without whom she had refused to move. 'You have your George and I have mine,' she had said. 'Everyone needs a George,' she had added, looking across at the blushing valet, and Edward had immediately concurred.

Edward and Marisol watched as the gardener and his sons transferred the eight trees to the terracotta pots inside the orangery.

'And now I am at home,' she said. She took his hand and squeezed it.

The gardener looked at them and smiled. 'These will soon be fruiting,' he said. 'I'll wager that you will have oranges for Christmas. It's a wonder they're so strong and healthy after the journey.'

'They are from my father's land,' she said. 'All of his trees are strong.'

'I'm sure they are, milady,' the gardener said, smiling more broadly. He looked at Edward. 'Well, sir, I shall be off.' He gestured to his sons. 'Come on, lads, time to go.'

'See you tomorrow, Hopkins,' said Edward. 'We have work to do elsewhere. I was thinking of a pond, perhaps, with water lilies.'

'As you wish, sir.'

When the men had gone, Marisol turned to Edward and hugged him around the waist until he cried out in simulated pain. 'You're squeezing the life out of me,' he protested.

'A pond!' she exclaimed. 'And flower beds, we must have acres of flower beds. We shall fill the house with flowers, Edward.'

He stiffened, against his will, and she let him go at once.

'I've done something wrong, haven't I?'

He took her into his arms and kissed her. 'Don't be silly. Of course you haven't.'

'Because you would tell me, wouldn't you, if I did?'

'Certainly I would.'

'Because we must have no secrets, you and I.'

He kissed her again. 'No secrets,' he said.

Later that day, driven by a sudden need to be with her, he walked into the small room Marisol had chosen for herself, decorated in yellow, the wallpaper a maze of leafy tendrils and improbable blooms, the furniture handpicked at Liberty during her first week in the city, a room that caught more light than any other in the house and seemed to hold it longer. She was sitting on a small rosewood nursing chair upholstered in amber silk that she had brought from home, and that had belonged to her mother, with Rosaria curled at her feet. The two of them were so absorbed in their conversation, not a word of which he could understand, that they only became aware of his presence when he coughed.

'What are you two talking about?' he said cheerfully.

'Families,' said Marisol.

'Homesick?'

'Not those families, silly.' She touched her stomach, and he was taken back so abruptly, so mercilessly to the cottage and to Settie making that same gesture that his vision clouded with sudden tears. His head swam. He thought he would faint. He rested his shoulder against the doorframe, praying that she would not notice. 'The families we plan to have,' she continued, with a smile.

Chapter Ten

'How strange it is that you have no friends in London, Edward.'

Marisol and Edward were sitting together in the breakfast room, overlooking the lawn, some newly prepared beds waiting to be filled with flowering shrubs and, at the far end of it, the orangery and patio. They had finished eating, Edward was folding his copy of *The Times* into four, and they were about to leave the table, Edward to go to his study and Marisol to her favourite room, when Marisol said these words. 'You're such an amicable person,' she added, when no answer was offered. 'And yet no one calls, no one visits.'

'I want to be able to devote all my time to you,' he said.

She smiled. 'You are very sweet to me, my dear. You always are. But I wonder if you are as sweet to others.' She was teasing him, he knew that, but that knowledge provided no escape from her questions, which, despite their apparent playfulness, required an answer. He knew Marisol well enough by now to understand when she was determined, and this was one of those occasions.

'I try my best,' he said. He stood up. 'Give me time. Not everyone knows I have returned to London and those who do know will also know that I have brought home my new bride and may wish to leave me in peace in order to allow me to enjoy your company undisturbed.'

'I should like to become acquainted with your friends,' she said firmly. 'You were at Cambridge. Surely you knew people there who are now in London.'

'Nobody I wish to see,' he said.

'Well, I should like you to find someone you do wish to see and then present him to me, or I shall begin to think you are ashamed of me.'

'Nothing could be further from the truth,' he said.

He found George cleaning his shoes in the scullery. He closed the door behind him. 'Has anyone looked for me since we came back?'

George raised his head from his work. 'I believe your return has been noted, sir,' he said.

Edward sighed, exasperated. 'For God's sake, George, a simple question requires a simple answer. I thought we understood each other by now.'

'I understand you perfectly, sir.'

'And that is why you're playing the offended maiden, is it? Because you understand me? Surely we can be honest when we are alone, at least.'

George grinned. 'If I am to be honest, sir, I don't think I would allow another man in the kingdom to call me a maiden. Offended or otherwise.'

Edward laughed. 'Thank you for that. Now perhaps you could tell me exactly who has noted my return, as you say.'

'Cards have been left,' said George. 'I have brought them to you.'

'And I have ignored them.'

'Yes, sir.'

'And who has left these cards that I have so rudely ignored?'

'Several people, sir. Some of them known to me, some not.'

'Well, perhaps we can begin with those who are known to you,

George,' Edward said, patiently pulling a stool out from beneath the table and sitting down.

'Your American friend,' said George. 'He has called three times.'

'Daniel Giles?'

'That's him, sir. A tall gentleman.'

'You didn't tell me.'

'You gave me specific instructions not to, sir. "I'm not at home to anyone and I don't want to know who calls, whoever it is,"' he quoted. 'Those were your precise words.'

Edward nodded. 'I suppose they were. Who else?'

'A Dr Bell. I seem to remember him from John Street, although I don't recollect his ever entering.'

'Just as well. *Persona non grata* in this house and, I imagine, many others.' Edward shook his head. The thought of the man pained him, filled him with an inchoate desire for revenge he did not wish to nurture. 'Who else?'

'Men without cards, sir. Rough types.'

'Rough types?'

'It's not for me to say, sir, but I think they may have been connected with your former mistress.' He lowered his voice for the last two words. 'One of them had a pair of dogs I would put money on in the right circumstances. Savage-looking beasts, they were.'

Edward said nothing for a few moments, then stood up. 'The next time Giles comes to the house, if he ever does come after I have so rudely ignored him, let him in. I should like to see him, and I think his company would also please my wife.' He paused by the door. 'She thinks I have no friends, and that makes her wonder what kind of man I am. I should not like her to think any worse of me than is necessary.'

'I have it on good authority that she thinks very highly of you indeed,' said George, vigorously brushing the toe of one of Edward's boots.

'And which authority would that be?' said Edward, amused.

'Rosaria, sir.'

'You have been gossiping with Rosaria? I didn't realise you had picked up so much Italian,' said Edward.

'Oh, we manage, sir,' said George, with another grin. 'Needs must, you know.'

That night, Edward was woken by what sounded like a baby crying. It seemed to be in the house, but that, he knew, was impossible. None of the staff had a child; he would never have allowed it. The crying was low, insistent, fretful, the type of lament his nanny used to condemn as grizzling. It must be coming from a neighbour's house, he decided, although the nearest house was a good fifty yards away from his and he had seen no sign of children there. Sound travels further at night, he told himself, but he wasn't convinced. The crying continued, like a wilful demand for his attention, until he thought he would go mad. He was anxious, he knew that. He had been anxious since he had seen Marisol and Rosaria chattering together the previous day and discovered that they had been talking about families. He couldn't erase from his mind the image of Marisol touching her stomach. She was so like Settie at times, the same slim figure, the same full lips and curtain of gleaming hair, and then, a moment later, she was utterly different, a child, both playful and demanding, and that was what had made him love her, that she was both like and not like Settie, as though her naivety and almost comical enthusiasm were an antidote to the rest. How could she become a mother? The thought was inconceivable. Was Rosaria encouraging her? The words of George, or what they suggested, came back to him. Perhaps Rosaria would be a mother first.

And then, as if it had never been, the crying stopped.

*

The following morning he told her that he was going into town and would be dropping in on his club. It was the first time he had left the house without her, other than to walk around the neighbourhood or venture onto the Heath and, even then, she tended to accompany him if the weather permitted. She had been warned about the vagaries of the English climate by several of her governesses, but was not prepared for driving rain and fog combined. On the two or three occasions he had left the house in these conditions, driven by an inner anguish only movement could quell, she had told him that he must be mad and he had ruefully admitted that she was probably right, had turned up the collar of his greatcoat and had set out, teeth gritted, head down, to walk the empty streets.

This morning, though, was a bright, crisp morning in early November. She watched as George helped Edward on with his coat, passed him his scarf, not saying a word until he was standing on the doorstep, about to put on his hat. 'Haven't you forgotten something?' she said.

'I don't think so,' he replied, but there was a teasing edge to his voice. 'Unless you're referring to the kiss I am about to give you.'

She smiled. '*Bravo*,' she said. She ran across the hall and threw her arms around his neck. They kissed.

'May I go now?' he said.

'Are you off to find some friends for me to meet?'

'That is my intention, yes.'

'In that case, you have my permission.'

'You're very gracious.'

They kissed again. He was turning to leave, when she caught his arm. Her expression had changed, darkened. 'Did you hear it?' she said.

'Hear what?'

'During the night. A child.'

'No,' he said.

'It was crying, Edward. It was so sad. All I wanted to do was hold it and make the crying stop.'

'There is no child here.'

'I know that. It must belong to someone though.' Shivering, she pulled her shawl around her shoulders and looked past him towards the upper storeys of the nearest house, visible beyond their garden wall. 'It sounded so close. I can't believe you didn't hear it.'

He was silent.

'Oh well,' she said. 'Perhaps it was my imagination.' She paused, looked at him closely. 'I have been thinking such a lot about babies recently. I expect that was it.'

He nodded and caressed her cheek with the back of his hand before slipping on his gloves. 'I expect it was,' he said.

Almost two years had passed since his last visit to the club, but it might have been yesterday. The same doorman took his coat and hat, asked him how he was, and informed him that Mr Poynter was in his usual small room near the dining room, reading the day's newspapers and taking coffee. Edward climbed the stairs and found his old friend half asleep, a copy of *The Times* sliding off his lap. Standing by the door, he coughed gently until Poynter opened his eyes.

'My God,' he said. 'A ghost.'

'On the contrary,' said Edward, walking over to shake the man's hand. 'I am solid flesh and bone.'

'And a married man, by all accounts.'

'You've heard?' Edward sat down. 'Yes, I found a hidden treasure in Sicily and brought her home. I am the happiest man in the world. I believe that's the appropriate expression in these cases.'

Poynter touched his knee, a look of sudden earnestness on his face. 'You have no idea how much pleasure it gives me to hear you say that, my dear boy.'

Neither man spoke for a moment.

'I was wondering if you'd seen Daniel Giles at the club recently,' said Edward eventually.

'Our young American friend? Why yes, if I'm not mistaken he dined here only last week. He is still in London, still on his father's business. He has frequently asked about you, you'll be pleased to hear.'

'I certainly am. I've been much occupied these past two months, since our arrival. Setting up home with a new wife is an arduous affair, I've discovered. But I should very much like to see him.'

'Other people have asked about you as well, you know.'

'Really? Who?'

'Any number of people.' Poynter paused. 'Bell, for one.'

'Oh really? I must admit that I have no great desire to see Bell.'

'I quite understand,' said Poynter.

'Well,' said Edward, standing up. 'I shall be getting off now. But do tell Giles that I have asked after him.'

'You can rely on me.'

'I have been rustling up some friends for you,' he told Marisol later that day. He had walked much of the way home, skirting the Regent's Park, through Camden and Kentish Town, until he reached the edge of the Heath. He had needed to walk, to clear his head. But the refrain would not be silenced. *She heard it too* accompanied every step he took, was taken up by the wheels of cabs as they passed, and reverberated in the click of iron on stone as horses drew their loads, and in the cries of vendors that transported him back, as they always did, to that night outside the music hall. Two years have passed, he thought, two years since I first saw Settie and was given a nosegay, and I am no nearer to forgiving myself. He noticed a man with a pair of dogs on a single leash walking down from Parliament Hill and remembered what George had told him, rough types he had said, and from that point on he became convinced that he was being followed. His walking speed increased and, with it, the rhythm of the words that wouldn't be hushed. *She heard it too.* And now she was standing in front of him and he knew that without her he would die. You are my second chance, he thought.

'I don't know what that means, Edward. I hope it's something pleasant.'

He nodded. 'It means we shall be having visitors, or so I hope.'

She clapped her hands in that childlike way he loved. 'How exciting!' she said. 'I shall bake cakes for them, if the cook will let me.' She lowered her voice. 'She refuses to trust me with knives,' she said in a conspiratorial tone. 'She thinks I might attack her with my stiletto.'

'Do you have a stiletto?' he said, uncertain.

'Of course I do,' she said. 'I'm Sicilian. All Sicilians have stilettos.' She smiled. 'I thought you knew.'

That night, Edward was woken by Marisol shaking his shoulder. 'Hush,' she said, before he could speak. He lay there in the moonlight, holding his breath, her hair in his face as she hung over him. 'You hear it,' she said, her voice urgent, edged with fear. He listened for the crying of the night before, but it was hard to distinguish anything above the howl of the wind. After a moment he heard what might have been a fretful child but the noise was so far away that it was hard to tell. He felt a wave of relief. She must have been dreaming, he thought. Perhaps she heard nothing after all. Perhaps there was nothing to be heard. She shook his shoulder a second time. 'There it is,' she said. 'Can you hear it now?'

This time he heard what she had heard. A sound like footsteps in the corridor, but not exactly footsteps, or not the footsteps of a man; a sort of shuffling noise as though small human feet swaddled in cloth were feeling their way towards the bedroom.

Edward rose from the bed and crossed the room. 'Don't leave me,' hissed Marisol, but he turned and put a finger to his lips, then gestured to her to lie back, be calm. She shook her head, her eyes wide open with fear, her hands pressed against her mouth to stifle a cry. He approached the door and paused, his hand on the knob. The shuffling in the corridor came to a halt as though whoever was moving there had also stopped to listen. As slowly and silently as he could, Edward turned the knob and opened the door.

The corridor was empty, but a wave of ice-cold air struck him as he left the room. The window at the far end of the corridor had been blown wide open by the wind. The floor of the corridor, from the window to their bedroom door, was strewn with the shrivelled petals of winter flowers.

Chapter Eleven

The following week, Edward was reading in his study, when he heard the doorbell ring. A few moments later, George appeared at the study door. 'Mr Daniel Giles to see you, sir.'

'Show him in, George,' said Edward. He put down his reading and waited, surprised to feel his heart beat more rapidly in his chest. George disappeared, footsteps were heard crossing the hall and the visitor was ushered in. Edward noticed George's raised eyebrow as he closed the door behind him and left the two men alone.

Daniel strode towards him, beaming with pleasure, his hand held out. 'My dear man,' he said. Edward, as unexpectedly soothed by his presence as he had been troubled by the anticipation of it, stood up and grasped his friend's hand.

'How good it is to see you,' he said. He held the hand longer than was necessary, looked into Daniel's eyes for a hint of what their conversation might bring. Daniel met his gaze.

'You look well,' he said. 'I was anxious for you, having heard of your return from Italy and then, well, nothing at all. Nothing but club gossip of the worst kind.'

'I expect Bell was behind that,' said Edward.

Daniel smiled. 'Yes. But he was not alone. When someone disappears from one week to the next, without a word, people are bound to talk. And people have such vivid imaginations. Several people thought you had left for Africa in search of an *obambo*.'

'Including Rickman himself, I imagine.'

'You haven't heard? Rickman has been otherwise engaged for some six months now.'

'Really?'

'He was foolish enough to allow himself to be blackmailed by a stable boy and then to speak to an acquaintance of his at Scotland Yard, by all accounts a fellow pederast, in an attempt to have the boy dissuaded. He hoped for a sort of solidarity among thieves, so to speak, but was soon disabused of that hope. The acquaintance decided that his own career and reputation were worth more than those of Rickman and promptly had Rickman arrested for buggery. He is now believed to be picking oakum in Newgate.'

'Oh dear,' said Edward. 'That seems rather harsh.'

'Other misdemeanours pale in comparison, I've heard people say,' said Daniel. 'Only Poynter has a good word to say about him.'

'Other misdemeanours?'

'We have all made mistakes,' said Daniel. He was about to say more when a woman's voice interrupted him.

'Good morning, Edward, my dear. I see you have a friend.'

Both men turned to the door.

'Marisol.' Edward sprang to his feet and took both his wife's hands in his. 'Allow me to introduce you to my very good friend, Mr Daniel Giles.'

Daniel clicked his heels and gave a little bow. 'How do you do?'

She gave him her hand. 'How do you do, Mr Giles. I would love to say that my husband has told me all about you but he has been unnaturally secretive about his London friends. I was beginning to wonder if he had committed some awful unspeakable crime and was now beyond the pale. That is the expression, isn't it?' she said, turning to Edward.

'It certainly is, my dear.' He smiled. 'Your English is as

impeccable as ever.' He turned to Daniel. 'My wife comes from Sicily. She is a princess.'

'You do that island, and your rank, great credit,' said Daniel, his eyes moving over her and then to Edward. 'I had heard that you were married, but no one had prepared me for such a magnificent apparition as your wife. You have all my congratulations.'

'You're American,' she said.

He nodded. 'A free citizen,' he said. 'A citizen of the world.'

She took his arm then turned to Edward. 'I should like to show your free citizen friend my orange trees.'

'As you wish. May I come with you?'

She thought about this for a moment and then, to his surprise, shook her head. 'No, my dear, I'd prefer to have him to myself for a little while. I intend to become better acquainted with him before he leaves. You have so few guests, Edward, I may not be given another chance. And I would like to ask him some rather impertinent questions.' She smiled at Daniel. 'Don't be shocked. I see my husband disapproves, but we are allowed to take these liberties as foreigners, don't you think? And I am also a princess,' she added, with a sardonic nod at Edward, speechless by his desk.

Daniel let himself be led from the study, throwing an amused, slightly mystified glance over his shoulder towards Edward as they left.

'What did she want to know? She refused to tell me however hard I insisted. I tried to coax her, I played the aggrieved husband, I even risked belligerence. Nothing. You'll have realised yourself, I imagine, that she is a born tease. It is one of her many talents.'

Edward and Daniel were sitting together at the club a few days later. Edward had passed those days in a state of anxious tension he had done his best to conceal from Marisol. He was not entirely sure that he had succeeded, and this only increased his anxiety.

If she genuinely thought he had something to conceal she would never be at peace, and neither would he. His tone with Daniel was deliberately light-hearted, and would remain so until he had decided how much he was prepared to share with the other man, and how much the other man already knew.

'She is an extraordinary woman. A natural princess, regardless of her rank. I hope you realise how fortunate you are.'

'I do.' He paused. 'So what did she want to know?'

Daniel shook his head. 'She told me about her father, how much he had wanted her to be independent, how happy he was that you should have arrived at just the right moment. The perfect English gentleman, he called you. She asked me about me and my business here in London, about my father. I answered her questions as completely as I could. I think you may have a new recruit to the cause of racial harmony in your family.' He tapped Edward's knee. 'You have nothing to worry about, believe me. The only thing she said that might have disturbed you if you had been there with us was that she would like to know your father. She said that your dislike of him was understandable, but unnatural. She sees you as lonely, and my impression was that it pains her. No family, no friends. She said that she wasn't sure that she would always be enough for you; she worried that you would lose interest in her and be left with nothing. I think she was telling the truth when she said how concerned she had been that you might have no friends.' He smiled. 'She told me several times how relieved she was to have met me.'

'She said a great deal, it seems.'

'I suppose she did.'

'And what did you say? When she asked you about me.'

'She didn't ask about you,' said Daniel. 'Not directly.' He paused. 'But she became very serious at one point. To be perfectly honest, she scared me a little. We were in the orangery and she was talking about the trees, about the risk of bringing them to England, how afraid she had been that they might die. They are like my children, she said, and then she looked almost as if she were about to cry.' He hesitated for a moment. 'And then she said that she would like to give you a child.'

'She is a child,' said Edward.

Daniel shook his head. 'You do her wrong, Edward. She is no child.' He paused again. 'She wanted to know what I thought, if I thought you would want her child. I was shocked, I admit it. The question was so unexpected, and so unsuitable, coming from a woman I barely knew. I didn't know what to say. I said that any man would be happy to have a child with her, and then felt that I had overstepped the mark, that she might think I was making love to her. That was not my intention, Edward. I would never do that.'

'She wants a child?'

'Yes. I think you can safely deduce that.'

'I see.'

Daniel was clearly waiting to see what else Edward might say, but Edward remained silent. The only thought in his head was that his last few nights had been interrupted by the incessant crying of a child he could not locate, that belonged to none of the neighbouring houses as far as George could ascertain. Had Marisol heard it too, as she had that first night? He hadn't dared ask. The muffled footsteps outside their door had not returned or, if they had, he had slept through them, but twice the corridor window had blown open during the night, despite its being shuttered and closed with care the previous evening; twice the air had been frigid and the floor of the corridor strewn with withered petals. On both days, the morning after, the upper floors of the house were filled with an inexplicable scent of flowers that only Edward, as far as he knew, could distinguish. She has come back, he thought. She has come back to haunt me. But the idea was too absurd to be considered.

He had asked George in as offhand a manner as he could manage if any part of the house had a different odour from usual and George had looked at him, bemused, and shaken his head. I can set traps, he had said, assuming rats, but Edward had dismissed that idea. He had said nothing to Marisol; once again he hadn't dared ask. If her answer had been yes, she would have wanted to know more. He would have had to lie to her and that, while knowing that his silence was also a sort of lie, was something he could not bring himself to do.

'You have told me nothing about your travels,' said Daniel finally.

Edward shook his head, as if to free himself physically of his thoughts.

'I set off not knowing where I would go,' he said. 'I knew that I had to go, and that was all.'

'Edward?'

'Yes, my dear?'

They were sitting together in the morning room. Marisol put down her book. 'I want you to do something for me.'

'Anything, my dear,' he said, not looking up from his newspaper. 'You only have to ask.'

'I should like you to write to my father and ask him to send me Concetta.'

'Concetta?' He had heard the name before, but couldn't recall from whom.

'Concetta was my wet nurse.'

'But why would you need a wet nurse?' he said, without thinking.

'I don't,' she said. 'I need Concetta.'

'I don't understand.'

'Concetta brought me up. She was with me from the moment of my birth. My mother was busy with my father's affairs and then she died. I was raised by Concetta and by my governesses. She is like a mother to me, and I shall need her.'

'But you have Rosaria,' he said, stubbornly refusing to understand.

'Rosaria is a sister, if you wish, but not a mother. She has no experience of babies.'

'You mean——?'

Marisol stood up and walked across the room until she was standing in front of his armchair. There was something unruly about her and something that recalled a supplicant. How beautiful you are, he thought. Daniel was right. How fortunate I am to have you. As rapidly as the image of Settie rose he tamped it down. He was silent, waiting for his wife to speak, knowing already what she would say. She gave an anxious smile and placed her hand on her stomach. 'I mean that I shall be having a child,' she said. 'Our child.'

He stood up and embraced her.

'You are happy?' she said.

'I have never been happier,' he said.

He wrote that day to his father-in-law. 'It will be better if it comes from you,' she said. 'I know the way my father thinks. I shall write a separate letter to Concetta. She will be afraid of the journey, I know, but I shall reassure her.' She smiled. 'She would do anything for me. It broke her heart when I came away with you, you know.'

'Why did I never meet her?'

'That was her choice. After my birthday she decided to move to one of our estates in the country. Perhaps she thought she would fall in love with one of the people working there and make a new life for herself.'

'And if she has?'

Marisol shook her head. 'She will come. She promised me that all I had to do was ask her.'

Later that day, Edward went to look for Marisol. She was alone in the orangery, standing in the shadows between two trees.

'Hopkins was right. They will soon bear fruit,' she said.

'I couldn't find you,' he said.

'I am warm here,' she said. She pulled her shawl more closely around her shoulders. 'I always knew that winters in England were cold – my governesses warned me – but I had imagined something else.' She laughed. 'Something less cold and dark than this.' She took his arm. 'It is barely afternoon and already the sun has abandoned us.'

'Let me take you back to the house. There will be a fire, and tea.'

'Oh yes,' she said. 'Tea.'

They were walking across the lawn when he paused. 'You are homesick today,' he said.

She took his face in her hands and kissed his lips. 'As long as I have you,' she said, 'I shall not be homesick. You are my home. Besides, we are not alone. We shall never be alone again.' Stepping back a little, she stroked his cheek. Her face took on a pensive look. 'I will admit though, Edward, that I would be even happier than I am already if I had some friends in my position, some other young women like myself. If only you had a sister,' she said, not noticing the shadow cross his face. He had never talked to her about his sister and the circumstances of his mother's death. 'But the only friend you have introduced me to is a bachelor. How strange you English are. Do you know no married men at all?'

He shook his head. 'I don't believe I do, my dear. All of my few acquaintances are confirmed bachelors.'

'In that case I shall have to be satisfied with you and Rosaria.' She thought for a moment. 'Perhaps we should look for the child we have heard crying. He must have a mother, all children do. They must live near here somewhere. Would they be glad of our company, do you think, as I would be of theirs?'

'Are you scared?' he said suddenly. He had not known he was about to say this until the words were spoken.

She started to walk ahead, towards the house; he caught up with her, took her elbow in his hand. She stopped and turned her head to look at him.

'Of course I am scared,' she said.

That evening, as though she had played through their conversation in her mind, she asked him about his mother.

'I barely remember her. I think if I had seen her in her final hours I would at least have had a face to hold in my heart, but my father kept me from her. I heard her scream. She called my name. I shall never forget it.'

'And that is why you hate your father,' she said.

'I don't hate my father, although I used to think I did. I'm sure that he hates me. In either case, we're better apart.'

'What was your mother like? I mean, was she beautiful?'

He shook his head. 'I have no idea. I wish I did. I imagine she must have been. My father is a collector of trophies. He would never have chosen a woman who wasn't worthy of the world's attention.'

'How did she die?'

When he told her, she took his hand in silent apology. 'How sad it is to have lost her,' she said. 'To have lost her like that. Sometimes, I think, it is as though people have never been, unless they leave something. Do you have anything of hers? Anything she owned, some possession to remember her by?'

He shook his head and then nodded. 'Yes,' he said. 'I have a ring that belonged to her.'

'May I see it?'

He went to his study and took the ring from his desk. It was the first time he had looked at it since the night Settie died. Holding it in his hand, it seemed still to contain her warmth. I don't know if I can do this, he thought, but he closed his hand around the ring and carried it across the hall and into the sitting room as though he had no will left to do otherwise, as though possessed. Falling to his knees beside her, with the heat of the fire on his face, he unfolded his fist and held out the ring, the two rubies glinting like small dark stars in the flickering light.

'Give me your hand,' he said. 'This ring is yours.'

That night, Edward was woken by the cry of a seagull, so loud it seemed to be in the room with them. He opened his eyes. The window shutters had been left open and the curtains drawn back because Marisol hated to wake up in the dark, and the room was bathed in moonlight. He raised his head a little to see if Marisol had been disturbed, but she was fast asleep, her lips slightly parted, her breathing a soft purr. Her loose hair covered the pillowcase, a black so dense it seemed to contain its own source of light rather than merely reflecting the light of the moon. When the room became suddenly dim, he thought a cloud must have passed before the moon, but then he heard something whipping against the glass of the window. He turned his head and saw the seagull, barely balanced on the sill, beating its wings for balance, its beak wide open as if it sought purchase on something solid. It squealed a second time and then seemed to fall away but before it fell it left something on the sill. Edward lay there, rigid with shock, as the spread wings of the bird swooped across the window a final time, its head turned towards the room, its beak splayed wide, and then flew off. When his breathing calmed, he rose from the bed and crossed to the window, lifting the lower section as carefully and silently as he could, shivering as the cold air entered the room and touched the bare skin of his face and arms.

On the sill was a piece of bleached white bone, the length of a finger, with a thread of bloodless flesh attached to it. Suppressing a shudder that had nothing to do with the cold, he pushed it away and closed the window.

Chapter Twelve

Concetta arrived two months after Edward's letter had been dispatched, on a cold afternoon in February. Edward and Marisol went to Charing Cross Station to meet her. Edward had been expecting, for no good reason other than preconceived notions of Italian wet nurses, a small, robust woman dressed in black, and was startled when Marisol shrieked in his ear with joy, waved both arms in the air, picked up her skirts and ran down the busy platform with no regard for others until she came to a halt beside a tall, imperious character in an elaborately tailored dark-green cloak with matching hat and furled umbrella, busily giving orders in Italian to a porter who clearly had no idea what she wanted. Marisol hugged the woman, laughing and crying at the same time. The woman eased her away and looked her up and down, her eyes lingering on the lower stomach, although there was still no sign of the incipient child. When Edward reached them, Marisol had already told the porter to take the bags and small trunk from the platform to the waiting cab and was busily interrogating Concetta on her journey. Concetta's eyes were moist with the emotion of seeing her young charge, now a married woman, and so far away from home, or so Edward imagined. He had been studying Italian since their arrival in London the previous year, with Marisol as his relentless, painstaking and often severe tutor, and prided himself on the rapidity of his learning. He put into practice what he knew on Rosaria sometimes, to her amusement, and he suspected from remarks that George had made that he was not the only person in the house to be doing so. But listening to the two women now, as they made their way across the teeming station to where their cab was waiting for them, his heart sank. He might have caught one word in five, or possibly four, but even that was uncertain. He would return to his copy of Verga's short stories, a wedding present from his father-in-law, with increased dedication, he decided.

The two months before Concetta's arrival had passed quietly, in an odd state of suspension, as though the life of the house revolved around the promise of what was to come and had no other business. The orange trees had borne their fruit. Christmas had come and gone without much fanfare; Marisol had insisted they celebrate the Epiphany, and Edward had been content to do so. Daniel Giles had become a regular visitor to the house and the friendship established with Edward had deepened and expanded to include Marisol, whose only regret, she told him, was that she had no suitable friend to whom he might be introduced. 'You would be an ideal husband,' she said, then looked at Edward, 'although not quite as ideal as you, my dear.' Only once, when Marisol was absent, did Daniel refer to Edward's previous life, obliquely, by saying that no other woman would have been as perfect a companion as Marisol, however much he might have thought so. He had seen Edward pale with shock and immediately apologised, but Edward had wondered, as he had so frequently in the past, how much was known about Settie's death. Assuming Bell knew the truth, had the man been foolish, or brutal, enough to talk about it with others, an anecdote to be shared in Edward's absence, as Rickman's disgrace had become, a moral tale of the most salacious kind? On another occasion, after a second bottle of claret had been drunk, he had been on the point of telling Daniel about the crying and the noises in the corridor, about the petals blown in through the open window, if for no other reason than to remind himself how ridiculous it had been of him to give such nonsense weight. But he could not be sure of that. At other times he felt that whatever force lay behind the crying, and the scent, and the looming sense of a presence that could not be borne, was biding its time, was waiting in abeyance for the right moment to make itself heard. The house was being lulled into a state of somnolence that only he did not deserve, and he feared that what came when the calm was interrupted would be all the more terrible for it. There was intention behind the silence, he thought, and this scared him more than anything.

He would have spoken about even this to Daniel if he had not been put off by the suspicion that his friend might think him sane and take the stories seriously. He thought back to their first few meetings, to Rickman's absurd yarns about *obambos*, to the music hall and the séance, to the reckless stupidity of that sordid underworld, to Daniel's credulity; but inevitably these thoughts brought with them memories of Settie, and were pushed aside.

Concetta busied herself with the organisation of the household from the day of her arrival. The room they had chosen as the nursery was summarily dismissed as it faced north-east. 'Children need warmth and light,' she informed them, Marisol acting as her interpreter. She said this with a contemptuous glance towards the window, as though the weather had refused to cooperate. What remained of February was cold, with flurries of snow and freezing fog, and the month of March offered days that were only slightly warmer. 'The nights are too long here,' she announced one morning. 'Why did no one think to warn me?' Marisol sighed and nodded and translated what she had said, and Edward wished for everyone's sake that he could somehow increase the length of English days, and enhance the feeble, utterly inadequate heat of the

English sun, which was as pale as his own English skin, according to Concetta, who examined him with the same dissatisfaction she had directed at the original choice of nursery. The room she chose for the child was next door to their bedroom, and the one beyond it she elected as her own. She installed her rosewood nursing chair and arranged her needlework materials on a small table at its side. When Marisol caught Edward examining the chair with a bemused expression on his face, she shook her head and mouthed to him not to worry. She covered her left breast with a hand and then tapped herself, to say that she would be feeding her child. The nursery itself had a cot, chosen by Marisol, with Concetta's guidance, at Liberty, her favourite shop, and an armchair placed to catch the light from the window, where Marisol had decided she would sit while the baby slept. A second nursing chair was purchased and, at Edward's insistence, a rocking horse. The cot, of painted wood, was installed in the room between the fireplace and the window, in a corner without draughts, because, Concetta insisted, even the smallest draught could kill a newborn child in a matter of hours. Left alone in the nursery, Edward rested his hands on the upper edge of the cot and looked down into it, imagining his own child lying there, wanted and loved and looking up at him, its plump arms raised in recognition. He ran his fingers across the bars of wood that made up the side of the cot. How like a cage it was, he thought, and shivered.

Leaving the room, he found Marisol in the corridor. She seemed to have been waiting for him. They were hardly ever alone these days; either Concetta or Rosaria seemed always to be with her, as though she had withdrawn, or been drawn back, into the life she had known before they met. Sometimes he felt uncomfortable with her, a stranger almost. Now that the two of them were alone in the corridor, she took his hand, and pressed it to her stomach, and the gesture seemed almost illicit, exciting. 'Can you feel it?' she said.

He nodded, the thrill of the barely perceptible movement coursing up his arm. 'I hate saying *it* but I don't know what else to call it,' she said, with a nervous laugh. 'He. She. I suppose you want a son. Most men do.'

'I want what you want,' he said. 'It makes no difference to me whether I have a son or a daughter, just so long as it is ours.'

She looked behind her, as if afraid she might be overheard. 'Sometimes,' she said, her voice low, 'I have the strangest sensation. It's as though there might be two of them inside me. I don't know how to explain it.'

'Twins?'

She nodded. 'Yes,' she said slowly, unconvinced. 'I suppose that's what I mean.'

Later that day he found her with Concetta and Rosaria, the three of them sitting together in Marisol's sitting room, singing a song he had never heard. When they had finished, he asked Marisol what the song was.

'It's a song to send children to sleep,' she said. 'A lullaby. In Italian, we say *"ninnananna"*, which I think is prettier.' She smiled at Concetta who, hearing the Italian word, nodded her approval. 'Concetta sang it to me when I was a child, and Rosaria's mother sang it to her. And I shall sing it to our child when the time comes.'

'It's very pretty,' he said. '*Una ninnananna bellissima.*'

Concetta nodded once again, acknowledging the effort he had made.

'Concetta knows all sorts of things that go back generations. Lullabies, songs, *filastrocche*. I don't recall how you say that. Little poems for children.'

'Nursery rhymes,' he said.

'Of course. How silly of me.' She laughed, then lowered her voice a little. 'She even knows some magic spells that will protect us against all kinds of things. Maledictions. Curses. The evil eye.

Don't you, Concetta, dear?' She translated this for Concetta, who smiled briefly, cast a warning glance at Edward and shook her head.

'She knows that I'm only teasing,' Marisol said. 'She takes no notice of me when I tease her.' Once again, she translated this. Concetta looked at Edward impassively, studying his face until he turned his eyes away.

In July, when the days had lengthened and the air warmed up sufficiently to satisfy even Concetta, Marisol gave birth to a boy. Edward waited outside the room, sitting on a chair he had carried from his study, flinching when he heard Marisol scream out with pain, relieved to hear the firm, comforting voice of Concetta. Rosaria came out and told him that all was well, and then returned to the bedside of her wailing mistress. An eternity later, when Edward was about to open the door, and be damned, he heard a final inhuman screech, followed moments later by a new sound that shook him to his core – the howl of a newborn child. His hand was already on the doorknob when he felt it turn. Rosaria, her face wet with sobbing, stood before him. She tried to block his way, or so it seemed. Oh my God, he thought, not again. Anything but that. He moaned out *No*, an abjuration from the very depths of him, and pushed the girl to one side.

Concetta had already done what had to be done. Marisol was sitting up in the bed, her hair lifted from her shoulders and twisted into a loose knot, her skin gleaming with sweat, her whole face wreathed in smiles. She had a small white bundle in her arms. She held it out to him. 'Meet your son,' she said. Rendered distraught by relief and joy, he burst into tears. He rushed to the bed and took the bundle from her. A tiny red face, wrinkled as a walnut, stared up at him.

'He's beautiful,' Edward said.

*

120

They called him Tommaso, after his Sicilian grandfather. This had been Edward's idea. He wrote a brief note to his own father, under pressure from Marisol, and received an equally brief note back, in which his father expressed pleasure at the news and a promise that he would lay down a crate of port for his grandson. Apart from that, what went on in the house was women's business, conducted in a language that was not his. He found himself increasingly in George's company. Sometimes, they would amuse themselves by trying to communicate with each other in Italian. Edward was surprised, and not entirely pleased, to discover that George's efforts with Rosaria had proved more beneficial than his own with Marisol. In a moment of unguarded intimacy he asked George if he intended at some point to make an honest woman of Rosaria and George had replied rather sharply that Rosaria already was, and would continue to be, an honest woman. Edward smarted under the reproof.

It was almost impossible to spend time alone with Marisol. Tommaso was proving a difficult child, she told him, her voice exhausted. Concetta had insisted that she stay in bed, sometimes with Tommaso in her arms, more often alone, with Rosaria sitting at her post by the window in the stuffy room, and the child being carried backwards and forwards between his mother and the nursery by Concetta. The window remained firmly closed, despite Marisol's pleading. At one point, Edward insisted it be opened to allow some fresh air to enter the room but Concetta had positioned herself in front of it, her arms crossed, her expression ferocious. 'Don't insist, Edward,' Marisol pleaded. 'She's right, a draught can kill.' He stepped away, his thoughts flying back without his volition to the corridor and the petals that had stirred in the rush of chilled air from the open window. Even now, with the memory of those nights fading into what he had now decided was a morbid fantasy, a sort of self-delusion, he caught the scent of flowers at unexpected moments in different corners of the house, and he would draw in his breath and feel her there before him, her warm hands holding his face, her eyes on his. The commonest flowers, he would find himself saying, are the sweetest-scented.

'How is he difficult?'

She was briefly silent, as though deciding whether he should be trusted. Concetta is to blame for this, he thought. 'He takes my breast,' she said finally, 'and feeds, and is happy. I can see that, I can feel it, Edward, it is like a bond. And then he changes – I don't know how to find the words for what happens – he pushes me away, and his eyes move away from mine. He is looking for something else, Edward, something more than I can give him, and I don't know what it is.' Her eyes filled with tears. 'I don't know how to satisfy him.' She paused, then leant forward and took his hand. 'Yesterday, I was trying to feed him and Concetta had given me a piece of bread – I was suddenly hungry – and he reached up and tried to take the bread from me. He was staring up at me, and his mouth was closed, refusing me, and I didn't recognise him.' She let him wipe her tears away. 'And then today he was my baby again, he was Tommaso. Does that make sense to you?'

'Babies are capricious creatures,' he said, hoping that this would suffice to comfort her.

She laughed through her tears. 'You know nothing about babies, my dear Edward, but I thank you, and I love you. And everything will be all right.' She squeezed his hand. 'And now I need to sleep.'

The baptism was arranged six weeks after Tommaso's birth. Concetta produced from her trunk the baptismal gown that had been worn by Marisol almost twenty years before, an explosion of linen and lace at least twice the length of the child. Tommaso wriggled and cried as the gown was slipped over his head, but calmed down immediately when his mother carried him to the carriage. It was his first trip outside the house and he seemed almost preternaturally curious, reaching towards the window and gurgling with excitement until Marisol lifted him nearer so that his hands could grip the lower edge of the frame.

The baptism was to be held at their local Catholic church, St Joseph's. Marisol and Rosaria regularly attended mass there, but Edward had never entered the building before that day. The priest shook his hand and spoke to the three women in Italian, explaining to Edward that he had spent three years at the English College in Rome and welcomed any opportunity to speak the language. There were few guests. Other than the members of their household, only Daniel Giles, who had agreed to be the child's godfather, and Arthur Poynter, an unexpected but welcome presence, were there, taking their seats in the pew behind the family. Marisol, in particular, was delighted to find that Edward had more than one friend in London. She turned and offered her hand to Poynter, who raised it to his lips. 'My dear young lady,' he said, 'how delightful it is finally to meet you,' casting an accusing glance at Edward. 'And at such an auspicious occasion as the entry of a child into the body of the church.'

'I had no idea you were Catholic,' said Edward tersely.

'We all have our secrets, Edward,' said Poynter, leaning back in his pew as if to bring the conversation to an end.

The priest had just taken Tommaso from Marisol's arms when Edward noticed a flurry of movement at the church door. A man appeared briefly and then darted back or was pulled away, or so it appeared. Something about the man was familiar to Edward. Whispering a word of apology in Marisol's ear, he slipped away from the group around the font and hurried down the aisle until he was standing on the steps outside the church. The man he had seen was at the foot of the steps, his back to Edward, as though waiting for him. As Edward walked down the steps, with a growing sense of foreboding, the man turned to face him.

'Bell,' said Edward.

'Monteith.'

'What in God's name are you doing here?' said Edward.

'I had to see you,' said Bell.

Edward looked at the figure before him, barely recognisable as the man he had last seen more than two years ago. His clothes, of excellent quality, were soiled and unpressed, his hair and beard uncombed. But it was the expression on his old acquaintance's face that most unnerved him. What he saw, beneath the tangled beard and grime, was dread. Edward's anger at the man, nurtured daily since Settie's death, melted away.

'What on earth has happened to you?' he said.

'Are you the man behind it?' Bell said. His voice was tremulous but determined. 'Are you responsible?'

'Responsible for what?'

Bell glanced behind him. 'You have set them on me, I know you have,' he said urgently, his voice low as though afraid of being overheard. 'Just tell me the truth.'

'I don't know what you're talking about.'

Bell clutched his arm. 'They're her people, I know they are.'

'Who are?'

'Don't torment me, Monteith. They've done for Hancock, you know that, don't you?'

'I don't know what you're talking about,' Edward said, although the name of Hancock awakened an indistinct half-buried memory.

'Your little flower seller,' said Bell. His hand tightened on Edward's sleeve. Edward tried to shake him off. 'You wanted her dead, not I. Maybe she is behind this. I wouldn't be surprised. Her and her mother, that Gypsy witch.' He shook Edward's arm. 'They are using you, you know that, don't you?'

'Get away from me,' said Edward, his voice breaking. 'You disgust me.'

'They have dogs,' said Bell, pleading now, letting go of Edward's sleeve and folding his hands into the gesture of one in prayer. 'They have tried to set their dogs on me, Edward. For pity's sake, make them stop. I beg you.' His voice rose. 'Make them stop.' He grabbed the sleeve a second time, shook it as a terrier might shake a rat.

Edward would have struck him if he hadn't heard a sharp cry from within the church. He cast Bell off with a gesture of revulsion and ran up the steps. George met him halfway between the main door and the font. 'There you are, sir,' he said, relieved.

'What was that cry?'

George took his arm. 'Come with me, sir. Your wife needs you.'

Edward rushed up the final part of the aisle to where the group was gathered, as he had left them. Tommaso was once again in Marisol's arms, but she passed the child at once to Concetta and ran the last few feet towards Edward. 'Where were you?' she said, placing her hands on his shoulders and holding him at arm's length, her tone a mixture of concern and indignation.

'I needed some air,' he said.

'Air?' she repeated, astounded. 'You should have been here, Edward. You should have been here.'

'Please,' said the priest hurriedly. He looked at Edward, with an expression of apology. 'Nothing untoward has happened, Mr Monteith.'

'Nothing untoward has happened?' repeated Marisol. 'I can't believe you said that. If nothing untoward has happened, perhaps you can explain this.' She caught the priest's arm and lifted it to reveal a bright-red scald on his right hand.

'It's nothing,' the priest said.

'He tried to hurt my child,' said Marisol, on the verge of hysteria. 'The water in the font was boiling, Edward. Boiling. Do you understand that?'

'I don't understand anything of what you've told me,' said Edward, confused. 'He tried to hurt Tommaso, you say?'

She nodded. 'He put his hand in the water and it was boiling, Edward,' she said again.

Edward looked at the font then, cautiously, lowered his hand into the water.

'It isn't even hot, my dear,' he said quietly.

Marisol stared at him, unbelieving.

'He screamed with pain, Edward. Just see what the water did to him.'

The priest made a feeble attempt to conceal his hand, but Edward caught his arm and forced the priest to show the burn. Already the skin was blistering.

'I cannot baptise this child today,' the priest said.

'You must,' said Marisol. She held out her arms for Tommaso, but Concetta shook her head. She tore the child from her wet nurse's hands.

'My son must be saved,' she said.

Chapter Thirteen

S ome days after the unsuccessful baptism, Edward was walking
to his bedroom when he heard Concetta speaking in the
nursery. He assumed that Marisol was with her and went to join
them, but came to a halt at the door when he saw that Concetta
was alone with the child. She was leaning over the side of the cot,
talking to Tommaso in a low, insistent way. She had no idea that
Edward was there. As he listened to the words, which were Italian
but not an Italian he recognised, he wondered if she was reciting a
nursery rhyme, but something about the tone of her voice and the
manner in which certain phrases seemed to be repeated, as though
Concetta were mesmerised or in a state of trance, unnerved him.
He was about to steal away, pretend that he had seen and heard
nothing, when Concetta became aware of him. She raised her
head and looked towards the door, and towards him, but seemed
not to see him. Her face was pale, her eyes glazed over somehow.
Edward stepped back, shocked. Concetta blinked and shook her
head slightly, as if to clear her vision. '*Tommaso dorme*,' she said,
and placed her hands together in a gesture of prayer. Edward,
unsettled, walked away.

He found Marisol in her room, with Rosaria, sewing clothes for
Tommaso. He told her what he had seen. Marisol sighed and put
down her work.

'I confess that I worry about her. I've never seen her so fretful.'

'You are worried about Concetta? I am more concerned about our son.'

'You misunderstand me deliberately,' said Marisol. 'Of course I am concerned about Tommaso. But Concetta has been behaving strangely ever since the baptism.'

'I thought we had put all that behind us,' said Edward. 'Surely she doesn't still believe that the holy water in the font changed temperature by some sort of magic?'

'Not magic, Edward.'

'Then what?'

She sighed a second time. 'She senses evil.'

'She thinks our child is evil?' said Edward, his voice rising slightly with irritation.

'That is not what I said. Please don't be angry with me. I was there too, you know.' Her tone was accusing. 'I *saw*.'

'So you think there is evil in this house as well?' he said, increasingly exasperated, but, more than that, apprehensive.

Marisol hesitated before speaking. 'I don't know what to think. All I can tell you is that Concetta feels the presence of evil. Of death.'

'Good God,' said Edward. 'You'll be telling me all about the evil eye again if you carry on like this. I thought you said that was all foolish superstition, old wives' tales. The dead are dead, Marisol. Let's have no more of this nonsense.'

Slowly, she shook her head. 'The dead are not dead, Edward. They are always with us. They eat at our table. They sleep in our beds.' She picked up her work as if, for her, there was no more to say; the conversation had come to an end. Rosaria muttered something he failed to catch. More perturbed than before, he left the room.

*

One morning in Palermo, before they were married, Marisol had told him that there was a place she wanted him to see. She had been a perfect guide; he had seen the city through her eyes and found it wonderful. But today, she told him, we shall visit something different. You will be meeting an illustrious relation of mine. They left the city in a gig, with Marisol in charge of the horse and Edward marvelling quietly at her side. After a twenty-minute journey along increasingly dusty roads, they came to an anonymous two-storey building to their left. She reined in the horse. 'Here we are,' she said. She let him help her down from the gig, although there was no need, and then led him along the side of the building to a small door. There, she rang a bell and waited. When a friar opened the door she spoke to him for a few moments. Edward heard her mention her father, and watched in admiration of her authority as the friar stepped back to allow them both to pass.

They went down a narrow staircase, Marisol leading the way, and found themselves at the start of a long wide corridor, barely lit by windows set high in the outer wall. It took a moment for Edward's eyes to adjust. When they did, he saw that the walls of the corridor were lined by boxes and wooden trunks, stacked one on top of the other and, above these, by a row of what looked like mannequins dressed as friars, their heads dipped in prayer. Drawing in his breath, he looked more closely and understood that these were not mannequins, but cadavers, their flesh dried and shrunken to the bones beneath, their skulls held together by skin. Each friar had a label around his neck, with a name and date written on it. 'Some of them have been in these catacombs for three hundred years and more,' said Marisol in a whisper. She took his arm and led him into a second corridor. Here, each desiccated corpse was dressed in civilian clothes, and had glass eyes that seemed to follow Edward as he walked. 'These are professional men who have paid large sums to be here,' she said. 'Doctors and lawyers and so on. My own relations are further down, with the nobility.' She paused. 'You see that one?' She pointed to a finely dressed figure, held upright against the wall by straps, his still dark hair reaching down to his shoulders. 'He died in a duel,' she said. 'Over a woman. They say his eyes still move when a beautiful woman passes.' She smiled. It was obvious that Edward's reaction, a mixture of curiosity and revulsion, had gratified her. 'And now let us move to the married women.' She smiled, taking his arm once again. 'They are kept apart, both from the men and from the virgins, perhaps to discourage further duels.' Unlike the men, all of whom had been secured in standing position along the walls, the mummified bodies of the women were laid out on shelves, one above the other, in embroidered robes, their cheeks and lips coloured with rouge, their hair tinted black, their faces shrunk into hideous grins and pouts. Some of them had children pressed to their breasts. When he saw the first child, the size and form of a skinned rabbit swaddled in lace, Edward felt sick and thought he might faint, for the memories it brought back were so vivid and so painful to him. He would have left, but that would have called for an explanation he was not prepared to give. They walked on. In whichever direction he looked he saw mummies, more or less decayed, richly clothed, some of them arranged in tableaux as though dining or conversing together, some of them at work in some way. How could this be done to people who had once been alive and loved? he asked himself. How could this parody of life in death be tolerated?

Further down, they came to a chapel filled with dead children. Two neatly attired small boys were seated together in a rocking chair. A little girl stared up through the glass lid of a box. Others were stored in niches, as if waiting to be lifted down, to be played with, to be held and loved. He thought he would be sick.

'I have to leave,' he said.

'But first you must see my great-uncle,' she said, and he had let himself be taken deeper into the catacombs, into a part lit only by the lantern she carried as she led the way. 'For us, these people are not really dead,' she said. 'We celebrate their birthdays with them, we hold their hands and join with them in prayer.' She stopped before a man dressed in a frock coat and tailored breeches, with a silk scarf knotted around his neck. 'Allow me to present Count Ludovico,' she said. Much of his face was still intact, the mouth still filled with teeth, the skin still smooth, apart from the gaping hole where his nose had been. 'The dead are always with us,' she said.

On the drive home she told him about the processes that had been used, the removal of the organs and their replacement with bay leaves and straw, the dripping rooms where the fluids of the dead had gradually been extracted from them by time and gravity. When they were dried sufficiently they were exposed to the air, then washed in vinegar and dressed in the clothes that they, or someone for them, had chosen, and moved to their final home, where they would live forever. She told him all this with an edge of excitement in her voice, but also as though she were teasing him, as though none of what she was describing, nor death itself, could possibly happen to them. He heard her, but did not listen. All he could think of was Settie, his beautiful Settie, and the child that had never been, that he had killed.

'Did you notice the inscription over the door?' Marisol asked him when they were back in the heart of the city and he saw living people walk and speak and laugh, and he had begun to breathe with greater calm. He shook his head.

'"*Voi siete quello che noi eravamo, noi siamo quello che voi sarete. Tutti moriremo,*"' she said.

'I don't understand.'

'You are what we were, we are what you will be. We shall all die,' she translated, with relish, her eyes wide.

He did not sleep that night, nor for some nights after.

'I need to speak to Bell,' Edward said. He was sitting in their usual room at the club. He had needed to leave the house after his last conversation with Marisol. The image of Concetta's empty stare was still before his eyes. 'Do you have any idea where I might find him?'

Poynter shook his head. 'He has been behaving like a fugitive these past few weeks.'

'I saw him at my son's baptism.'

'He was there?' said Poynter, surprised.

'He was outside,' said Edward. 'You remember I left the church? He was waiting for me. He told me that he was being followed. He feared for his life, he said.'

Poynter showed no surprise at this news. 'A rum business altogether,' he said. 'Both inside and outside the church.'

'You're referring to that business about the water?'

'You must admit that it was rather curious.'

Edward sighed. 'A misunderstanding, that was all. The priest apparently had a touch of fever.'

'I think you have been the victim of a number of misunderstandings, my dear Edward, and Bell has all too frequently been involved in them.'

Once again, Edward wondered how much Poynter knew about Settie's death and how much he had deduced. Any knowledge he had must have come directly or indirectly from Bell, that was clear. 'Which is why I'd like to find him,' he said.

'You have tried his home?'

'Not yet. He gave me the impression that his home was the last place I would find him. He talked about dogs being set on him.

He was in a piteous state, dirty, unshaven. Against my will, I must admit, I felt a particle of pity for him.'

'Dogs, you say. Gypsies?'

'I imagine so. He seemed to think that I could help him, that I would be able to call his tormentors off.'

'And could you?'

'I wish I could.'

'And your connection with Gypsies?'

'I don't know what you mean.'

'How shall I put this? With the people to whom you were introduced at the séance in Stoke Newington all that time ago?'

'I have no connection with those people.'

'I see,' said Poynter. 'Because I do, you see.' He placed his hands together as though about to pray and lifted them to his mouth, looking at Edward in a thoughtful way.

'I have no connection,' repeated Edward.

'I have been studying the spiritual beliefs of Gypsies,' continued Poynter, as though Edward had not spoken. 'You remember our conversation about them some time ago, when you were enamoured of that young flower seller? They are quite fascinating, you know. They have much in common with those of other ancient cultures, as one might expect, but there are one or two intriguing notions that are quite unique. They are afraid of death, as are we all, but to an extent that goes far beyond the mere faint-heartedness of our own beliefs. They fear it actively, to such an extent that they will refuse to touch the body of the deceased for fear of contamination. In order to avoid such contamination, they wash and dress the person who is about to die in his or her finest clothes before death. If this cannot be done, some stranger must be called in to perform the task, an undertaker for example. It is also believed that evil spirits may enter the body after death. At times, to prevent this, the nostrils of the deceased are plugged with beeswax or pearls. There is a lovely abundance there, don't you think?'

'Why are you telling me this?' said Edward.

Poynter seemed not to have heard. 'Gypsies believe that the dead can come back to seek revenge on the living. The family of a dying Gypsy seeks forgiveness for any act they might have committed. If envy exists, or resentment, the deceased might return in the form of an animal, or monstrous being. He might be invisible or take on the semblance of a loved one in order to trick the living more easily. He might be indistinguishable from the way he was when alive, apart from some small detail, a missing toe or finger perhaps, a mole on the face. His purpose might be to punish or, in some cases, to protect. He returns as a *mulo*, neither alive nor fully dead, to settle debts.'

'A *mulo*?'

'That is the word they use.'

'An *obambo*,' said Edward.

'There are similarities certainly,' said Poynter.

'But it is all nonsense,' said Edward brusquely. 'The sort of thing ancient cultures, as you call them, invent to explain away what they cannot understand.'

'That may also be the case,' said Poynter.

There was silence for some moments. In his mind's eye, Edward saw the scalded hand of the priest. Now there is something I do not understand, he thought. What other stories must I invent to explain that away? No one, least of all the priest himself, believed in the story of the fever. It had taken time and money, and Daniel's help, to calm the man down. Edward had seen Marisol and Concetta outside the church, huddled together, speaking in low voices. Marisol had Tommaso in her arms, but Concetta constantly touched his chest and face. It took him a moment or two to realise that she was making the sign of the cross. He was walking towards the women, to take the child from them, or to drive Concetta away, when the woman turned her head in the direction of the church and raised her hand in a gesture he had seen her make before, with the outer fingers extended. When she saw that he was looking she hid her hand behind her back and whispered something to Marisol. He could still see the way Marisol smiled as she walked towards him, holding the baby out for him to take, and the way Tommaso wriggled in his arms when he held him. Be gentle, she'd said, as if he had ever been anything else, and he had nodded. Keep that woman away from him, he had wanted to say, but Concetta was already there beside them, slipping an arm through Marisol's and, with an almost unnoticeable pressure, drawing her away.

'I have no time for superstition,' Edward said now, more angrily than he intended.

Poynter lowered his hands. 'I believe I have offered my help to you before today, Edward, my dear boy. That offer remains open for as long as help might be required.' He paused. 'As for Bell, I suggest that you avoid him for as long as you are able to do so. I can assure you that he will bring you and your family nothing but pain. He is not a good man, and he has been a foolish man, and there is very little that any of us can do that might save him from himself or others.' He stood up. 'And now, if I were you, I would go home to my exquisite young wife and enjoy the love that only she can offer.'

That night, Edward was almost asleep when he heard a whimpering come from the next room. Tommaso rarely cried during the night. When he did cry he woke the entire house and only a hushed *ninnananna* from Concetta would send him back to sleep. But this sound was different, inhuman somehow, like the suffering of a trapped animal. Edward rose from the bed, careful not to wake Marisol, slipped on his dressing gown and went into the nursery.

Concetta always left a small oil light burning in the room.

He crossed the room, the noise of whimpering ever louder as he approached Tommaso's cot, and looked down. The light was behind him and his body cast a shadow into the cot as he bent over and reached down to lift his son and comfort him. He tried to slip his hands beneath the child, but something prevented him. He moved a little to one side in order to allow more light through the bars of the cot and saw that his son had been tightly wrapped in cloth, cocooned like a mummy, and that the white cocoon in which his child was restrained had itself been strapped down and attached to the bars of the cot. 'Good God,' he exclaimed in horror, and was about to begin releasing the infant from his bondage when he heard a voice behind him.

'*Lascia stare.*'

He turned and saw Concetta behind the open door. She must already have been in the nursery when he arrived. His Italian was good enough to know that he had been told to leave the child as he was.

'What in God's name have you done?' he said, little caring whether or not the woman understood.

'*Lascia stare,*' she repeated.

'Get out of here, damn you,' said Edward. He started to fumble with the knots that held the cloth down.

'What are you doing, Edward?' said Marisol. She was standing beside Concetta, in her nightgown, her hair loose, her fingers playing with the ring on her other hand.

'I'm freeing our child.'

Concetta began to speak hurriedly to Marisol, a hand on her arm to restrain her. Marisol shook her head, tried to break away, but Concetta refused to let her go. Her voice became even more urgent. Edward stopped what he was doing and tried to understand, but Concetta spoke too fast for him. Marisol seemed to lose force as she listened. She turned her face to Edward in a sort of plea, although for what he had no idea. Eventually, Concetta fell silent. She looked at Edward with an expression of pity, then left the room.

'She has to go,' said Edward.

Marisol walked across and lifted his hands from the cot. The whimpering had stopped by now, as though Tommaso had been listening. She put her arms around her husband and held him close. 'Don't be too hasty,' she said.

'Hasty? Have you seen what she's done?'

'She's trying to stop him hurting himself.'

'Hurting himself?'

'He moves too much, she says.' Marisol looked up at him, her eyes wet with tears. 'She kept saying that he moves too much. I don't know what she means, but she would never hurt our child, Edward, you must believe that.' She shuddered. 'It was the way she said it, over and over again. It isn't natural. I did it to stop him moving, she said.' She pulled away a little. 'She was scared, Edward, and now I am scared too.' She stroked his arm. 'Please don't be angry with her, or with me.'

'We'll talk about this tomorrow,' said Edward, trying to sound calm.

'Yes,' she said. She looked into the cot. 'Goodnight, my darling.'

'I can't leave him like this,' Edward said.

'Then free him,' said Marisol, leaving the room.

Edward slowly unknotted the strips of cloth, like bandages that held the bundle down, and then unwrapped the bundle itself until he had his son Tommaso in his arms. The child lay perfectly still, his eyes staring up, but unfocused. I wonder what he sees, Edward thought, and then: The woman is mad. Whatever Marisol says, she will have to leave. Surely a new nurse can be found somewhere here, in London. Marisol would come to understand, he was sure of that. He started to rock the child in his arms. He wished he had a *ninnananna* that he could sing, an English one perhaps, but he had no memories of being sung to sleep as a child, and no mother he could ask now. He closed his eyes for a moment, remembering his own mother, startled to feel the prickling of tears.

When Tommaso jerked in his arms, he opened his eyes sharply and looked down to see what was wrong. A cold wave of terror coursed through his body as he saw what he held. The baby that lay in his arms only seconds before had been reduced to a tangle of living bone, the skin distended across it, the flesh beneath the skin sucked out. It screamed from the hollow of its mouth. He gave a cry of disgust and threw the thing into the cot. Instantly, his child was back, and reaching up to be held.

'What's wrong?' said Marisol, rushing into the room. 'What have you done to him?'

Edward could find no words.

'You've hurt him,' she said, accusingly.

'I would never hurt my son,' Edward said, his voice shaking, his eyes turned towards his wife in a silent plea. 'You know that, surely.' He took a deep breath. 'I think I must have had a nightmare. A waking nightmare. Some sort of derangement of the mind. I don't know what happened.'

There was a noise behind him. He turned to see Concetta standing at the door.

'He moves,' she said.

Chapter Fourteen

Edward agreed with Marisol that it would be wrong to dismiss Concetta, who had proved her worth, in so many ways, and possibly harmful to Tommaso, for whom her care had become indispensable. Her intentions had always been good, they decided, despite her methods being somewhat old-fashioned. That word was Marisol's; Edward would have preferred barbaric. But he was in no mood to argue with his wife, still too shaken by what he had seen, eager to dismiss it as a momentary madness, keen to put the events of that night behind him. And so Concetta remained and a truce between the wet nurse and Edward was silently declared.

As the weeks passed, and no further signs of strangeness manifested themselves, the household settled down once again. The days grew short and the nights long, to Concetta's often voiced discontent, and the orange trees were hauled back into the orangery by Hopkins and his sons, and straw packed around their roots in case of frost. Tommaso became increasingly alert to the world around him, reaching out from his carriage by day as if to grasp each thing that passed. His gurgling took the form of nearly-words, as Marisol coined them, sounds that could almost be identified although no one could agree on the language that was being attempted, each preferring his or her own. At five months old, Tommaso rolled over onto his stomach and began to crawl, which surprised everyone. 'Surely he's too young to crawl,' said Edward, but Marisol saw it as a sign of his intelligence and independence and was thrilled. Concetta said nothing, but Edward saw unease in her eyes, and was inclined to share it. Daniel Giles, who continued to be a regular visitor to the house, declared every gesture the child achieved a source of delight, and relished the role of godfather that he had been given.

One morning in early December, Edward was in his study when he heard the doorbell ring. A moment later, George informed him that Mr Giles was outside the house and would like to speak to him.

'Well, tell him to come in,' said Edward.

George shook his head. 'He told me to say that he prefers to talk to you outside.'

Curious, Edward followed George into the hall. Daniel was by the door, waiting for him, his manner impatient. When Edward reached him, the American took his arm and led him down the steps.

'Let us walk,' he said.

Five minutes later, they had left the villas and shops of Highgate behind them and were on the Heath. Daniel had said nothing more since leaving the house and Edward, at first intrigued, was beginning to feel a rising sense of irritation. As they headed out towards the ponds, he came to a halt.

'You have something to say to me.'

Daniel was a pace or two ahead. He stopped and turned.

'We have never spoken about that evening,' he said.

'Which evening do you mean?' said Edward, his heart sinking.

'You know full well which evening, I mean, Edward. There's no point in pretending to me that you have no memory of it. It was almost three years ago now. It began at the club; we were drinking there with Bell. We drank too much, far too much in your case. You were horribly inebriated by the end of it. Maybe that was why you were indiscreet. Maybe you had drunk to find the courage, I don't know, and it is of no importance. You told us that your flower girl, whose name I no longer remember, was about to have your child.'

'Settie,' said Edward. 'Her name was Settie.'

'Settie,' repeated Daniel. 'Bell tried to convince you to convince her to abort. You were adamant that this would not happen.'

'You don't need to do this, Daniel, I remember perfectly well.'

But Daniel continued. 'I accompanied you to your house. We walked past some loose women and you were deeply perturbed by them, but refused to say why. Your valet let us both in and would have looked after you from that point, but I was concerned and remained with you.'

'I have no memory of that,' Edward confessed.

'You were rendered perfectly incoherent by alcohol,' said Daniel. 'I loosened your clothes and when I realised that I would get no more sense out of you, I left the house.' He paused. 'And that was the last I saw of you for almost two years.'

'Why are you dredging this up now, Daniel,' said Edward. 'I don't understand.'

Daniel ignored this. 'You disappeared for two years, without a word to anyone, and then reappeared with Marisol as though nothing untoward had happened. You now have a wife and a child, and, as far as I can see, no past. This is none of my business, and you may well decide to cut me off from your friendship for having spoken to you so frankly, although I sincerely hope you don't, but I can't help wondering what happened to Settie and to the child you were supposed to be having with her. And the reason I can't help wondering is that I think she may be dead.'

Edward was silent for some time. He walked away from Daniel and stared towards a distant grove of trees but saw nothing. His eyes were blinded by tears.

'I killed her, Daniel,' he said without turning round. 'I killed them both.'

'So Bell was right.'

Edward turned sharply back to face Daniel.

'Bell?'

'I saw him some nights ago, outside an alehouse in Pimlico. I was walking past and he reeled out and stumbled, as drunk as the lord he would probably like to be, practically landing at my feet. I tried to avoid him but he recognised me. He followed me to the Embankment, I couldn't shake him off. Eventually, I was obliged to listen to him. He told me that he lived in fear, that he was being tormented by the family of the girl you had killed. Those were his words. I asked him why they should be seeking him, and he told me that he had directed you – out of the goodness of his heart, he insisted – to a certain doctor in Whitechapel, and that the people who were seeking him had already settled their debts with the doctor and it would be his life next. He was confused, but that was the gist of it.' He paused and waited for Edward to speak, but Edward shook his head. 'I wasn't sure what to do,' Daniel continued, 'whether to believe what he had told me or not, whether to confront you with the sorry tale, as I am doing now, or whether to forget the whole business, put it down to the ramblings of a drunk with a guilty conscience. I wanted to think the best of you, Edward, for your sake and for the sake of your wife and child.'

'Please God, shut up,' said Edward, openly weeping.

Daniel took two newspaper cuttings from his pocket. 'And then I saw these in *Lloyd's Weekly.*'

MYSTERIOUS TRAGEDY IN
WHITECHAPEL
SUPPOSED MURDER OF A MAN

About twenty minutes to six o'clock this morning, David Jenks, who lives at 29, George-yard Buildings, Whitechapel, was on his way to work when he discovered the body of a man lying in a pool of blood in the alley behind his building. Jenks at once called in Constable D. Fletcher, who was on the beat in the vicinity, and Dr C. Greenwood, of Brick Lane, was communicated with and promptly arrived. He immediately made an examination of the man and pronounced life extinct, and gave it as his opinion that he had been brutally murdered, there being knife wounds to his face, chest and abdomen, and signs of throttling at the neck. The body was that of a man between 40 and 50 years of age, about 5ft 7in in height, with a pale complexion and dark hair and moustache, wearing black trousers and greatcoat, a white shirt and black boots of good quality. No disturbance of any kind was heard during the night. The circumstances of his death are mysterious and the body, which up to the time of writing had not been identified, has been removed to Whitechapel mortuary. Inspector Elliston, of the Commercial Street Police Station, has placed the case in the hands of Inspector Keeling, of the Criminal Investigation Department, and that officer is now instituting inquiries.

The second cutting came from a later edition and had no title.

At the inquest, Dr Greenwood, of 28 Brick Lane, stated that he was called to the deceased and found him dead. He examined the body and found nine puncture wounds, inflicted with a long, strong instrument, and evidence of severe throttling at the neck. The legs and feet also showed evident signs of

143

having been bitten, probably by one or more dogs of medium to large dimensions. The brutal treatment to which the deceased had been subjected around the face and throat rendered identification difficult. However, there is little doubt that the victim is Graham Hancock, 47, of Thomas Street, an ex-army doctor, erased from the medical register for misconduct, who nonetheless continued to practise his trade in the area by providing unfortunate and immoral women with female pills and the suppression of unwanted offspring. It is believed that the deceased was forcefully dragged, brutally ill-treated and then murdered in the alley, a long dark thoroughfare, in which he was found.

'This is the man,' said Edward. 'I recognise his name, and the address. The address is his. I shall never forget it.' He gave the cuttings back to Daniel. 'I am glad that he is dead.'

Daniel nodded. 'Was that your intention? That she should die?'

'Of course not,' said Edward. He dried the tears from his face with a handkerchief and told Daniel everything that he remembered from that dreadful night, in as much detail as he could recall. He told him about the phial that Bell had provided, and the low table, and the kettle bubbling on the hearth. He told him about the white apron, and his misgivings, and the moment at which he realised that Settie had died. He told Daniel that he had struck Hancock and then fainted and that later, when he came round, the house had been emptied. There was no sign of Hancock and no sign of Settie. 'It was as if she had never been,' he said. 'I knew that I had lost her, that I had lost everything.' He did not mention his mother's ring, or the severed finger, but he did not forget them; he would never forget them. The ring was a constant reminder of what he had done. He was crying again as he spoke. 'I have never forgiven myself.' He turned his agonised face to Daniel. 'She said that she would always be with me. They both would. I only now begin to understand what she meant.'

Daniel took his hand and held it between his own two hands. 'Of course you cannot forget her but what's done is done, Edward. You have a new wife and a new life. You must forgive yourself, for her sake, if not for yours.'

'I wish I knew how.'

'She must never be told about this, whatever happens,' said Daniel. 'This must remain your secret. You see that, don't you?'

'Yes,' said Edward. 'This is my secret. And now it is yours as well.'

They walked on in silence and had almost reached the house when Daniel came to a halt. 'What I fail to understand is why they should have spared you.'

'I have no idea. I saw Settie's brother, some months ago now. At least I think it was him.' Edward pointed towards Parliament Hill. 'He was over there with his dogs, evil-looking beasts, the kind that must have attacked Hancock. I believe he followed me back to the house. They know where they can find me if they want to.'

'They torment Bell, they drive him to the very edge of madness, and yet they let you live in peace,' said Daniel.

'Perhaps I am protected,' said Edward. Daniel glanced at him.

'Perhaps you are.'

At eight months, Tommaso took his first steps. At nine months, he spoke his first few words. Marisol was thrilled. She had been acquiring books on the education of children, books that Edward had no idea existed, and would read out sections to him over breakfast. By all the accounts of what a child might do and at what age, Tommaso was more than precocious. He was a prodigy.

'He's more like a two-year-old,' Marisol announced, when he stumbled across to her one afternoon in the orangery, reached out for a segment of the orange that she had picked and said 'please'. Rosaria clapped her hands in delight and tried to kiss Tommaso, but he wriggled out of her grasp. Concetta said something in Italian, her tone admonitory, and Marisol snapped at her. 'She wants our darling child to become like an English child, born to be seen but not heard.' Edward smiled, but shared Concetta's unease. Tommaso took the segment, examined it, nibbled a corner and spat it out, shaking his head in disgust. He muttered a word that Edward assumed to be Italian, but Marisol denied this.

'Maybe it's some strange local dialect,' he said, glancing at Concetta, who was sewing at a little distance from them. Marisol, with a smile, translated this and Edward was surprised by the vehemence of Concetta's denial.

'Spring has finally arrived,' said Marisol, stroking the nearest orange tree. 'My patient, sweet Sicilian friends. How happy it makes me to see you here. We shall soon be moving you out of your beautiful glass prison onto the patio.' She looked at Edward. 'Shan't we, my dear?'

'We shall indeed,' he said.

On other days, Tommaso seemed to slide back into infancy. He would lie on his back on a cushion beside Marisol's nursing chair, his plump hands waving above his head as if to grasp something only he could see. He refused solid food and wanted his mother's breast; the words he was using the day before seemed to stick in his throat and his small face creased with frustration as he tried to speak. It was after one of these days, when evening had fallen and dinner had been consumed, that Edward, walking along the corridor, heard a noise coming from the nursery that was neither crying nor whimpering, but a growling, it seemed to Edward, as though a dog had been trapped inside the room. His immediate thought was of the Gypsies and their lurchers, of what the dogs had done to Hancock's legs and feet. Fear clutching at his heart, he opened the door.

The first thing to strike him, apart from the sudden silence, was an overpowering stench of decay. The second, in the half-light of the nursery, was what looked like a loosely woven bag made of tangled bands of some pale substance, balsa wood perhaps or plaster, attached to the side of the cot and filled with rotting plants. This is Concetta's work, he thought, this primitive fetish. He vowed to himself that she would have to go. But then, with a barely discernible grunt, the bag moved. It lifted itself away from the bars and began to clamber with unexpected energy towards the cot's upper edge and it was then that Edward saw, with a wave of nausea and terror, that what he had thought was a bag of decaying leaves and fruit was a child stripped of its flesh, that the cage containing the putrid mess was an infant's thorax, the spine and ribs shining white in the moonlight. The thing was pulling itself up the side of the cot with the bare bones of its arms, its skeletal feet were striving for purchase against the wooden bars. Edward shuddered, let out a moan of horror. The thing froze, and turned its head towards him. The sockets where the eyes should have been seemed to focus on him for a moment and then, with the chattering noise an ape might make, the thing jumped down from the side of the cot and began to shuffle across the floor towards him with a terrible eagerness, its arms open wide as if to be picked up and held. Edward staggered back into the corridor, pulled the door shut behind him, shaking with fear. Leaning his back against the door, he struggled to control his breath, his whole being refusing to believe what he had seen. As if to convince him of its existence, the thing scratched at the foot of the door and made the same low growl as before, and then, to his horror, Edward heard what sounded like the word *dadda* in a high-pitched inhuman voice and his heart stopped. And then there was silence.

A moment later, he realised what he had done. He had closed the thing in the nursery with Tommaso, with his son. I have done it again, he thought, I have abandoned my child. He turned and reached for the handle, his palm slick with sweat. Slowly, faint with dread, he opened the door.

The thing was nowhere to be seen. The stench of rotting plants had disappeared and the air smelt of flowers, of orange blossom. He walked across to the cot and reached down inside it to pick Tommaso up. He held his sleeping son to his heart, his lips pressed against the child's bare head. 'My darling,' he whispered, feeling the soft hair against his lips, hugging the child as hard as he dared. He felt a stirring in his arms as the child woke, and a drowsy murmur. 'My darling son,' he said. 'Forgive me. I will never let you be hurt, my sweet one. I swear to you. Never again. I will always be here for you.' The arms of the child pushed hard against his chest and Edward lifted him away a little, to give him room. Tommaso looked up into his father's eyes, then raised his arms to hug him back.

Chapter Fifteen

'I need to speak to Rickman,' Edward said. He was sitting in the breakfast room at the club, watching his friends eat devilled kidneys. He had already breakfasted at home, or sat at the table as Marisol picked at a slice of buttered bread, and then, excusing himself, walked all the way from Highgate. His aim had been to clear his head of what he had seen the night before. He had walked fast, skirting the Regent's Park, hoping that the fresh, spring air would help him to forget what he had seen. But this had not happened. Now, in the overheated room, the scent of the kidneys filled his nostrils. He wrinkled his nose with distaste.

Daniel and Poynter looked at each other.

'Why on earth would you need to do that?' said Poynter.

'That's my business,' said Edward brusquely.

'In that case, I don't see why you are seeking our help,' said Poynter, visibly irritated. 'You know where he is, I'm sure. I imagine he's allowed visitors.'

'Forgive me,' said Edward. 'I have been through a difficult few days. I was ill-mannered and I apologise.'

'He will be pleased to see you, I'm sure,' said Daniel, placatory as ever. 'Nobody speaks of him since his fall from grace. He has few friends. To the world he once knew, he might as well be dead.'

'You are too generous to the man, Giles. He had few friends well before what you term his fall from grace,' said Poynter, clearly still vexed. 'I must admit that I saw little grace in his previous escapades, although I should not wish death on him, nor on anyone else. Perhaps a little oblivion will encourage him to temper his haughtiness.' He stood up and crossed to the sideboard, where he filled his plate a second time.

'When does his sentence end?' said Edward.

'Some time next year, I believe,' said Poynter. 'These kidneys are really rather excellent, Edward. You should try them.'

Edward ignored this. 'And then?' he said.

'And then he will go to the continent, where his particular style of depravity is looked on with less disfavour.' Poynter gave a sardonic smile. 'I've heard that the birthplace of your lovely wife is known for its tolerance as far as the so-called Greek vice is concerned.'

'I wouldn't know,' said Edward.

'Yes, well, I shall be getting along,' said Poynter. He threw his napkin on the table. 'Duty calls.'

'Duty?' said Edward.

'You are in a disagreeable mood today, Edward,' said Poynter. 'I shall leave you in the company of young Giles here, whose patience is no doubt greater than mine.' He sighed and stood up. 'I wish him luck.'

'Why do you wish to speak to him?' said Daniel when Poynter had left.

'You remember those tales he told,' said Edward. 'About spirits and ghosts and so on?'

'The *obambo*,' said Daniel, with a smile. 'I remember them very well. I have heard many similar tales from people my father helped.'

'And you believe them?'

Daniel spread his hands. 'One can believe or not, I'm not sure what difference it makes. The stories continue to be told. Some purpose must be served by them. Those who have seen an *obambo*, or think they have, will tell you it is real. Whether they can be trusted is another matter. Perhaps we should give them the benefit of the doubt.'

'Poynter's right about you, Daniel. You are a generous man,' said Edward. 'Perhaps too generous. Not everything that can be seen is real. If the opposite were true, if everything we saw or thought we saw were real, the road to madness would be short indeed.'

'You have seen something that has disturbed you?'

Edward paused before speaking.

'How much does Poynter know?'

'About?'

'About that night.'

Daniel shrugged. 'I have no idea. More than he would confess to, I'm sure of that. He is omnipresent, like a bad penny. His duty, such as it is, is to know the business of other people.'

Edward laughed, for the first time. 'He is that disreputable? Surely not. Poynter is the most respectable of men.'

'You're right.' Daniel smiled. 'I may have been unfair to him. He is an infinite source of erudition, if nothing else. You remember his talking about Gypsies again some nights ago, about their spiritual beliefs, if I remember correctly. There is nothing that doesn't seem to stimulate his curiosity. He is entitled to our respect for that, at least.'

That afternoon, Edward set off for Newgate. He had passed before the large dark granite-built building that housed the prison a hundred times but never imagined that one day he would need to enter. The doors were iron, studded with iron, with a small grating in the upper half, and padlocked bolts. He rang the bell and waited until the head of a warder appeared behind the grating. He made his request and was told to wait. Several minutes passed before a second head appeared to tell him that someone in authority would be along in a while. He continued to wait. Eventually, when Edward had been standing outside the prison for a good half-hour, the door opened and he was admitted into a long bare corridor. A man in his sixties, in a grey dress coat and black trousers, approached him, introduced himself as the Governor of Newgate Prison and asked him the nature of his business with the prisoner. 'He is a friend of mine,' said Edward. The man raised an eyebrow, then called a warder over. The warder led him down the corridor and into an exercise yard, the walls around it tipped with iron spikes. He unlocked a metal door, took Edward along a second corridor, unlocked another door, locking each door carefully behind them as they advanced into the prison. Further doors and corridors followed, and Edward had the sensation that he was being led into the centre of hell itself. Only the ever increasing coldness of the air disproved this. Distant cries were heard, and the sound of other doors being closed. The walls were black with soot and grease. Eventually he found himself in a vaulted room divided by two rows of iron bars. A warder sat between the rows, within hearing distance of the chair to which Edward was directed. He sat and waited until he heard a key turn in a lock and saw a door beyond the furthest row of bars swing open to admit Rickman.

Edward wouldn't have recognised him. He had lost at least a stone in weight, his skin was pale, and his prison clothes were streaked with dirt. He stumbled rather than walked, as though he had hurt an ankle. He had a straggling beard and his hair had been savagely cut. As soon as he saw Edward he began to weep. He grasped the iron bars, the skin of his hands disfigured by blisters and calluses, the nails broken and bleeding. He had not been provided with a chair, and Edward immediately sprang to his feet. The warder sat between them, an eye on the clock.

'My dear man,' Edward said. 'It breaks my heart to see you reduced to this.'

'You are my first and only visitor,' Rickman said through his tears, his voice breaking.

'The world has been cruel to you,' said Edward, not knowing what else to say, aware that he would not have come here himself without a purpose.

Rickman glanced at the warder. 'I have only myself to blame.'

Edward nodded.

'How is everyone?' said Rickman. 'Bell? How is Bell? I had hoped he might come to see me in my disgrace. Of all people, Bell.'

'I haven't seen him for some time,' said Edward. 'I have been away.'

'I heard,' said Rickman, gathering his strength. 'You have been in Europe, I believe.'

'Yes,' said Edward. 'I am married. I have a wife, from Sicily. And a boy. I have a child.'

'You are a fortunate man,' said Rickman, with feeling. 'I envy you.'

Edward paused. 'What will you do when you can leave this place?'

'I shall do what you did,' said Rickman. 'I shall run away.'

So Rickman knew, or suspected, the reason for his departure, Edward thought, and that made it easier for him to come to the point of his visit. 'You will return to Africa?' he said.

'Or nearer home,' said Rickman, with another sideways glance at the warder. 'Some place where I may be allowed to live in peace.'

'Do you remember that evening we spoke about spirits? At the club. Poynter was there, and Bell too.'

'I do indeed.' For the first time, Rickman gave a hesitant smile. 'Such times, my dear boy. If only I had appreciated them as fully as I should have done.'

'You spoke about an African spirit,' said Edward slowly. 'A skeleton filled with rotting plants. An *obambo*, you called it.'

'Ah yes,' said Rickman, a touch of warning in his voice. 'But maybe here and now is neither the place nor the time to discuss this. I am living a God-fearing life, you see. I have learnt the error of my ways.'

Edward ignored this. 'You said you had seen an *obambo*, and you had done what it requested of you,' he said, his tone increasingly urgent. 'You built it a home. I want to know how you did that.'

'Did I really say that? I wonder what possessed me to talk such nonsense.' He paused. 'And you believed me?'

'Yes,' said Edward. 'I did.'

Rickman shook his head. 'Old wives' tales, Monteith. Nothing more.'

'You never saw an *obambo*?'

'My dear boy, of course not. What do you take me for? A witch doctor?'

'You lied to us?'

'I entertained you, that was all. I gave you material with which to dream. I fed your imaginations.' This speech seemed to exhaust Rickman. He slumped against the bars.

Edward turned to the warder. 'Can you fetch my friend a chair?'

'He don't have a right to no chair,' the warder said complacently. 'He's supposed to be picking oakum not chatting to a gentleman. He's a right malingerer, is this one.'

'*Ils me tuent,*' Rickman said, his voice low. '*Vous devez m'aider.*'

The warder stood up, rattled his truncheon along the bars. 'Enough of that filthy foreign lingo. Time's up.' He called for Rickman to be taken away, but before the warder arrived on that side of the bars, Edward was escorted from the room. His last glimpse of Rickman was of the man being half led, half dragged away by his keeper.

*

'He said they were killing him,' Edward told Daniel the following day. 'He asked for our help.'

'I'm afraid that there's very little we can do for him,' said Daniel. 'But did he provide you with what you were looking for?'

Edward hesitated. 'He denied that he had ever seen an *obambo*, or anything like it. He said it was all hearsay, food for our imaginations. But I cannot be sure that he was telling me the truth. There was a warder beside us throughout the visit. It was awful, Daniel, to see him reduced like that. You cannot imagine the degree of humiliation to which he has been subjected. And not only his spirit, which is utterly broken; his body as well. His hands were bleeding, Daniel.'

'Picking oakum does that, I believe.'

'The warder listened to every word he said. He was lying, I think. I hope to God that he was lying to save his skin.' Or mine, thought Edward.

'But did he tell you what you needed to know?'

Edward shook his head.

'Maybe you should talk to me about what you saw,' said Daniel.

And so Edward did. When he had finished, Daniel grasped his shoulder.

'Listen to me,' he said. 'What you have seen is impossible. Such creatures do not exist. You have a perfect son and a perfect wife, and you must put these thoughts away. Rickman was right when he said that he had fed your imagination. He has fed it with dross and poison. He deserves to be where he is, not for what he has done to the lad who put him there, but for what he has done to you.'

Edward listened, but with half an ear. He had never seen Daniel so pale, as though the blood had been drawn out of him, whether from fear or anger it was impossible to tell. He nodded.

'Thank you,' he said.

*

In the following weeks, Edward watched Tommaso with anxious eyes, but the child showed no signs of disturbance, other than the fits and starts of his unsettling precocity, and gradually the fear that had transfixed him began to fade. Just over two months had passed since the apparition, as Edward had decided to classify it, when Marisol came to his study in tears. It was early afternoon. The last he had seen of his wife and child they were sitting in the garden with Rosaria playing a game with string he remembered from his own childhood. He had watched them with pride and pleasure before re-entering the house. Now, less than an hour later, she stood before him, wringing her hands, fidgeting with her ring, as though its presence irritated her.

'I don't know what to do with him, Edward. There are times he doesn't seem to know me. I worry so much that he might be ill in some way. He is so clever, so advanced for his age. He walks, he talks, he is barely one year old. He shouldn't be able to do these things, Edward, and I don't know if I should be proud of him, because I am proud of him, or frightened, because I am also frightened. Sometimes I am very frightened. He is not natural. Concetta says nothing, but I know that she shares my fears. Sometimes I think that she is more afraid than I am.'

'Let me speak to him,' said Edward.

Rosaria and Tommaso had abandoned the string game and were playing together on the patio outside the orangery, throwing pebbles at a larger stone. Tommaso's pebble struck the stone and he clapped his hands with delight. Marisol is right to be concerned, thought Edward. Surely he is far too young to be doing this sort of thing. They walked across the lawn. When Tommaso saw them, he trotted across. Edward's knowledge of children was limited but even he felt that this was wrong, this directed energy, the sheer *will* of the child. He stood back as Marisol bent over to scoop him up, but Tommaso pushed Marisol to one side with a gesture of irritation and tottered towards his father, his arms lifted. Edward had a moment of dread. The child stood at his feet, straining to be held, then spoke. 'You know who I am,' he said. 'Take me home. Take me to Mamma. Real Mamma.'

Edward recoiled.

'You see,' said Marisol, her voice breaking.

Edward sank down on his haunches and took hold of the child by his shoulders. He wanted to shake him, but something held him back. 'What do you mean?' he said.

The child seemed to soften in his hands, to soften and shrink. 'I'm sorry,' he said. He began to cry. He wriggled until Edward let him go and then turned to his mother. 'Mamma, Mamma,' he cried. Sobbing, she picked him up and held him to her, pressed his head against her breast. 'My child,' she said.

'Let us go into the house,' Edward said. He put his arm around her, around them both. 'We are tired. It has been a long day.'

Chapter Sixteen

Marisol was distant after that afternoon. She responded to anything Edward said as briefly as she could. She snapped at Concetta. Even with Rosaria, her manner changed, as though the girl were no longer her childhood friend and ally. She withdrew into herself, into her room, leaving the care of Tommaso to the wet nurse, and to Edward, who had begun to observe his son with greater attention. He studied Marisol's books on child development, discovering fuel for his deepest fears. But, as though aware of this, Tommaso became a one-year-old again. Edward spoke to him and was met with smiles and gurgles, to such an extent that he wondered if his son might be impeded in some way, and new anxieties set in. When the child tried to walk, he would take three steps, stumble and fall into a crawling position, exploring his surroundings on all fours and behaving exactly as he should, according to the books, until Edward started to believe that they had all been mistaken about the child. They had taken mere sounds for words, infantile gestures for intentions. In the nursery, at times Edward sniffed the air to see if there was any trace of rotting plants, and then mocked himself for his foolishness. He spoke to Daniel about his fears, but to no one else, and Daniel listened, but said nothing.

One day, in late July, Edward and Daniel were sitting in the garden, with Tommaso squatting on a blanket between them, playing with some coloured blocks of wood that Daniel had given him. 'He will be an architect,' he said, as the child piled the blocks up. 'Or an iconoclast,' said Edward, when he knocked them down. They laughed. They talked about books while the child played at their feet. Daniel had returned to his study of Thoreau, out of nostalgia for the country in which he was born, a country he had not seen for some years now. Edward, on the other hand, had been reading the Apocrypha in order to keep up his Greek. 'There is no single truth,' he said to Daniel, 'and the Apocrypha are proof of that. Everything we believe, or think we believe, is a mishmash of stories told by the dead. I begin to think that stories obey the laws of evolution, according to Darwin,' he said. 'The fittest survive by adapting to their habitat, by meeting its needs. They breed and beget offspring that are stronger and that last longer than they would alone.' He sat forward in his chair, enthusiastic, ignoring the sceptical smile on Daniel's face. 'Parts of the oracles of the sibyls, for example, describe the same events as those in books in the Hebrew tradition, not all of them included in the Bible. The flood is all over the place, Daniel, as one might expect, I suppose; it is such an excellent story it was bound to survive. The same ideas but developed through time, adapted to circumstance. I recently came across an extraordinary collection of texts from Ethiopia of all places, translated into German, called the Book of Enoch.'

He was interrupted by Tommaso, who knocked down the edifice he had so carefully constructed with a single blow. He struggled to his feet, swaying forward until he had found his balance, then grasped Edward's leg and tried to scramble up onto his lap. 'You know me, Papa,' he said. 'You know me. You know my name.'

'Enoch?' said Edward, his voice trembling.

The child had tears in his eyes. He heaved himself up until he was kneeling on Edward's legs, then threw his arms around his father's neck. 'Papa,' he said.

'Now you understand,' said a woman's voice from behind them.

They turned and saw Concetta. She held out her hand, palm down, the middle fingers folded, the outer fingers extended, then spat and walked back towards the house.

Daniel looked at Edward. 'What did she mean by that?'

'The first time I saw her do it, I asked Marisol what it means,' said Edward. 'She didn't want to tell me to begin with. She said it was nothing but silly superstition, but I could tell she was upset. I had to insist until finally she told me.'

'And what did she tell you?' said Daniel, curious.

'That it was the sign people use to protect themselves from the evil eye.'

'She believes in the evil eye?'

'Marisol?' said Edward. 'Of course not.'

Marisol waited until Daniel had left before approaching Edward in his study. Tommaso was sleeping in the nursery.

'Concetta told me what she heard and saw in the garden,' she said.

'What did she tell you?'

'That Tommaso has another name.'

'That's nonsense.'

'You called him by another name and he responded. He recognised it, Edward.' She paused. 'What was the name, Edward?'

'I don't know what you mean.'

'Don't lie to me, Edward.'

'I wish I could answer your question,' he said, imploringly, 'but I have no idea what happened. One minute he was playing with blocks and the next he was on my lap and calling me his papa.'

'So Concetta is lying?'

'What does she say?'

'She says that he is not my son, that my son has been taken from me and replaced by a *trovatello* – I don't know the word in English

160

— a child that has been abandoned and found by someone else, not by his parents.'

'Foundling,' said Edward. 'The English word is foundling. But what she says is nonsense, my dearest. You know it is. Tommaso is our son, and no one else's.'

'I know that,' she said. She slumped to the floor at his feet, rested her head on his knee. 'I don't know what to think, Edward. Sometimes I am so unhappy, I wish that I were dead.'

'You must never say that,' he said, shocked. 'If you were dead, I could not live. And then our Tommaso would be an orphan, and would have no one to cherish and protect him as we shall always do.' He stroked her hair. 'You have such beautiful hair,' he said.

She raised her head to look at him. Her eyes were damp. 'Tommaso loves my hair,' she said. 'He told me so. I was pinning it up only yesterday and he was sitting on my dressing table to watch what I was doing, because he loves to do that, and he caught my hand to prevent me. He told me that he wanted my hair loose.'

'He said that?'

She sighed. 'Not exactly. I don't recall the words he used. But I remember thinking that they were too adult. I think he said, this is how I want you, but I can't be sure. Even the way he touched my hair, the way he played with it, it was as though he had discovered something, as though it reminded him of something. I don't know how to explain it.'

'And so you left your hair loose,' he said. 'You never told me about this.'

She sighed. 'I wanted him to be happy.' She put her hand over his, held it against her head as if for comfort. 'I wonder sometimes if Concetta should return to Sicily.'

'It would break her heart,' he said, although his own heart exulted.

'You are a good man,' she said. She stood up. 'It's time I woke

Tommaso up from his siesta,' she said. 'Rosaria and I plan to take him onto the Heath in his carriage. The fresh air will do us all good, I think.'

Leaving his study, she halted at the door and turned back to look at him. She studied him for a moment. 'You do love me, don't you, Edward?'

He was shocked. 'Of course I do.'

She nodded, apparently satisfied, and left the room.

George came to his study ten minutes after Marisol and Rosaria had taken Tommaso out of the house. 'May I speak to you, sir?' he said.

'Of course you may, George,' said Edward. 'Come in.' He gestured towards a chair. 'Sit down.'

'Well, thank you, sir,' said George. 'If you don't mind, I will.' He sat down, examined his nails while Edward waited for him to speak, something he seemed reluctant to do.

'So, tell me, George,' Edward said eventually. 'How can I help?'

'It isn't you that should be helping me, sir, but the other way around. Only I don't know how to start without seeming impertinent.'

Edward smiled. 'We have known each other too long and too well for you to need to worry about impertinence, George. Come on now, let the cat out of the bag.'

'Very well, sir. It's about something Rosaria said. About the mistress.'

'You gossip about us,' said Edward. 'Your Italian must be improving rapidly.'

George gave a sheepish smile. 'We manage, sir. But it isn't gossip, exactly. It's more concern, if you will.'

'Concern?'

George nodded. 'She says that the mistress is unhappy.'

'She worries about Tommaso,' said Edward.

'I know that,' said George. 'But that isn't the only thing that makes her unhappy.'

'I don't understand.'

George looked directly at Edward, embarrassed. 'She thinks you may not love her as you should.'

'I'm sorry?'

'That there may be another person you love, as you love her, but more so.'

'She thinks I have a mistress?' said Edward, incredulous.

George nodded. 'She has said to Rosaria that she can smell another woman on you.'

'She has said what?'

George repeated his words, adding: 'On your skin, sir.'

'I don't believe this. Are you sure?'

'Yes, sir. She says there are times your body smells of some other woman's perfume.'

'What nonsense is this?' said Edward, agitated.

'A flowery scent, she says.'

Edward looked at George, for the first time in anger.

'You have spoken to Rosaria about why we left London, about what happened here?'

George shook his head, adamant. 'I would never do that, sir. You do me a great wrong to even think so.'

'Forgive me, George.' Edward was immediately contrite. He had trusted George with every secret he had, apart from one, and never had reason to doubt his valet's good faith. They were as close as brothers, he had often thought. Whatever George might want, he only had to ask. 'So she knows nothing?'

'If she knows anything about what happened, she has learnt it from someone other than me, sir.'

Edward sighed deeply. 'Do I?' he said.

'Do you what, sir?'

'Do I smell?'

George tried unsuccessfully to conceal a smile. 'Not that I've noticed, sir.'

'And has Rosaria noticed this woman's smell on me?'

'No, sir, not as far as I know. If she has done, she has kept it to herself. But I know for a fact that she thinks the mistress is mistaken and has told her so more than once. I have heard her.'

'They have spoken about this in front of you?'

George smiled again. 'The mistress doesn't credit me with knowing even a little of their language.'

'I wish I were as competent a student as you have proved, George.'

'I have had more incentive to learn, sir, what with Rosaria not speaking our lingo. The mistress's English puts mine to shame.'

Edward was silent for a moment, lost in thought. Finally, he spoke. 'Have you noticed anything strange here, George, in the house?'

'Yes, sir,' said George. 'I certainly have. Noises I can't account for. I've smelt flowers too, although not on you, sir. Ever since the young master was born. Not all the time, just now and then. Before that there was the crying at night. I couldn't sleep. I thought at first it was coming from your room.'

'You never spoke.'

'It wasn't my place to speak, sir.' George paused. 'And not only in the house.'

'What do you mean? What else have you heard?'

'Not heard, sir. Seen. One evening, in the garden. I was bringing in some cushions that had been left out there and I saw something inside the orangery, something moving around. I thought it might be a fox that had got trapped in there, so I went to look.'

'And what was it?'

'Well, it wasn't no fox, sir. It looked about the size of a chimpanzee and that's how it moved, sort of low, with long arms, but, well, I don't know how to describe it, sir.' He shook his head, as if still in disbelief. 'It looked hollow, it was just bones, sir, bones walking.'

'And inside the bones, was there nothing inside?'

'Green stuff, sir. Dead plants, they looked like. Flowers, but withered up.'

'What did you do?'

George looked ashamed. 'I did nothing, sir. I brought the cushions up to the house and I locked my bedroom door. I didn't sleep that night.'

'You've seen nothing since?'

'No, sir.'

A noise came from the hall. Marisol and Rosaria had returned from their walk with Tommaso. Edward heard laughter, and was relieved. 'Thank you, George. I appreciate your honesty.'

'It was my pleasure, sir.' He hung back a moment. 'Only I wouldn't want Rosie to have to leave, you see.'

Rosie, Edward noted. He smiled. 'I shan't let that happen,' he said.

He caught up with Marisol in the nursery. She was lowering Tommaso into the cot and didn't hear him enter the room. When he slipped his arms around her waist, she stiffened and then relaxed. 'You scared me,' she said.

'I love you with all my heart,' he said. 'You know that, don't you?'

She turned in his arms until she was facing him.

'Of course I know it,' she said.

'You must trust me,' he said. 'Always.'

She pulled a little away from him. 'Why are you telling me this?' she said.

'Because I'm frightened you love me less than you did,' he said. 'I couldn't bear that.'

She wriggled free. 'I'm sorry,' she said. 'I'm in no mood for this.'

Edward didn't understand her mood at first. He looked into the cot. 'Has our little son been difficult?'

She shook her head. 'It has nothing to do with him.' She bit her bottom lip, a gesture he loved. 'I think we were followed.'

'Why do you think that?'

'Because I saw two men when we reached the Heath. They were standing some distance away. I might not have noticed them but they both had dogs, and you know that I distrust dogs. I pointed them out to Rosaria, and they moved off. But ten minutes later I saw them a second time, and then again as we were leaving.'

'They might have been exercising their dogs.'

'Of course they might. But they weren't, Edward.' She sighed. 'I don't expect you to believe me. Why should you?'

'Of course I believe you,' he said. 'Just as you believe me.'

She looked at him then. 'Have you ever loved another woman, Edward?'

'Why do you ask?'

'Because I need to know, Edward.' But before he could answer, she continued: 'I could tell on our wedding night that I wasn't the first. I expected that, and I was glad of it, if you wish to know the truth. I was scared you might know as little as I did about what needed to be done.' She smiled, as if remembering. 'But that isn't what I mean by love. You know what I mean, Edward. You have always been honest with me, as I always have been honest with you. Please don't lie to me now. I could not bear it.'

It was impossible not to tell the truth. 'Yes,' he said, his heart thumping in his chest. 'Yes, I have loved another woman.'

'And where is she now? Is she here, with us?'

'Good God, no.' The idea was too awful to be contemplated.

'She is dead,' he said. 'She died before I met you.'

'You're sure of that?'

He bit back a cry of pain and rage. 'Of course I'm sure of it. What are you saying?'

Nervous, she tugged at the ring on her finger. 'There are times when I feel that we are not alone, that someone is with us. A woman, Edward. I feel her presence. She is like a warmth in the air sometimes, sometimes a coldness. I can't explain. Sometimes I feel that she is inside me, inside my body, that she is using me to look at you, to be with you, that I am being pushed to one side to make room for her. I smell her sometimes, the scent of her. I thought it was on you, but now I'm less sure. I think the smell is on me, on my skin.' She shuddered, then brushed one hand with the other, as if to knock something off. 'What was she like? Was she beautiful?'

Edward nodded. He thought his heart would break. 'Yes, she was beautiful.'

Marisol considered this. 'Did she look at all like me?'

'Why are you doing this to me?' he said, his voice tormented. 'I can't bear it.'

'I look like her, don't I? You married me because I look like the woman you loved, the woman you say is dead.' This was no longer a question.

'You look like you, like no one else,' he said. He took her hands, felt her resistance, held them until she yielded, surrendered to his will. 'I love you with every breath of my body, every beat of my heart. I don't know what else to say.' He let her go. 'You must believe me. I shall die if you don't.'

She was about to respond when George appeared at the door. Edward wondered how long he had been there.

'Excuse me, sir,' he said. 'But Hopkins is in the garden. He wishes to speak to you. He says there is a problem with the orange trees. He thinks they may be dying.'

Chapter Seventeen

Marisol gathered up her skirts and ran down into the garden, with Edward and George behind her. She caught sight of Rosaria as she passed her room and called for her to follow. The four of them arrived together at the door to the orangery. It was late afternoon by this time, the sun still streaming through the windows, casting long shadows on the floor and walls. Hopkins and his sons were standing by one of the trees nearest the door, examining its bark. They turned as one when Marisol approached them, gasping for breath.

'What is the matter with my trees?' she said.

'I don't rightly know, ma'am,' said Hopkins. 'Not being familiar with citrus plants. But look at this.' He pointed to a part of the bark that had started to flake off. The wood beneath was streaked with red and oozing, as though the tree had bled. Around the base of the trunk were dark-brown patches of hardened bark. 'I've never seen the like of it.'

'Can nothing be done?' she said. She looked around her. The floor of the orangery was littered with fallen fruit. 'And the other trees? Are they affected too?'

'Afraid so, ma'am. But this one is the worst.'

'You say they are dying?'

He shrugged. 'I cannot say they are not dying, ma'am.'

She cast a helpless glance at Edward.

'Fresh air,' he said. 'They need fresh air and sunlight. Are you sure we shouldn't have moved them on to the terrace, Hopkins?'

'As I said, sir, I'm no expert.' He looked at the eldest of his sons, who nodded. 'We can but try.'

The pots were manhandled out of the orangery and lined up along the terrace. Marisol examined every tree, delicately touching each patch of wounded bark as if afraid that too heavy a hand might cause the tree pain. The job was half done when Edward saw that Concetta had brought Tommaso down into the garden, to watch. He waved her over, expecting her to join them, but she shook her head and took the child back into the house.

Marisol came over to him and took his arm. 'I don't know what I'll do if they die,' she said, her voice breaking. She was near to tears. 'They are all I have of my home.'

'I shall find an expert gardener for you,' he said. 'They have an orangery at Kew. We shall save your trees, my darling.'

She took his hand and led him across to the nearest tree, reaching into the mass of leaves to pick a forgotten fruit from a branch. With a cry, she pulled back her hand. The fruit she had plucked fell to the ground and burst apart, its inner pulp already decayed.

'You've hurt yourself?'

'There was a thorn,' she said. 'I didn't see it.' She held her hand out to show him as a wounded child might, in a way that touched his heart. There was a bubble of blood on the tip of her ring finger. He kissed it clean.

'There shouldn't be thorns on these trees,' said Hopkins. 'It's gone back to its wild state if there are thorns grown on it. That's something I do know about these blighters, if you'll excuse my language, ma'am.'

'Do what you can, Mr Hopkins,' she said. 'I beg you.'

'I shall do my best, ma'am. I promise you that.'

*

169

That evening, Marisol complained that her whole hand was throbbing. 'If only I could get the ring off,' she said, 'but I think the finger has swollen.'

Edward looked and saw that the point at which the thorn had pierced the skin was an angry red, with a point of yellow at its heart. 'You have an infection,' he said. 'We need to wash the wound.' He called George and told him to tell Rosaria to prepare a warm bath for her. 'You have had a tiring day,' he said.

'But I want to see Tommaso,' she said, in an agitated way. 'Before he goes to sleep.'

'Let Concetta care for him,' said Edward, taking hold of her arms in an attempt to pacify her. 'You can see him later, after you've attended to yourself. He won't be asleep. If he is, you can sit beside him for a while. He will know you are there.'

He helped her undress and put on a robe. He was gentle with her and he felt his gentleness work upon her; she became softer in his hands, more yielding. When Rosaria came to accompany her to the bathroom, he told her that he would take care of his wife that evening, and Rosaria smiled and backed away.

Marisol lowered herself into the water, with Edward's help. He had never seen her so exhausted, as though the life force had been torn out of her, to leave her ragged and frail. She winced when her hand touched the water. He knelt beside her. 'You are so beautiful,' he said, his voice low, almost as though he were talking to himself, as he carefully sponged her back, then moved around the tub to wash her arms and shoulders and breasts. Her skin was the colour of pale caramel, dark against the paleness of his own hands. 'You are mine,' he said when he touched her shoulder and, silent, she leant forward to let him bathe her hair. 'All mine,' he said, his voice so low it could barely be heard. He scooped up the water with a jug, time after time, tipping it slowly onto her bent head, until the whole luxurious mass was gleaming jet-black and full, then lifted it and let it separate and fall through his fingers, time and again, a gesture that was both affectionate and hypnotic. 'I have never loved anyone as I have loved you,' he said. What a relief it had been to talk to her that afternoon, he thought, to have told her, finally, the truth. That he had loved before.

That was when he heard the moan. At first, he thought he had imagined it, until he heard it a second time, a low, almost animal whimper. He had no idea where it came from; it seemed to have been made by the air itself. And then she moved her head a little, raising it from the water and he realised that it came from her, from beneath the dark wet curtain of her hair. He fell back. 'Teddy,' she said. She turned her head towards him. He saw her face, or what was left of it, skin drawn across bone, only the eyes alive. 'Teddy,' she said again. He shook his head in horror, and denial. 'No,' he cried, and, as though nothing had happened, Marisol was looking at him, her expression alarmed, water dripping from her hair, her hands on the edge of the tub to raise herself from it.

'What on earth is the matter, my dear?' she said.

Marisol's finger grew worse during the next few days, despite the attentions of Concetta, who applied a series of evil-smelling packs to the infection. When Edward asked his wife what they contained, Marisol told him not to worry. 'Concetta knows what she is doing,' she reassured him, but he was not convinced. He had neither forgotten nor forgiven her making the sign of the evil eye. All his attempts to speak to her, in Italian or otherwise, had been met by silence or the fewest words necessary to bring the conversation to a close. He had asked George if Rosaria knew what the woman was doing, but George said that his Rosie refused to speak about it. The mistress is in a bad way, he said, and Edward was grateful for his valet's candour. It was clear that Marisol, whatever she thought, needed something other than her wet nurse's mumbo-jumbo. When Daniel came to visit, Edward asked him if he could suggest the name of a competent doctor. Daniel was startled by the request.

'You have no doctor?'

'I have never had need of one in London,' Edward said.

Daniel raised an eyebrow. 'When push came to shove, I suppose there was always Bell,' he said.

'That was unnecessary.'

'You're right,' said Daniel. 'Forgive me.'

Edward nodded. 'You're forgiven,' he said, although his tone contradicted this. 'In any case, I'm not the patient.' He told Daniel what had happened to Marisol.

'My, that does look painful,' Daniel said a few minutes later, when Marisol showed him her finger. It had swollen even more, the final phalanx was round and red as a plum. 'I have heard speak of a doctor, a compatriot of mine recently arrived in London to deliver a series of lectures on new techniques of anaesthesiology. He may be the man you need. I shall contact him immediately.'

'You think it is serious?' she said.

'I am not a medical man, so I really wouldn't know. But caution in these cases is always advisable, don't you think?'

Marisol looked at Edward, comforted, despite the anxiety in her eyes.

'Everything will be fine,' he said. 'You'll see.'

That afternoon, when Marisol was resting and Rosaria was playing with Tommaso in the garden, George came to find him. 'I think you should come with me, sir,' he said to Edward. 'There is something you should see.' Edward put down the book he was reading and followed George from the house. Neither man spoke. They walked down the drive and through the gate that led onto the road. As soon as the gate was closed behind them, George nodded to his left. 'Down there, sir.' Edward glanced down the road and saw a huddle of Gypsy women at the corner, looking his way. 'They've been hanging around here all day, sir. I asked them what they wanted a little before lunch and they told me that what they did was none of my business and that I should leave them alone, although their language were a little more choice than that.'

'I'll deal with this,' said Edward. He strode towards the women, with George a pace or two behind him. As they approached, the group broke up and formed a line of four stoutly built women, arms crossed, feet placed firmly apart, that blocked their path. He came to a halt some yards away, with George at his heels.

'Good afternoon, ladies. I hear you have been here for some time,' he said. He touched the wall at his side. 'This is my property. Perhaps I can help you.'

'We want what's ours,' one of the women said.

'I don't understand. I have nothing that's yours.'

'Give us what's ours and we shall go.'

'I don't know what you're talking about,' said Edward, feeling himself flush with fear and rage.

'You bring to us what's ours and you shall have what's yours,' the woman said. The others nodded.

'I know you,' a second, older woman said. 'And you know me, if you will only look.' Moving closer, he recognised Settie's mother. Madame Arlette, she had called herself then. He wondered what name she went by now. He had thought that he would never forget her, and he had been right. His stomach lurched in fear. 'You were quite the young gentleman then, if I'm not mistaken,' she said, with grim satisfaction. 'With your fine clothes and your fine friends. I remember them all, just as well as I do you. You wanted me to tell you what I knew about the dead, what they knew about you.' She smiled, without affection. 'Well, my dear, by now I think you may know a little more than you did then about the dead. And there is more to come, my fine young man. The dead are everywhere you look.'

'I know you, yes,' he told her. 'I know who you are.' What had Marisol once said, about the dead being always with us?

'Of course you know me,' she said. 'You stole my daughter from me, my youngest child that I had made with Enoch, my husband, God rest his soul. You had a good woman and look what you did to her.' Her voice rose. 'Look what you did to her and to what she gave you, with her own blood.' She took a step forward. Edward quailed before her. *Enoch*, he thought. He understood now. Settie had called her son Enoch, after her father. 'Bring to us what's ours,' the woman said again as a sort of invocation, as though the words had been rehearsed a thousand times, 'and you shall have what's yours.'

'Sir,' said George urgently, touching his shoulder. Edward turned to see what he wanted and saw, outside the gate to the house, Rosaria and Tommaso. Rosaria was trying to control the child, who was fighting against her, pummelling her chest with his fists. When he began to scream, she put him down, shocked. He fell on all fours and began to scuttle towards Edward and the group of women. There was something deformed about him, about his gait, as though his body were being strained beyond its natural limits. It was horrible to see. George fell back, then ran to meet Rosaria, who was following the child, both hands over her mouth in a failed attempt to stifle a cry of revulsion, and of pity. Edward forced himself to remain still, to calmly receive his son, beginning to sink to his haunches and open his arms, his blood running cold, but the child darted past him and came to a halt in front of the women. Settie's mother reached down, her arms spread wide, and spoke to him in a language Edward had never heard before. The child paused, as if to consider what she had said, and then, in babyish tones, replied in what sounded like the same tongue. The woman looked irritated, turned to her companions and muttered beneath her breath, too quietly for Edward to hear. But the child must have heard, because he backed away until he was beside Edward. He clutched Edward's leg. 'They want me,' he said, and the voice was Tommaso's. 'They want to take me away,' he said, and Edward thought, how can this be? How can this child be mine, twice over? 'They are not my mamma,' the child said, turning his head towards the gate.

Marisol was walking towards them, a shawl thrown hurriedly about her shoulders, her hair loose. Edward picked the child up and hugged him to his chest, but he began to wriggle once more and beg to be put down. When Marisol reached them, he looked at the women and then at her, before starting to cry. She bent down to comfort him, holding the women at bay with a raised hand. 'My darling,' she said. 'Mamma's here.' His whole body trembled for a moment and then went limp. Lifting him, wincing with pain as his body brushed against her finger, she turned to the women. 'You will pay for this,' she said. 'This child is mine.'

Edward took her arm. 'It is time we went home,' he said.

Walking along the road, Marisol hummed a *ninnananna* to Tommaso, her lips pressed close against his soft dark curls as he began to stir from his lifelessness. The child had inherited his mother's hair, his mother's skin, his mother's language. He had nothing of Edward. On the house steps, she passed the child to Rosaria and told her to take him to the nursery. She said that she would join them later. 'And tell Concetta that I shall need her as well,' she said. Rosaria and George went upstairs together, talking quietly to each other, the child alert now and staring over Rosaria's shoulder at his mother.

They were in the hall before Marisol spoke to him.

'Why did those people come to the house?' she said. 'What do they want from us?' Her tone was cold with rage. 'The men with the dogs, the men who followed me, they are all the same people, are they not? You have some connection with them. Don't lie to me. They know you, don't they?' He touched her arm, but she shook him off. 'You have many more secrets to tell me, I think.'

'The woman I loved,' he said. 'She belonged to them.'

'But she is dead, you said. What do they want from you now?'

He took hold of her more firmly, ignoring her efforts to free herself, his hands on both her arms. He made her turn to face him. 'Look at me,' he said, tightening his grip until she raised her head. He had never used violence of any kind with her; he was not a violent man. Shocked, she looked into his eyes.

'Whatever they want, I will make sure they have, I will do whatever they require, and then they will leave us alone, I promise you. I will make sure of that. My only thought is for you and for our son, Marisol. You must trust me,' he said. 'If you do not trust me, if you think I am lying to you or doing less than is necessary, I can do nothing. I will save you, at whatever cost, and I will save Tommaso, our only child.'

She nodded. 'I trust you,' she said. 'I am alone here, Edward. I have no choice.' Almost at once, she seemed to realise how cruel this sounded. When he relaxed his hold on her, she leant forward, stood on tiptoe and kissed him on the mouth. 'I have to go to Tommaso now,' she said. 'He will be waiting for his mother.'

Chapter Eighteen

Concetta was standing over the cot, her hands moving rapidly above the child in a series of circles, as though describing a spider's web. When Marisol and Edward entered the nursery, she put a finger to her lips, then tilted her head to one side and placed her hands together beside her cheek to indicate that Tommaso was asleep, and should not be woken. Crossing to the door, she gave Edward a perfunctory nod before whispering a few words to Marisol. Marisol shook her head rapidly. Concetta sighed, then left the room.

'What did she say?' said Edward.

'Nothing of importance,' said Marisol. 'Just that he was calm now.'

'You seemed to disagree.'

'No,' said Marisol, 'but sometimes she worries too much and then I become anxious.'

He was not persuaded. 'What was she doing with her hands?'

'Something to keep him safe.'

'Safe?' said Edward. 'Safe from what?'

'I have no idea,' said Marisol, with a note of irritation. 'Pay no heed to her, Edward. It is all nothing but foolish superstition. Concetta is of the people. She believes in demons and omens and the evil eye. She believes in ghosts.'

'Do you believe in ghosts?'

She looked at him. 'I believe that we are stronger than any ghost.'

Two days later, Daniel arrived at the house with Dr Andreas Licht, a wiry middle-aged man with a grey beard and a ready smile, carrying a leather bag. 'I am here to examine your wife's finger,' he said when he was introduced to Edward. 'Our friend here,' he added, indicating Daniel, 'is an extremely persuasive young man. He has convinced me that I am the only physician in the capital of England capable of treating the finger in question.'

'I am deeply grateful to you, sir,' said Edward, indicating that Licht should take a seat. He sent George to ask Marisol to join them in his study.

'You are well placed here in Highgate,' said Licht. 'The London air is utterly poisonous, as I am sure you are aware.'

'You are more accustomed to the wide open spaces of an entire continent, I imagine,' said Edward.

'Hardly that,' said Licht, with a smile. 'I live on the island of Manhattan and rarely leave unless it is to visit Europe. I am a creature of cities. I feel more at my ease in Berlin than I would do in the wilds of California.' He took a cigarette from his pocket and lit it. 'To be frank, I am perfectly at home in London, and will find it hard to leave.'

He might have said more but was interrupted by the arrival of Marisol. She had brought Rosaria with her, as though needing an ally in the virile atmosphere of Edward's study. Licht sprang to his feet and gave a little bow as he took Marisol's hand. He raised it briefly to his lips and then examined it.

'This is not the hand in question, I presume.'

Marisol shook her head. Reluctantly, as though she were ashamed of it, she showed him the wounded hand.

'Oh my dear girl,' Licht said, visibly shocked. 'I was expecting a simple whitlow, but this is rather more serious.' Edward followed his eyes and was appalled to see how much worse the finger looked than it had done only hours before. The nail seemed to be on the point of detaching itself from the skin beneath, the colour of which ranged from deep red to a single point of black where the thorn had entered. From the second knuckle to the tip the flesh was swollen to the size of a small egg, completely engulfing the first knuckle. Marisol had begun silently to weep.

'When did this happen?'

'Just over a week ago,' Edward said. 'A thorn from an orange tree.'

'And you have done nothing?'

'My son's nurse has treated it,' said Marisol through her tears. 'With traditional remedies. Herbs and suchlike. She is Italian, as I am.'

Licht looked sceptical. 'Traditional remedies are all very well when they work,' he said. 'But in this case, I am afraid they may have worsened the situation. You see this point here?' he said, taking a pen from his pocket to indicate. 'This looks like the initial stage of necrosis.' He sighed. 'Before I try anything else, I shall have to lance it.' He looked at Edward. 'I shall need some water boiled, clean cloths of some kind and a table.'

'The kitchen,' said Edward. 'Rosaria?'

Rosaria nodded and left the room. They joined her a few moments later. Marisol had regained her composure, but her face was creased with pain. Edward had taken her by the arm. At one point she stumbled against him. 'I am so afraid,' she whispered. 'I'm here beside you,' he said, but could not hide his own foreboding. She carried the wounded hand before her, raised like some awful trophy.

Licht sat her down beside the table. The cook had been dismissed to another room, but Concetta had been invited to assist, if necessary. She stood before the window, blocking the light, until Licht asked her to move away. Grudgingly, she obeyed. Edward sat beside Marisol, holding her free hand. Daniel and Rosaria, with George behind them, were waiting just outside the kitchen.

'All this fuss,' said Marisol, sniffing, her cheeks still wet with tears.

Licht opened his bag and took out a small bottle containing colourless liquid, and a scalpel. 'I shall try to make this as painless as possible,' he said. He uncorked the bottle and poured some liquid onto the blade, then made a small incision in the swollen finger. Marisol gasped, but whether from pain or from the sudden stench that filled the room it was impossible to say. Edward, retching, covered his mouth and turned his head away as a dark green pus-like substance oozed from the cut. 'I am sorry, my dear girl, but this is even worse than I expected,' said Licht. 'Hot water and a cloth,' he said, and Rosaria ran over and carried a bowl of water across to the table. He probed with the tip of the scalpel. Marisol's grasp on Edward's hand tightened and she let out a low whimper of pain. Licht extracted the scalpel. 'There is some rather curious material in there,' he said. He took some tweezers from his bag, wiped them with the same liquid as before and used them to slowly ease out a knot of what looked like vegetable matter, tangled and crushed. The stench grew worse. Rosaria ran down the corridor, crying, followed by George. Bending down, Licht peered inside the cut, then pulled away. 'I have never seen anything like this before,' he said slowly, looking at Daniel and then at Edward, avoiding Marisol's eyes. 'I think it may be the work of a parasite, too small to be seen by the naked eye, but more than that I cannot say.' He paused. 'What I can say is that the finger cannot be saved.'

'What do you mean?' said Edward.

'To judge from the state of this infection, and the effect it has had on the actual bone of the finger, the ring your wife is wearing has almost certainly saved her life,' he said. 'But I fear I must tell you that it has not been able to save her finger. The finger must be removed.'

Marisol turned to Edward. 'He is going to cut off my finger?' she said.

'I have no alternative,' Licht said. 'If you had waited another day I might have been too late.'

'You mean you intend to do it now?' said Edward.

Licht nodded. 'It is now or never.'

'Here? In the kitchen?' he said, aware that the question was absurd.

'It is as good a place as any.' Licht gave a reassuring smile to Marisol, whose face had drained of colour. 'I have everything I need, my dear. You will feel nothing.'

'But I will have no finger,' she said stupidly. She turned to Concetta, her face like that of a child who has stumbled and scraped a knee, unsure if the pain she feels warrants tears. '*Mio Dio*,' she said, '*O mio Dio*,' and Concetta took Marisol's head between her hands and pressed it to her bosom, as she would a child, to comfort her. Sitting helplessly beside his wife, Edward had never been so thankful to have Concetta with them. He felt Licht's eyes on him, patient, questioning. He nodded.

Licht had been right. There was no pain. He used ether and then cocaine around the point at which the cut was made. The sutures were neatness itself. He gave the ring to Edward. When Marisol came round she looked at her bandaged hand, and then at Edward. He embraced her, covered her face with kisses, told her how brave she had been. 'It's all over now,' he said, and she looked at him as though she had no idea what he meant. She did not ask him about the ring.

*

181

'I will have those trees destroyed,' Edward said the following day, when Daniel came to inquire about Marisol. He had left the house with Licht the previous afternoon. 'Reduced to firewood and burnt until nothing of them remains.'

'I think that would kill her,' Daniel said.

'You seem to know a great deal about what would kill my wife,' Edward said.

Daniel waited for a moment before speaking. 'You know that I am right. You brought her here as your bride when she was little more than a child, an extraordinary child, but a child still. You brought her to a country that is not hers, and her grasp of the language, extraordinary though it is, only conceals the fact that she is foreign. She has grown up in a different country, far from here, with different customs, and she has put those customs to one side for you.'

'You defend her wonderfully.'

'I understand her, Edward. She has no need to be defended. She can more than defend herself if that's required. But in order to live in your world as she wishes, as completely as she wishes, she must have something that belongs to her, to her world.'

'She has Rosaria,' said Edward. 'Good God, Daniel, she has Concetta.'

'She has her trees, Edward.'

'She has her child, for God's sake!'

'Does she?'

'What do you mean?' Edward was shocked.

'I'm sorry,' said Daniel. 'I should not have spoken so unwisely.'

'I'm not interested in whether you're wise or not,' said Edward, furious now. 'I want to know what you mean.'

'Very well, if you insist,' said Daniel. 'But whatever I say and whatever you think of what I say, you must remember that I speak to you now as your friend, perhaps your only friend, and as the friend of your wife. Do you promise me that?'

'Of course,' said Edward tersely, apprehensive.

'There is something about Tommaso that puzzles me. No, more than puzzles; that unnerves me. And it is something that I have also seen in Marisol. In the garden that day, when you were talking about the Book of Enoch and Tommaso responded to the name as though it were his. It is as though there were two boys in him. One of them is a normal child, who is learning to speak and walk as normal children do, and is a joy, and is *your* child, but the other one is older and more knowing and answers to the name of Enoch, and I wonder whose child he is. And it is hard to know which child has the upper hand.'

'You've seen that in him?' Edward was cautious.

'Yes,' said Daniel. 'And I believe I've seen something like it in his mother. She is distant sometimes. At first I thought she was dreaming of her home, but it is more than that. She is not dreaming; it is as if she were waiting. There are times she almost seems possessed.'

Edward was silent. When he spoke, his voice was low. 'Before Settie died she told me that she and our child would always be with me, would always be by my side. I thought it was the most loving thing I'd ever heard. It was like the marriage ceremony. Till death do us part, I thought. I never imagined that she would die.' He paused. 'And I never imagined that death would make no difference.' He stared into Daniel's eyes, his expression haunted. 'She is still here with us,' he said. 'I have seen her.'

'Where? In the house?'

Edward shook his head. 'I have seen her in Marisol.'

Their conversation was interrupted by a cry from upstairs. It seemed to come out of the nursery. Edward sprang to his feet. 'Come with me,' he said to Daniel. 'Whatever is happening I want you to be there.'

Concetta was leaning over the cot, dressed in a long black robe that Edward had never seen before. She was chanting what seemed to be some sort of incantation, words that he recognised as Latin, but transformed by centuries of use into a mystifying demotic. She had a small glass bowl in one hand and a wooden cross in the other. She was dipping the cross into the bowl and flicking drops of water onto the child below, who was wriggling and screaming. Marisol stood by the window, watching the scene with such intentness that she only became aware of Edward when he crossed the room and pulled Concetta away. She turned towards him with a howl of anger and struck his face with the cross. '*Via!*' she shrieked. 'Go!' He staggered back, his hands flying up to his cheek. Marisol restrained him as he rushed towards Concetta, ready to pull her away once more. The room was racked by the screaming of the child. 'Leave her alone,' she said, bursting into tears. 'Let her finish what she has started.' He pushed his wife away, but found his arms pinned down as Daniel took hold of him from behind. 'Get that damned witch out of here!' he cried. 'I shall kill her before she harms our child.'

'Have you understood nothing?' wept Marisol.

'I want her out of this house tomorrow,' said Edward, wriggling to free himself from Daniel's grasp. He felt blood trickle down his cheek as Daniel pulled him from the room and pinned him against the wall of the corridor.

'Listen to me,' he said. 'You will calm down.' He waited for Edward to answer him. When no answer came, he continued. 'When you have calmed down, I shall release you and we shall talk about this with your wife. Do you understand?' He waited until Edward made a reluctant nod. Marisol had left the room and was standing beside him. She touched Daniel's arm.

'Thank you,' she said.

'You lied to me before,' Edward said. 'When she was in there with Tommaso two days ago. She was doing the same thing, wasn't she? Casting some sort of spell.'

'She was doing it because I told her to do it.'

'You told her to bewitch our son?'

'You don't understand. Bewitching has nothing to do with it. You've seen him. You know that what is happening to him is wrong. He is being destroyed from within.' She gestured to Daniel to step back. 'Do you remember when I thought I might be carrying twins, but I wasn't sure. I could not find the words then, and I do not think I can find them now. But the child inside me was doubled in some way. And now I have seen him, I have lived with him and fed him and loved him this past year and more, and I am more convinced than ever that I was right. He is one child but he has two souls, Edward, and one of those souls is evil. He scares me sometimes and that is when I know. You have seen him do things no normal child can do. The women outside the house knew that. They knew *him*, Edward.'

'I don't want her in the house,' he said.

She brushed this aside. 'Edward, my trees are dying,' she said. 'There is something evil in this house and it is not Concetta. And it is not our son, although it may have taken refuge in him.' She lifted her bandaged hand, where the finger had been. 'Whatever is killing them has done this to me. It has taken my finger and it is taking my trees, and sometimes I feel that it is taking me, but it will not take my son.'

She put the hand against his cheek; he felt the roughness of the cloth and, beneath it, the absence. Let her live, Settie, he thought. Let her be happy as you were happy. Let her be loved as you were loved. Forgive me.

Marisol lowered her hand and stepped back. 'I think you know who they are, and why they are doing this, and what they want.'

'What can I do?' he said. His tone was penitent, helpless.

'You can put it right,' she said.

Chapter Nineteen

The following day, Edward and Daniel made their way to the Lea Valley. They left their cab in Clapton and crossed the river on foot. Edward thought that he could remember where he had seen the camp but now, almost four years later, there was no longer any trace of it. He started to walk aimlessly, beating at bushes with a stick he had picked up, cursing under his breath, until Daniel caught his arm and pointed out that Gypsies were nomads. 'They might not even be in London,' he said.

'So now what shall I do?' said Edward. The previous day had left him exhausted, without resources now that his anger with Concetta had passed. All he knew was that he had to save Marisol.

'You could ask Poynter,' said Daniel. 'It was Poynter who arranged the séance in the first place. I believe he is still dabbling in Gypsy lore when he is not philosophising at the club to anyone prepared to listen. I expect he is there as we speak. He may know where his erstwhile spirit guide has set up shop.'

'Then let us find him,' said Edward.

As Daniel had predicted, Poynter was sitting in one of the smaller rooms at the club, the usual copy of *The Times* about to slide from his sleeping body to the floor. He woke up when the two men sat in neighbouring chairs. 'What a pleasant surprise,' he said.

'I'm not sure about that,' said Edward. 'We need your help.'

'Whatever I can do,' he said. He sat up. 'Is this about Bell?'

'Why should it be about Bell?' said Daniel.

'Because I hear that he has been admitted to an asylum, although I imagine one should not say that. Men such as Bell prefer more genteel names for such places. Let us call it an institution for people with nervous exhaustion.'

'Why should we want to help Bell?' said Edward.

Poynter shrugged. 'Because he once helped you?'

Edward blenched, then glanced at Daniel, who made a gesture that he should continue. He looked back at Poynter. '*You* once helped me,' he said, 'and I should like you to help me again.'

Poynter sat forward. 'Willingly, my dear boy.'

'I am looking for the medium whose séance we attended. Madame Arlette.'

'In that case,' said Poynter, with a smile, 'you are speaking to the right man.'

The camp was on the far side of Parliament Hill, in a part of the Heath that Edward had never seen, as distant from the city as could be imagined. The Gypsies' tents and caravans had been arranged in a sheltered valley between two small copses of oak, with a stream running along one side of the camp, and open countryside before it. Edward and Daniel had left their cab a mile or so behind them, where the road petered out, and followed Poynter's directions, increasingly dubious about their accuracy until they saw a plume of smoke in the air. 'There they are, damn them,' said Edward, a note of exhausted triumph in his voice. He accelerated his pace, with Daniel trailing behind him.

They were within hailing distance of the camp when a man approached. Edward recognised him at once. 'We meet again,' he said. 'Where are your dogs?'

'Elsewhere.' The man took off his hat and wiped his brow with his sleeve. He glanced at Daniel, then gave a wry smile. 'You have brought *your* dog with you, I see,' he said.

Edward turned to Daniel. 'I believe this man is Settie's elder brother. His name is Bartley. I am right, am I not?'

The man made no answer to this. 'What do you want with us?'

'I should be the one to ask you that question. You have been hounding me for months. You have driven an acquaintance of ours into a lunatic asylum. And that is not all.'

'We are free men. We can do as we wish.'

'I do not doubt it. But I am not here to talk to you. I wish to speak to the person I believe to be your mother. I know her as Madame Arlette.'

The man turned his back on them both and walked away. After a few steps, he stopped and looked over his shoulder. 'Are you coming, or not?'

They followed him down to the camp.

Their visit had been expected, or so it appeared. As they neared the camp, people began to emerge. Men and women, boys and girls climbed down from the darkness of their wagons or crawled from the low earth-coloured tents to gather together around the fire. By the time Edward and Daniel reached the heart of the camp, where the fire had been made, thirty people or more were waiting for them, the men with their arms crossed, handkerchiefs knotted at their throats, the women standing together a little apart, barefooted children hanging on to their skirts. It was hard to read their expressions, hard to distinguish aggression from curiosity. The air smelt of the horses tethered beside the stream, and of burning wood. The silence was unnatural, thought Edward, unnerving. And then a little girl began to cry to be picked up and he was taken back to the first nights with Marisol in their marriage bed, and the scent of flowers.

He did not see Madame Arlette at first. He was about to ask

someone if she might be fetched when the group of women parted to let her through. She was dressed in the same full patchwork skirt as the others, but more heavily embroidered. Her blouse had long full sleeves, with ruffles at the wrists and collar. Over her head she had tied a bandanna, knotted behind her neck, her long grey hair hanging beneath it in two loose plaits. She wore a necklace of gold and bracelets that sparkled in the light of the fire when she moved her hands. Her ears were weighted with more gold, twisted and encrusted with glinting stones. For the first time he saw a likeness in the mother to her daughter, to Settie, less from this tawdry display of wealth, this unwonted magnificence, than from an air of power the display had given her, the knowledge of her own splendour, a splendour that in Settie had been innate.

'You have come to us,' she said. 'Finally.'

'Yes,' Edward said. 'I have come to ask for your help.'

The woman laughed, a rancorous, scornful laugh, then looked about her, at her people, as if to seek confirmation of what she had just heard. Some of them nodded, others remained impassive. The little girl began to cry again, wishing to be put down. Finally, when Edward was about to repeat his request, she turned, her expression contemptuous, to face him. 'You gorgios have no shame. You murder my daughter, you murder my grandchild, and then, as if nothing had occurred, you come here to our homes and ask us for our help.' Some of the men unfolded their arms and took a step forward. She raised a hand to stop them, spoke to them in their language. They stepped back, but Edward sensed that his safety, and that of Daniel, depended on her. He wished that he were alone. The thought that he had allowed Daniel to become involved in this was bitter to him. His conscience could not bear another death. He steeled himself. All I can do, he thought, is tell the truth.

'I did not want your daughter to die,' he said. 'You must believe me. I would have given my own life for that not to have happened.'

189

'Your life is of no use to us,' she said dismissively. 'If we had wanted your life we would have taken it by now, as we have taken others.' She turned towards the group of men and said a few words. Before either Edward or Daniel had time to move, four of the men broke away from the group and interposed themselves between the two friends. Daniel was half led, half dragged away by two of the men, while the other two held Edward. He struggled for a moment, but the men's grip tightened on his arms. He cast an agonised glance at Daniel, who was far away from him now, his initial resistance having been replaced by submission.

'I know that you are capable of murder, and that justice is on your side,' he said as calmly as he could. 'I must thank you for allowing me to live.' He paused, afraid his voice might break. 'But I would beg you not to harm my friend, who is entirely innocent in this matter.'

The woman nodded slowly. 'You wish to live. That is your right. But it is too late for my daughter.' She turned then to her people and raised her arms. 'Our daughter is dead,' she said. An angry murmur rose from the crowd. 'Our daughter is dead at your hand.'

Edward felt the grip tighten once more on his arms. He strained his eyes to find Daniel, but he had been led behind the caravans and could no longer be seen. Desperate, he decided that he would play his final card.

'Are you so certain that she is dead?' he said. 'Because I have sensed her presence.' He waited to see if the woman would react. 'I have seen her. I have seen her in the body of my wife.'

The woman nodded. She seemed unsurprised. 'That is my daughter's work,' she said.

'I cannot bring her back to life,' Edward said. 'And yet she will not leave me in peace.'

'She will not leave you in peace because she knows no peace. You say she is not dead and what you say is true. She will not be dead until she is united once more with her people. Until that is the case she will continue to seek to return and she will never leave you in peace, or otherwise. Your task, and your only hope for peace, is to bring her home to us.'

'How can I do that?' he said.

'Bring us her earthly form,' the woman said, 'and she will rest.'

'You want me to find her body?' said Edward, sickened by the thought.

'She must come home to us,' the woman said again, raising her voice for the first time. She lifted both arms in the air and wailed, the noise of an enraged, wounded beast. The men began to stamp their feet, the women took the howl and modulated it into a song that seemed to come from the earth, a round of pain and anger, of anguish and revenge. Edward's blood ran cold. He struggled against the grip of the men holding him, called out at the top of his voice for Daniel, was rewarded by his own name being called out in return. He imagined the body of Settie, the state it would be in by now, and was repulsed by what he saw in his mind's eye. He had no idea where she was, no notion how he would find her.

'I will find her,' he shouted above the noise. 'I will find her and bring her to you.' The blood-chilling chorus of the women died down, the men interrupted their dance and stood as they had stood before, menacing in their stillness. He waited until there was silence, and then addressed the woman in as low and level a voice as he could muster, as though the two of them were alone. 'Give me my friend and let us go. If we are harmed, if *he* is harmed, or a single hair on the head of my wife or child, believe me, you will never see her again. I promise you that.'

The woman lowered her arms. During the wailing her face had been flushed but now had lost its colour. She seemed to consider Edward's words, and then called for Daniel to be brought back. 'We would bring her home ourselves but we do not know where she is,' the woman said and, for the first time, Edward heard a new note in her voice, a note of pain, of regret, a plea to which he might be able to respond. He recalled Settie's words, at the cemetery, at their first meeting. *If we are buried elsewhere we cannot rest.* Had she been telling him even then what he must do?

He waited until Daniel stood beside him. 'If I can find her and bring her to you, will she rest then?' he said.

'Yes. I give you my word. Find her and bring her to us, and she will have peace. We shall all have peace.'

'Prepare whatever is required,' said Edward. 'I swear to you that I shall find her.'

'Now, tell me once again every detail you remember about that night,' said Daniel. They were seated together at an alehouse near the Heath. They had walked from the camp to the road in silence, until Edward found the strength to apologise to his friend for what had taken place. Daniel had shrugged his apologies off. He had put his arm around Edward's shoulders, a gesture of conciliation and affection that had moved Edward and augmented his sense of guilt. 'Thank you,' he had said, 'I don't deserve you,' before lapsing once more into silence. When Daniel had suggested they return to the house, where Marisol would be waiting, he had shaken his head. 'Not yet,' he had said. 'I need to think.' Now, he raised his empty glass and called for it to be filled, for both of their glasses to be filled.

'You woke up—' prompted Daniel.

'I've told you already a dozen times,' replied Edward, who felt that he was about to weep with frustration. 'I came round after collapsing and the house was abandoned. There was no sign of the doctor, no sign of Settie. The rooms were empty. I searched the entire place, every floor, every room. I looked behind curtains, under beds. I was desperate, Daniel. I had lost everything I loved.'

Daniel was thoughtful for some minutes, an eternity it seemed to

Edward, who already regretted having snapped at him. Eventually he spoke. 'There is one person who might be able to help us.'

Edward raised his eyes to the ceiling, lowered them with a sigh. 'Bell?'

Daniel nodded. 'Bell.'

'And to find Bell, we need to speak to Poynter again.'

'I'm afraid we do.'

'I wonder sometimes how much he knows about that night, about Settie,' said Edward.

'Oh, I think he knows everything,' said Daniel. 'And whatever he does not know, he has imagined. He is a devious man, and not always in a good way.'

'Is there a good way to be devious?'

'I would like to think that there is not,' said Daniel. 'But there is an ocean of difference between what is good and what is useful.' He was about to stand up when Edward told him to stay where he was.

'Let us have one more drink,' he said. 'If only to strengthen my resolve. Because I don't know how I shall be able to go through with this, Daniel, even with your help. You have been more than a brother to me, and I thank you for it with all my heart.'

Fresh glasses arrived. Daniel raised his. 'Let us drink to friendship, and to the usefulness of devious men.'

Edward smiled and raised his glass. 'I can drink to that,' he said.

Poynter wanted to know if they had found Madame Arlette, and was delighted to hear that the information he had provided had been valuable. 'She is an extraordinary person,' he said. 'And I genuinely believe that she has a gift. She speaks to the dead. As I believe her daughter does,' he added, throwing an arch glance at Edward. 'She has seven children, you know, and is herself a seventh child.'

'She had seven children. Her youngest is dead.'

'Ah yes,' said Poynter. He placed the tips of his fingers together and raised his hands in a parody of prayer. 'I imagined that to be the case.'

Edward rose to go, but Daniel caught his arm. 'You said that Bell had been placed in an institution,' he said.

'I believe that he placed himself there,' said Poynter. 'To protect himself.'

'We should like to speak to him about a certain matter,' said Daniel, looking at Edward as if to warn him not to speak. 'Perhaps you can tell us where the institution is.'

'I believe he is there incognito. I'm not sure that he would appreciate a visit from people he used to know.'

'What he would appreciate is neither here nor there,' said Edward sharply.

'Quite,' said Poynter. He named a street in Maida Vale. Edward and Daniel stood up and were about to leave when Poynter called them back. 'Be sure to give him my regards,' he said. He looked at Edward. 'No one is beyond forgiveness, you know. Whatever they may have done.'

The road Poynter had indicated was lined on both sides with white four-storeyed stucco buildings. The street number took them to a double-fronted structure with a deep portico supporting a balcony. There was no indication of the nature of the building outside and Edward hesitated a moment before ringing the bell. Almost immediately the door was opened by a middle-aged woman in a grey dress, buttoned up to the neck, with a white cap on her head.

'Good afternoon, gentlemen, what can I do for you?'

'We wish to see Dr Frederick Bell. I believe he is a guest here.'

'Who gave you this information?'

'Arthur Poynter, a mutual friend.'

'Do you have cards?'

'Of course,' said Edward.

The woman took them, read the names and looked both men over, as if checking for hidden weapons. 'You may wait inside,' she said finally, stepping aside to let them enter a spacious hall, empty of all furniture apart from a hatstand made of twisted antlers, the hollowed-out foot of an elephant containing a selection of rolled umbrellas, and a single straight-back chair. Paintings of hunting scenes adorned the walls. She went upstairs, her skirts swishing against the rails of the bannister. A few moments later she came down and they were told to follow her. She led them along a corridor until she reached the final door, knocked and, without waiting for a response, opened the door. Standing back once more, she ushered the two men into a large sunlit room. Bell was sitting at a desk beside the window in a silk dressing gown. He smiled nervously, and stood up to greet them, his hand held out.

'How pleased I am to see you,' he said. 'Poynter informed you that I was resting here, I gather.'

Daniel shook Bell's hand. 'That was what he said, yes.'

'They are all very good to me here,' he said, throwing a glance of unctuous gratitude at the woman as she left the room. He turned to Edward, who also briefly took his hand, but did not speak.

'Please, do sit down,' Bell said, indicating two armchairs, one at each side of the fireplace. 'I shall call for tea, if you wish. I am afraid I can offer you nothing stronger. Alcohol has been deemed too great a stimulant to my nerves in my present condition.' He gave a wry smile. He had put on weight since the last time Edward had seen him, and benefited from the attentions of a barber, but there was a pastiness to his skin and his eyes were dull; even his movements seemed to be slower than before, as though the mechanism of his self were winding down.

Edward shook his head. 'We are here to ask you for your help,' he said.

Bell seemed to wake up at this. 'Really? Surely I have helped you enough already,' he said, with an edge of sarcasm. 'I should have thought that my help was the last thing you would need. For my part, I see no reason why I should help you in any way. It is entirely thanks to the help I have already given you that I find myself here.' Each time he used the word *help* the pitch of his voice rose a semitone. 'If I had refused to help you resolve your problem with that damned Gypsy girl I should never have found myself hounded into this hateful place.' He was on the verge of hysteria by this point. 'I have been threatened, and deprived of my freedom and my belongings; I have been chased from one end of London to the other; I have lost my friends and been deprived of my profession. Why in God's name should I wish to help you?'

'We have been to speak to the people who tormented you,' said Daniel in a soothing tone. 'That is why we are here.'

Bell shuddered. He looked at Edward with malevolence. 'Why do they not kill you as they killed that poor devil in Whitechapel?'

'That is what we are here to talk to you about,' said Edward. 'I know there is no love lost between us. If the truth be told, I despise you as heartily as you despise me. But that poor devil in Whitechapel, as you call him, is the only one who can save us all.'

'He is dead! For God's sake, he is dead!' cried Bell, rising from his chair.

Immediately, the door opened and the woman who had let them into the building rushed across. 'I think it is time you gentlemen left,' she said. 'You have upset him. He is very frail. I will not have it, do you hear?'

Edward ignored her. 'What did he do with the women he killed?' he said, because there were no longer any secrets. He had had enough of secrets. 'I would wager good money that she wasn't the first unfortunate girl to die at his hand. I am right, am I not? You know that I am right. Where did he hide them?'

Bell flapped his arms in terror, then covered his ears. The woman stood between Bell and Edward, then pointed to the door. 'Leave. Leave these premises immediately.'

Edward pushed her to one side and grabbed Bell by the collar, then shook him with all the strength he had. 'Where did he hide the bodies?'

'I don't know,' Bell sobbed, the breath knocked out of him.

'I think we should go,' said Daniel. The woman tugged at Edward's coat, but he pushed her off a second time.

'If we find her, you will be free,' said Edward. 'Do you understand? You will be free.'

Bell looked at him, as if trying to understand. 'They killed him and they will kill me. They will kill us all.'

'If we find her, we shall all be free,' said Edward. 'They will never harm you again.'

'The cellar,' gasped Bell. 'Look in the cellar.'

Edward released him with a gesture of disgust. 'We have what we need now,' he said to Daniel. 'It is time we went.'

Chapter Twenty

It was later that evening, sitting alone in his study, that Edward remembered the prophecy of Madame Arlette. The smell of fruit gone bad, the cold earth floor, trodden down by indifferent feet. The cellar, he thought. That must be it. Something rotten that only love could heal. You will know love, she had said, and you must cherish it. And blood, she had talked of blood, of blood being left to flow and cleanse. Marisol had asked him where he had been all day and he had remembered his vow that there should be no more secrets, but he had still not found the courage to tell her everything. She had given him her bandaged hand and he had kissed the place where her finger had been while she stroked his head, and there had been a sort of peace between them that felt, to him, unwarranted, undeserved. He had talked about freedom so much these past few hours, freedom from fear of reprisal, freedom from guilt, freedom from the spirit of his first true love, now rotten thanks to him, and needing blood. He wondered if he would ever be truly free.

He crossed to the window and looked out. Marisol, with Tommaso in her arms, was walking towards the orange trees in the darkening garden. He watched her set the child down to touch the leaves of one tree, and then another. She is talking to them, he thought, urging them back to health, the trees that are all she has of her home. The man from the gardens at Kew had said that little could be done, but she had not given up. His heart filled with love for her. He left his study to join her, walked across the hall and along the corridor that led to that part of the garden. His hand was on the handle of the door when he heard Marisol's voice from the floor above, the floor of Tommaso's nursery. She was singing a *ninnananna* to their son; he knew the words by heart, he had heard it so often.

His hand trembling, he opened the door. Behind him, he heard a movement in the corridor. He turned and saw George, a tray in his hand, two glasses and a decanter on the tray. He looked sheepish, as though he had been caught out. 'Come with me,' he said. George glanced around for somewhere to put the tray. 'Don't worry about that,' snapped Edward. 'I need you with me now.'

The woman and child he had seen from his study window were on the terrace, by the orange trees. He walked towards them, his heart in his mouth. They didn't seem to be aware of him at first. The woman continued to touch the leaves of each of the trees, stroking their underside, muttering words in a language he didn't know, but now understood were words not of healing but of blight. He had almost reached them when the woman turned her head slowly towards him and he saw that her face was what was left of Settie's face. Her mouth opened, a void in the void. He was about to scream when she spoke, in a voice that was the shadow of a voice, filtered through darkness and pain. *Free me*, she said. She touched the child beside her, and he saw the thing he had seen on the side of the cot, and smelt the same foul stench, like a flower of bone and rotting flesh. *Free us*, she said.

George was standing beside him when he came round. He looked to see where he was, saw with relief that he was back in his study.

'How long have I been here?'

'Five minutes, no more than that,' said George. 'You stumbled, sir. When you didn't get back onto your feet, I picked you up and carried you back into the house.'

'You saw them?'

George looked surprised. 'I'm sorry, sir.'

'You saw them,' insisted Edward.

'I don't know who you mean, sir.'

'On the terrace,' said Edward.

'There was no one in the garden but ourselves, sir,' said George, an anxious note in his voice.

Edward threw his head back and stared at the ceiling for a moment. He took a deep breath. *You must leave them alone. They do not belong to you.*

'I'm not sure what you mean, sir.' George looked around the study, as if for guidance. 'Let me get you a drop of brandy, sir.'

Edward sat up. He looked at George and there must have been something terrible in his look, because the man shrank back.

'Say nothing of this to anyone,' said Edward.

'As you wish, sir.' He stepped back. 'Is there anything you need, sir?'

'No,' said Edward. 'Thank you as always, George.'

George was walking towards the door when Edward called his name.

'Yes, sir.'

'Forgive me, George.'

'There is nothing to forgive, sir,' said George.

'You are always there when I need you, George. I would not have managed these past few years without you.'

George's face reddened. He gave an ironic little bow. 'At your service, sir. Whatever is required.'

Edward paused, and only spoke when George was on the point of leaving the room. 'In that case I shall need you tomorrow evening, George, for a rather delicate job. It will not be pleasant but it must be done, for the good of us all. Are you willing to help?'

'Of course, sir. Whatever needs to be done, you can rely on me.'

Edward nodded.

'Goodnight, George.'

'Goodnight, sir.'

Daniel met them outside Hancock's house in Whitechapel just before eleven o'clock the following evening. Like them, he was dressed in black. He had arranged for a cab, with a driver that could be trusted, to pass by the house after midnight. The street was deserted, the nearest gaslight some distance away. Edward and George had arrived a good thirty minutes earlier and had used that time to decide on the best way to enter the house. They had discovered, parallel to the road, a passage that ran along the back of the terrace to which Hancock's house belonged. From there, it was easy enough to force a window and climb into the scullery, from which the rest of the house could be reached. Five minutes after Daniel's arrival, the three men stood in the darkness of the interior. They had an oil lamp, spades and a pick, some rope and a large, deep sack filled with sheets. The preparation had been left to Daniel; Edward could not have done it without attracting the attention of Marisol.

Edward had explained to George what needed to be done during their journey from Highgate. George had shown no surprise; he had nodded and said that he was ready to do whatever was required of him. 'Rosie says the mistress will be glad when all this is over,' he had said, and Edward wondered how much Rosaria knew, and how much George had decided not to tell him. 'We shall all be glad,' he replied. Now, as they stood together in the room that must once have been the kitchen, he wondered if he had been right to involve George. The house had an evil feel to it, but that was just him, he told himself, and what he knew. Although maybe not; he had been worried that the house might have been sold, or occupied, but he thought now that every brick and tile and floorboard would repel anyone foolish enough to want to live there. The house remembered, he thought. The house knew. He hoped to God that none of its evil would rub off on Daniel and George.

He looked around him. There was a sink and a range. The air was stale, the floor was deep in dust and something adhesive that clung to their shoes as they moved. Cobwebs dangled from the ceiling, visible when Daniel lit the oil lamp. A rat scuttled somewhere out of sight behind a skirting board. There was no furniture of any kind, apart from a broken chair that looked as though it had once been used to hold the door shut. Edward remembered this room, and every other room in the house as though he had never left, as though his heart and soul had been imprisoned there since that night. He led the other two into the hall.

'There must be a way into the cellar from here,' he said.

'You didn't go to the cellar?' said Daniel.

Edward shook his head. 'It didn't occur to me that there might be a cellar. Oh my God, Daniel, she might still have been alive. I was sure she was dead but maybe I was wrong, maybe I was too hasty. I might have been able to save her.'

'There is no point in thinking like that. If she had been alive, you would have known.'

At first they could find no door leading down from the ground floor. It was George who finally spotted a break in the wallpaper beneath the stairs. 'Come over here,' he said. 'This must be it.' He pushed his fingers into the crack until he had gained purchase. Edward joined him, running his hands around the hinged panel until it could be eased away from the rest of the wall. The panel ran from the floor to just above waist height and was no more than thirty inches wide. It couldn't have been easy to manoeuvre a body through such a space, thought Edward, as he stepped through the hole and put his feet on the first step of a narrow staircase leading down into the cellar. Daniel had given him the oil lamp to light his way down. At the foot of the stairs, he held the lamp up so that his companions might follow. When the three of them were standing together, with the tools they had brought, Edward swung the lamp around so that they could see where they were.

The cellar stretched the width and depth of the entire house. The walls were rough brick, the ceiling the underside of the beams and wooden floors above their heads. The air was rank, stifling. Filled with trepidation, Edward lowered the lamp to see what lay beneath their feet and saw pressed earth. 'She must be here,' he said. 'But where do we start?' He put down the lamp and sank to his haunches in despair.

'We can't give up now, sir,' said George. 'Can we, Mr Giles?'

'Of course not, George.' Daniel put his hand on Edward's shoulder. 'Come on, my dear fellow, we shall do what we have come here to do, or be damned trying.'

Edward gave a wry laugh. 'Rarely has a word been better chosen,' he said, straightening up, his momentary weakness behind him. He picked up the lamp again and began to walk slowly around the cellar, looking for signs of moved earth. 'We need more light,' he said, frustrated. He took another step. 'Look,' he said, crouching down, 'here you can see a sort of scratching, but what does it mean? That some rat has tried to dig a hole here? It might just as well be the way the dirt was thrown down in the first place.'

'Look over here,' said George.

Two lines were inscribed in the dirt, as though a box had been dragged across it.

'It's on the surface,' said Edward, disappointed. 'There is no sign of digging.' He began to lose heart once again. 'I wonder how many people have been buried here,' he said. 'If we do find anything, anyone, how shall we even know that it's Settie? He must have murdered more than one woman in his career. I'm glad that he's dead, you know, and I only wish he knew that.'

'Wait a minute,' said Daniel suddenly. 'What's that over there?' He took the lamp from Edward's hand and carried it across to the furthest corner from where they stood. 'Just look at that,' he said, pointing down.

The two men looked to where he was pointing and saw the skin of dark earth move a little, as though a wind had lifted it from the harder surface beneath. As Edward watched, a cavity seemed to form in the shape of a human footprint, no longer than the palm of a hand. A second footprint appeared in the same way, and a third. 'There,' he said. 'You see.' But the other two men were staring at him, perplexed. Step by step a trail was made, as if by the feet of an invisible child, until the far wall was reached, at which point the footprints stopped. *You have led me to your grave*, Edward thought, *and I thank you for it*. The temperature in the cellar had fallen but Edward barely noticed as he took a spade and scraped the surface dirt away and began to dig.

It took them ten minutes to reach her. In the years since her death, dampness had consolidated the earth of the cellar floor; despite the sudden cold, the three men were sweating by the time they caught a glimpse of soiled white cloth emerging from the heavy clay. Edward fell to his knees beside the hole they had made and began to scrape the cloth free of what covered it with his bare hands. When Daniel tried to lift him away, he immediately protested. 'She's here, I know she is,' he said. 'He's wrapped her in this. This is her shroud.' He found the edge of the cloth and pulled it to one side, but the fabric resisted and then tore. The piece of cloth that was left in his hand he threw behind him in a fit of rage. 'Give me the spade,' he said, continuing to lift the cloying earth away until finally a lozenge-like form became visible, encased like a mummy by bound and rotting sheets. Edward passed the spade back to George and, with his bare hands, began once again to tear at those points where the cloth looked at its weakest, dark stains where the blood had soaked through, patches of mould, a hole that seemed to have been made by a scavenging rodent. Eventually, the cloth gave way to his efforts, tearing along a fault line that ran from head to foot of the body concealed within. With a cry of triumph, Edward ripped the sheet away.

The first thing he saw was the hair, the hair he had loved, as black as jet, as strong and lustrous as it had ever been, longer now than he had ever seen it, as though it had continued to grow after death. It reached her shoulders and breasts, and formed a cushion beneath the upper part of her body. It framed a face that was still somehow *her* face, despite the cheekbones that poked beneath the dried skin, the empty sockets where her beautiful eyes had once lived, the teeth that seemed to have grown out of all proportion. He *recognised* her. Hancock had left her dressed and the rags of what she wore that night still lay on her, discoloured, mouldy, a shroud within a shroud, but beneath them, as he stripped them away, he found her body, reduced to nothing, to skin and bone in the most literal sense, but hers, and only hers. He'd expected the stench of dead flesh, and he was ready for that, but there was nothing, no odour of any kind; the air of the cellar seemed strangely cleansed by her presence. He worked with scrabbling hands at the scraps of cloth, of skirt and blouse, of underclothes, until she was naked, indifferent to the company of the other men, who had fallen back, in horror or disgust he neither knew nor cared. He worked until nothing stood between them. He lay on her then, his whole body pressed against hers, his living face against the taut stretched skin of her cheek, his mouth in her hair, as soft as it had always been, silk to his touch. I will never leave you, he shifted his head and whispered into the hard shell of her ear, the hoop that pierced its lobe still there, warm gold against his lips. You will always be mine. He reached for her hand and found it and felt the space where the finger had been and all the horror of that night came back to him, the sound of the scalpel, the gush of blood, and with that, the presence of Marisol, his living wife. He lay there and wept until Daniel and George lifted him from the corpse and out of the makeshift grave into which she had been tipped. 'I'm sorry,' he said, to Settie and to Marisol – he no longer knew to whom – as they sat him on the last step of the stairs, 'I'm so sorry.'

'The cab will be arriving,' Daniel said gently. 'We need to prepare her to be moved.' He paused. 'We can do this without you if you prefer.'

'No,' said Edward, standing up. 'I wish to be with her to the last.'

They found the child after Settie had been lifted from the hole and placed on the fresh white sheets that Daniel had brought. It had been hidden beneath her, bundled up in bloodstained rags, the size of a dead cat, thought Edward, his mind going back to the carcass on the beach, the furious seagulls wheeling above his head. So small a thing, to have barely lived and to have died like this. The moment he saw the bundle he remembered the same wretched rags in Hancock's hands, still fresh with Settie's blood. He took it now from George, who had raised it from the hole, and held it to him as he had held the child's mother, as though his beating heart could instil its own life into them. How light it is, he thought, a breath of air, a handful of dried leaves, a gust of wind in a bag. 'My unborn Enoch,' he said. He thought of the footprints that had led him to them and wrapped what felt like a tiny half-formed foot in his hand. 'Thank you, my child,' he said. Settie had already been laid out on the sheets and Daniel was just about to lift one side to cover her body, but Edward gestured to him to stop and placed the bloodied faggot where it belonged, still swaddled as a newly

206

born baby might be, on the breast of its mother. Standing back, he closed his eyes for a moment, as if he had seen enough and could take no more, then shook his head and told Daniel that he could continue. He watched in silence as the other two men finished the job.

Chapter Twenty-one

They put the body in the orangery, concealed behind a screen. By the time they had finished Edward, despite his exhaustion, had no desire to sleep. He showed Daniel to a bedroom and left him there to rest, wanting to spend some time alone before Marisol woke and asked him where he had been. He had told her that he would be late back the previous evening and she, understanding that he had a secret, had asked no further questions. But he suspected that her reticence would soon be replaced by curiosity and that he would be expected to satisfy it. He sat in a chair on the terrace, surrounded by the dying orange trees, remembering what he had seen there less than two days before, the woman and child walking slowly from tree to tree, less real than the woman and child he had exhumed that night, and yet more real too, walking and speaking as though they were as alive as he was, spreading their blight. He had thought they were Marisol and Tommaso, and he had been right to think that, although the idea of it scared him so deeply he had to resist the urge to drag the bodies out of the orangery and burn them, a funeral pyre both interrogation and final judgement. You had no right to make us suffer like this, he said, as though Settie were standing before him. I had no wish to hurt you. But the cruelty of this struck him as soon as the notion had formed. You came to me in supplication, he thought. You asked me to free you, and that is what I shall do.

'What are you thinking?'

He turned and saw Marisol beside him.

'I was thinking that I don't deserve you,' he said.

She sat down next to him. 'I couldn't sleep,' she said.

'I'm sorry,' he said. 'I had to be somewhere else. I shall tell you about it one day.'

'No,' she said. 'That wasn't it. It wasn't your absence that disturbed me, I mean. It was something else. I was unsettled, literally. I felt that I was being moved, manhandled, that is the word, isn't it? I felt that I was not myself.' She leant over and took his hand. 'Tommaso was the same. He cried for hours and then suddenly went to sleep as though someone had comforted him.' She looked into his eyes. 'I don't know where you were, and I don't believe that I want to know, but I think that you were doing something that will make us feel safe, that will make us feel free. You don't need to tell me if I am right, because I know that I am.'

'Everything I have done and will do,' he said, 'I do for you.'

The same cab that had brought them back from Whitechapel was waiting for them outside the house three hours later. Daniel had slept a little, and was ready to leave. Edward had decided that George's presence would not be necessary and, despite his insistence, he was told to remain at the house. Marisol had busied herself with Tommaso all morning, preferring to stay out of the way, but she had made it clear that she had some idea of what was taking place when she presented Edward with a quilted silk counterpane, richly embroidered in gold thread, that she had brought with her from Palermo, a family heirloom that she had always refused to use, deeming it too precious. Now, she stood before him with the counterpane in her arms. 'She deserves better than a cotton sheet,' she said when he took it from her, overwhelmed. 'Let her be buried in this.' She turned and walked away before Edward had a chance to speak.

He took it to the orangery where Daniel was waiting for him by the screen. Gently, the two men enfolded Settie in the counterpane and carried her to the cab. Edward was struck once more by how light she was, how insubstantial the process of death had made her, as though what mattered of her had been dispersed elsewhere. He remembered as he crossed the lawn, with Settie's shoulders weightless in his hands, what Poynter had said about the spirit of the dead seeking revenge. What was the word he had used? Yes, *mulo*. The *mulo* of Settie and their child had fled this shell and left it as empty as the brittle husk cast off by a moth. Where are you now? he wondered. You will soon be altogether free, he said in a whisper, lowering his head towards the covered head beneath him. He glanced up at the house as they crossed the drive and noticed a woman at one of the second-floor windows, a woman holding a child, and was convinced, for the briefest moment, that it was Settie, watching the scene of her own removal, cradling Enoch in her arms. But then, as the woman moved closer to the glass, he recognised Concetta, with Tommaso. Did she feel the *mulo* of Enoch being drawn from the flesh of her small charge, as a splinter might be drawn from a wound? He saw the child wave, and smiled up, hoping that the smile could be seen that far away. He wondered where Marisol was and felt a tremor of foreboding.

The cab moved off as soon as both men were seated inside. When they had arrived at the nearest possible point to the camp, Edward told the driver and Daniel to wait. 'We have to make sure that we do this as it should be done,' he said.

He followed the same path he had followed only days before until he reached the camp. Men and women left their caravans and tents to watch him as he approached, expressionless, with that edge of threat he had felt on his previous visit. Once more, he was greeted by the man he knew as Bartley, Settie's brother. He had his dogs with him this time. They seemed to know Edward, sniffing with interest around his heels. 'I have her with me,' Edward said. 'I have brought her to you.'

The man nodded. 'You have done well.'

'She is in a cab, back there on the road,' Edward said, pointing behind him. Help me, he thought, I cannot do this by myself. We must share this burden now.

'I shall fetch a horse and trap,' the man said. 'The earth is rough, but it is better that way. We cannot touch her. Wait here for me.'

He walked off, his dogs behind him. A few minutes later Edward saw him return with a trap, a second man sitting beside him. 'Show us where she is,' he said.

Edward walked back to the cab, with the horse and trap following him. He remembered what Poynter had told him about contamination, how the body of the dead contained a poison of the spirit. When they reached the road, the two men dismounted and he and Daniel lifted the body onto the trap. It was a little too long and had to be bent to fit, a final indignity, thought Edward, sick to the stomach at the thought of what they had done and still had to do. Settie's brother stood back, the blood drained from his face by the proximity of death, while his companion turned the horse and trap and began to lead it back to the camp. A hundred yards away, he brought the horse to a halt.

'You will wait here,' Bartley said. 'We have certain things to prepare.'

'How long will that take?' said Edward.

'When we are ready for my sister you will know.' They walked down to the camp, leaving Edward and Daniel at the trap.

'So Marisol knew,' said Daniel.

'What?'

'The counterpane,' said Daniel.

'Yes,' said Edward. 'I don't know how. I suspect that George has spoken to Rosaria, her maid. He is head over heels in love with her, and will tell her anything she wants to know, and she will tell Marisol. Love knows no secrets.'

'So you intend to talk to her yourself?'

'When all this is over, yes.'

'She deserves no less,' said Daniel. 'And so do you. I was wrong to think otherwise. She deserves your trust.'

Edward turned to his friend. 'I have been so frightened,' he said. 'I thought I could put the past behind me, but I was wrong. Poynter told me that Gypsies believe in the spirits of the dead coming back to seek revenge, that the dead are not always dead, that they hunt down the persons who caused their death, and I thought of that story that Rickman told us, do you remember? About the *obambo*? But what the *obambo* sought was not revenge so much as a home, a place to live, and I wonder if that is what Settie has been searching for all this time. A place to live. She had every right and every reason to seek revenge, God knows, but I cannot bring myself to see her as evil, Daniel, I simply cannot. I think she still loves me and it breaks my heart that I cannot love her back, as she deserves. I can only hope that she will find her home today.'

Daniel was about to answer when they heard a shout. The horse pricked up its ears and began to trot down the hill towards the camp, with Edward and Daniel walking swiftly in an effort to keep up. The horse came to a halt at the heart of the camp, where the fire had been. It was now empty, and looked as if it had been swept clean in preparation for their arrival. They stood beside the trap, uncertain what to do, whether to lift Settie from the trap or let her remain there until someone appeared to tell them what should be done. Edward was about to call out when a low hum came from the caravans and tents surrounding them. The hum became louder, transformed itself into a wordless chant as the men and women of the tribe slowly emerged from the darkness. Edward had expected them to be dressed in black, but both women and men were wearing red and white, the men red trousers and white shirts, the women red floral skirts and shawls and blouses in white lace and red silk, a shocking brightness in the late-morning light. They gathered, the chanting of the women breaking up and becoming a deep, guttural weeping, but orchestrated as the chant had been, with the voices of the men providing a counterpoint. As if she had been summoned by the weeping, Settie's mother climbed down from a caravan and took her place at the head of the group. She wore a deep-red dress, as though dipped in blood, with a white shawl over her head and covering her shoulders. She had a stick in one hand. She added her weeping to the rest. Agitated, the horse whinnied and scraped its hooves against the grass. Gradually, with a slow and measured step that had the quality of a dance about it, the tribe encircled the two men and the contents of the trap, closing in until Edward felt a tremor of fear, an urge to break through the tightening ring and flee. Settie's mother came to a stop before him. He could see the pores of her nose, the fine hairs on her upper lip. The gold around her neck would have weighed a lesser woman down. He looked at Daniel, who was pale, his face set. Daniel caught his eye and, with the slightest gesture of his head, told him to stay where he was.

The lament escalated as Bartley stepped forward to take the bridle of the fretful horse. The people standing before them parted to make a passage that would allow the trap to leave the circle and gently, with the men and women of the tribe flowing back into the wake of the trap and carrying Edward and Daniel with them, Bartley led the horse towards one of the copses that flanked the camp. The procession fell in behind him, Edward and Daniel walking on either side of Settie's mother. At the edge of the copse, Bartley brought the horse to a halt. Edward saw a hole prepared in the ground for Settie and beside it a coffin.

Bartley approached him. 'There is one more thing you must do for us. We cannot touch her with our hands. It is forbidden. You will place her in the coffin for us. That is the last thing we shall ask of you.'

Edward nodded and stepped forward but Settie's mother caught his arm.

'What have you done to her? What is she wearing? What are these cloths in which she is wrapped? Are they hers?'

'Yes.'

'I have never seen them. You gave them to her?'

'They are rightfully hers,' said Edward. 'They belong to her and will accompany her to her final rest. That is her wish.'

The woman considered this, then acquiesced with a nod. 'I need to see her.'

Bartley spoke to his mother, sharp urgent words, but she brushed them off. 'She is my child. I need to see her,' she said again. She gestured to Edward. 'Take these cloths off her. Show her to me.'

Edward and Daniel did as the woman wished. Slowly the body of Settie was revealed. Everyone but her mother had fallen back long before the final layer was removed. Even Bartley had turned his face away. She lay there still, as she had done when they uncovered her the night before, but this time the bundle of the child was where it belonged, where Edward had placed it, on her breast.

'And the child,' Settie's mother said, gesturing towards the bundle with her stick. 'I wish to see the child. No grandchild of mine shall be buried in those filthy rags.'

Edward looked at Daniel, who bent to pick the bundle up, but the woman used her stick to stop his arm. She pointed with the same stick at Edward. 'He is your son,' she said. 'This is for you to do.'

Reluctant, heartsick, he took his child and felt for a way to remove the cloth, rotten and clinging to the tiny corpse within. He found the edge of the material and scratched until it came free. The blood the cloth was soaked in had set into a kind of glue that was stronger than the cloth itself. It came away in hunks until all that was left was the tiny skeleton of an unborn child, dried skin barely covering the bones, with the vestige of a tail and the tiniest hands and feet imaginable. A third of its length was the head, a third the ribcage, round as a ball, its limbs like tangled twigs. It looked nothing like the thing he had seen in the nursery, thought Edward. But of course not; the thing had grown as this pale leathered shell had not. He lifted it to his face to see if it had a scent of any kind, of rotting vegetation, of creeping vine; there was nothing but the faintest trace of mould. He held it up for the mourners to see and a cry of horror rose from them. '*Mokadi*,' they said. 'Unclean,' translated Bartley.

His mother called two women across to her. They were carrying clothes, an embroidered gown, a shawl and red leather shoes, which they placed at her feet. 'You will dress her in these,' she said to Edward. 'They are the clothes she wore when she was last here, before she was taken from us. They are the finest clothes she had.' Edward looked at Daniel, appalled, but Daniel picked up the dress and nodded to the woman.

'It shall be done as you wish,' he said. He indicated to Edward to lift Settie's head and shoulders and he did so, shocked to find that they were warm to his touch, as though life still beat in them, but brittle, as though a careless hand might break them. Daniel eased the gown past her head and the nape of her neck. 'Now you must lift her arms,' he said, adding, in a low voice, 'We shall do this, Edward. We have no choice.' Edward did as Daniel bid him. He took Settie's hands in his and slowly raised the arms, first one and then the other, expecting stiffness, unnerved to find a compliance in them, a willingness to help him in this unbearable task. He lifted her hips and the gown slid beneath and down her legs until she was dressed, and whole, and Edward's heart was broken a second time. 'No, let me do it,' he said as Daniel was about to ease the

215

shoes onto her feet. He took the shoes and held them in his hands for a moment. She had worn a pair of shoes like these when they were in the cottage, he remembered; he had held them as he was holding these shoes now, imagining her living feet inside them. He thought of the second time he had seen her, at the séance, and the prophecies, as though they had been spoken by her; the blood washing blood, the cold, hard earth. The earth will be kind to you this time, he whispered. You will always be loved. Carefully, he slid a shrivelled foot into each shoe, tears blurring his vision. He straightened up and was about to step back when a cry from the woman stopped him. 'Wait,' she said. 'She is incomplete.' She poked at Settie's hand with the tip of her stick. 'Where is her finger?'

Edward was about to speak when Daniel touched his arm. 'Leave this to me,' he said. He took something from his jacket pocket and held it out. 'It is here,' he said, holding out a small cylindrical object wrapped in a handkerchief. 'It was removed by the man who murdered your daughter, but I have recovered it.' He shook the handkerchief and a finger fell out of it onto the counterpane. The woman moved back with a cry of horror. Bartley came close to see what she had seen, a human finger, the skin still pink, the flesh still soft upon it, the wound still visible but clean of infection, as though it had been healed. 'Bury her,' he said. 'Do it now.' Edward was frozen where he stood, but Daniel picked up a long side of the counterpane and began to cover the body once again. 'Leave that,' snapped Bartley. 'We want none of that. That is not hers and will be destroyed. Put her in the coffin as she is, with the child, and close the lid. Do it now, I tell you, before we are further defiled.' He turned and held his mother then, to comfort her.

Daniel had to shake Edward to make him do as Bartley had bid them. The two men lifted Settie from the ground and lowered her into the coffin, then placed the naked child on her breast. He was naked because he had never been born. He had never been dressed, nor fed, nor loved, thought Edward. He shuddered when Daniel picked up the severed finger from the counterpane and dropped it into the coffin beside the disfigured hand. For a moment, Edward thought he saw it writhe, like some blind worm, as if seeking its rightful home.

Together, they lifted the lid and rested it on the coffin. 'Wait,' said Edward. He looked on Settie's face for the last time and saw it as it had been, her dark eyes, her skin the colour of dusk, of roses, her hair so black and yet lit from within, by its own light. And that was when he remembered. He put his hand into his trouser pocket, took out the ring that had once belonged to his mother and dropped it into the coffin.

'You can close it now,' he said.

Chapter Twenty-two

Throughout the journey back, Daniel sat silently on his side of the cab, watching the road as it passed beneath their wheels. Edward waited for him to explain why Marisol's severed finger had been in his possession, but no explanation was given and Edward did not have the heart to ask him. When the cab came to a halt, he rested his hand for a moment on Daniel's sleeve.

'I don't know how to thank you,' he said. 'I could never have done what we have done without you.'

Daniel nodded and smiled, a wary smile, as though he had expected something else. 'We are still friends,' he said, his tone determined that this should be so. Edward squeezed his arm.

'We shall always be friends.'

Marisol was waiting for them at the open door of the house. When they walked through the gate she ran down the drive and threw her arms around Edward's neck. 'My darling,' she said. 'I have been so anxious.'

'Everything has been resolved,' he said. He hugged her to him, kissed her cheek. It was damp against his lips. She has been crying, he thought, and was once more filled with regret at the pain he had caused her. He had so much to tell her, but that could wait.

Without letting go of Edward she held out a hand towards Daniel. 'My dear friend,' she said when he took it. Edward turned his head to see Daniel perform a little mock bow, clearly gratified by her attention, and understood for the first time the depth of Daniel's feelings for his wife. How stupid I have been, he thought. He wondered how much of what Daniel had done had been done not for him but for her, out of love for her, but dismissed the doubt at once as both idle and ungrateful. Without Daniel he would have achieved nothing.

'Come with me,' she said, taking both men by the hand and leading them into the house. They looked at each other; there was something in her tone that made Edward apprehensive. She called for Rosaria and told her to take Daniel into the garden and to serve him coffee and anything else he might wish for. 'I have to talk to my husband,' she said when Daniel looked surprised. 'I know that you have become part of our family and I can imagine how much we must owe you, but I am sure that you will be patient. We shall join you very soon.' Daniel gave another bow and followed Rosaria. As soon as they were gone, she turned to Edward. 'And now we must talk, you and I,' she said, her tone stern, but with an edge of irony. 'You have a great deal to tell me and I intend to wait no longer.'

So that was it. His plans to delay the conversation had been thwarted. He could hardly blame her. He led her into his study. 'Sit down,' he said. He pulled an armchair across to face her, sat down opposite her and took both her hands in his.

'Her name was Settie,' he began.

When he had finished, when he had told her everything from their initial meeting outside the theatre to their final farewell that morning, she took her eyes off his for the first time. 'You loved her very much,' she said. He nodded, but did not speak. 'And do you love me as much as you loved her?' He nodded again. His eyes were filled with tears.

'I do,' he said. 'I think I love you more.'

219

She dismissed that with a wave of her hand. 'Do you think she forgave me?'

'I hope so,' he said. 'I believe so.'

She sighed. 'I felt something leave me this morning. You will understand, I think. I have felt a sort of oppression for some time now, an oppression within myself. Concetta would call it possession, but I have not given her that opportunity. I have spoken a little of this to Rosaria, but to no one else. I have felt her within me, watching me, guiding me sometimes – I don't know how else to describe it. She has taken control of me sometimes. There were times when I was sure that Tommaso wanted her rather than me and I may have allowed it to happen. I may have stood aside for her. Does this make sense to you?'

'Yes.'

'And then this morning, when you were at the camp, I felt a lightening. It was physical, Edward. I felt her leave my body. It was almost like a birth, but without the pain, without the effort. She was simply there and then not there and I was free. And the strangest thing was that, as she went, I felt that she wished my happiness. I felt as though I were being blessed by her. She had been waiting to be released as I had; no, more than I had. Far more than I had. She was waiting to finally die and I was waiting to be fully alive. I did not understand until you told me what had happened to her – how could I? But now I think I do. I think I understand how desperate she was to be gone.'

He stood up and pulled her from her chair into his arms. They were kissing, laughing, sobbing together when there was a knock on the door. Before either of them had a chance to speak, the door opened.

'Come with me,' said Concetta, followed by some words in Italian. Edward looked at Marisol, waiting for clarification.

'She says there's something wrong.' She shook her head, as if to remove an unwanted, troublesome thought. 'With Tommaso.'

*

Tommaso was lying on his back in his cot. His eyes were closed and his mouth slightly open. Concetta had covered him in a light blanket although there was no need. The room was already overheated, the windows kept closed to guard against draughts. He was breathing normally and seemed fast asleep.

'What's wrong?' said Edward. 'I don't understand.'

Marisol spoke rapidly to Concetta, who snapped back in an affronted way, as though she had been unjustly accused. When Marisol insisted, she shook her head, then spread out her hands to say that she had no answer. She seemed to be on the point of tears. Edward had never seen the woman like this; he was struck once more with apprehension.

'What does she say?'

'She says that she cannot wake him.' Marisol reached into the cot and gently touched Tommaso's shoulder. When he failed to respond, she took hold of the shoulder and jiggled it a little, but without result. She pulled the blanket off him and picked him up, shook him softly, whispering. 'Wake up, my darling,' she said. '*Svegliati*. Wake up.'

'Here,' said Edward. 'Give him to me.' Before she could say no, he had taken the child in his arms and begun to rock him, slowly at first and then more vigorously.

'You'll hurt him,' she said.

Edward looked at Concetta. 'You have given him something to make him sleep.'

The wet nurse, not understanding, turned to Marisol. When she heard what Edward had said, she was vehement in her denial. '*Amo il bambino come fosse il mio*,' she said, her voice breaking.

'She would never do anything to harm him,' said Marisol. 'She loves him as if he were her own son.'

Edward, who had understood, held the child away from him,

221

hands beneath his arms. He hung there like a boneless doll, his head lolling, his eyes still closed. He has been drugged, thought Edward; there is no other explanation.

'We need a doctor for him as urgently as possible. I shall ask Daniel to contact Licht.' He headed towards the door before anyone had the chance to stop him and hurried down the stairs and into the garden, where Daniel and Rosaria were sitting with George.

'Good news,' Daniel said with a smile, but his expression changed immediately when he saw Tommaso. 'What on earth is wrong?' he said.

'He's sleeping and nothing will wake him,' said Edward. 'We need a doctor. How quickly can you get hold of your friend, Licht?'

'I shall leave at once,' said Daniel.

He was walking away when Edward asked him what he'd meant by good news.

'This is not the moment for good news, sir,' interrupted George. 'May I take the little chap for a few minutes? We have played together often. He may remember me and wake up.'

Edward, at a loss, glanced at Marisol, who had joined them minutes before. She nodded. George took the child and sat down with Tommaso balanced on his knee. He bounced him up and down, whistling. 'There's my little chap,' he said. Rosaria bit her bottom lip, then turned away, eyes welling up with tears.

Marisol watched George try to wake the child, her hand over her mouth. 'You'll make him sick if you carry on doing that,' she said finally, before starting to cry, long deep sobs that shook Edward to the core. 'I can't bear it,' she said. 'Not now. Not now that we are safe.'

Daniel came back after twenty minutes to find Edward and Marisol still in the garden. 'I sent a telegraph to Licht. He has replied and is on his way. He should be here very soon. He is aware of the urgency of the situation.' He looked at Tommaso, who was lying on Marisol's lap. 'No change, I see.'

She shook her head. Her eyes were red with weeping. 'I thought it was all over,' she said, 'but I was wrong.' She looked at Edward, who was sitting near her, his face in his hands, and had not so much as glanced at Daniel. 'You promised me, you swore to me, that it would all be over,' she said. 'And I believed you. I believed every word you told me.' She turned her gaze on Daniel. 'I trusted you both.'

Edward waited for Daniel to speak, to defend himself, but his friend, taken aback by this unexpected assault, seemed lost for words.

'He has done what he can,' Edward said. 'You cannot blame him.'

'I do not blame him,' she said. 'I blame you.'

'You are right to blame me,' he said, not raising his head, his voice muffled by tears and his cradling hands.

'I do not think I wish to stay here any longer,' she said.

Edward's head shot up. 'You don't mean that,' he said. 'You can't mean that.'

She began to cry again. 'I don't know any longer what I mean. Sometimes I wish that I had never met you, that you had never come to Palermo. And then I remember what we have done, the love we have shared, and I blame myself. Do you hear that?' She laughed, a bitter, mocking laugh. 'I blame myself.' She was about to say more when a cry burst from her. 'Oh!' she said.

'What is it?'

'He moved, Edward! He moved.'

Edward jumped up to see as Marisol lifted the child from her lap. It was true, his arms were lifted and seemed to be pushing something, or someone, away; his face, the eyes still closed, was anguished, and then angry. He made a sound that was almost a word, and then, as if nothing had taken place, went still and was limp once again, expressionless, in his mother's arms. She gave him to his father. 'I can't bear it,' she said, running into the house. 'I can't bear this any more.'

Licht arrived shortly after. Edward and Daniel heard his feet on the gravel of the drive. Edward sighed with relief. Tommaso, lying across his knees, had not moved again. The doctor was brought around the side of the house by George, Rosaria hovering in the background. He put his bag down on the table and turned his attention to Edward.

'This is your son,' he said, pulling a chair over in order to sit facing Edward and opening his bag. He lifted Tommaso's dangling hand to hold in his, felt for his pulse. 'How long has he been in this state?'

'For hours. There is nothing we can do that will wake him.'

'Has he been administered drugs of any kind to make him sleep? Alcohol?'

'Nothing at all. He normally goes to sleep without any effort, and wakes up in the same way. This has never happened before.' Licht took a stethoscope from his bag and listened to the child's chest for a moment, his face expressionless. He told Edward to turn Tommaso over and listened to his back. He lifted both eyelids and looked at each eye as it stared up towards him. He felt the throat and the stomach and between the legs. Finally, when Edward was about to demand some sort of response, he shook his head. 'There is nothing wrong with your son,' he said. 'He is in excellent shape.'

'Then why won't he wake up?'

Licht shook his head again. 'I have no idea. I have seen cases of narcolepsy in adults.'

'Narcolepsy?' said Daniel.

'From the Greek words for numbness and to be seized,' said

Licht. 'It has only recently been identified as an illness, in France, I believe, although cases have also been recorded in Germany. It induces periods of diurnal sleep. But the sleep is normally of short duration, unlike the case we see here.' He lifted the eyelids again. 'Have you seen any signs at all of movement since this began?'

Edward hesitated.

'Tell him,' said Daniel.

'There was a moment a little while ago,' said Edward. He described what had taken place. Licht listened attentively.

'Dreams are common in states of narcolepsy,' he said. 'And this sounds very much like the external manifestation of a dream.' He stood up. 'I see your wife is arriving,' he said.

Edward turned and saw Marisol walking across the lawn, with Rosaria and Concetta at her side. 'Good day, Doctor,' she said. Her voice was level and determined, almost cold, it seemed to Edward. He had never seen her in this mood before today. 'You have examined Tommaso, I see. What is your opinion of my child's state? What can we do to wake him?'

'I am afraid I can offer no solution, other than to wait, my dear child.'

She bridled at the word child, but then looked distraught as she took in fully what he had said. 'Wait, you say? And how long must we wait?'

'I wish I knew.' He put his stethoscope back in his bag. 'How is your hand?'

Marisol had clearly not expected this. 'The condition of my hand is the least important thing at the moment,' she said tersely, but Licht approached her.

'I understand your concern,' he said, 'but I can assure you that your son is in perfect health, as far as I can ascertain. Doctors, even the best doctors, may know a great deal, but the human body is always one step ahead of us, my dear, and all we can do is follow and try to learn. My experience tells me that your son will be with us all again very soon, unharmed, and that, I fear, is the only consolation I can offer.' He paused, then held out a hand. 'And now perhaps you would like to show me your finger.'

Reluctantly, Marisol allowed him to remove the bandage. When the wound was revealed he stepped back, visibly shocked.

'This is impossible,' he said.

Marisol held up her hand to her face. Edward stood up, Tommaso in his arms, and saw that where the finger had been removed the skin had healed completely. There was no sign of the incision Licht had made, nor, more surprisingly, of the sutures he had used to close the wound. The stump that remained of the finger seemed even to have grown a little.

'You have removed the stitches yourself?' Licht said.

Marisol shook her head. 'I don't understand,' she said. 'The bandage is as you left it. I have touched nothing.'

'There is something at work here,' said Licht, his voice shaking. 'I am a man of science, but I tell you, there is something at work in this house that I cannot explain.' He picked up his bag, avoiding all their eyes. 'I bid you farewell and I wish you and your child good fortune, from the bottom of my heart.'

'I must leave as well,' said Daniel. Marisol looked at him with anxious, pleading eyes. 'But I shall be back tomorrow.' He stood up.

'I'll walk to the road with you,' said Edward.

They had left the garden when Daniel stopped. 'I suppose you want to ask me about Marisol's finger.'

'I suppose I ought just to be grateful and leave it at that,' said Edward. 'Without it, we might never have finished our business there. But yes, I do want to ask you.'

'It's very simple,' said Daniel, with a trace of embarrassment. 'I left with Licht, you may recall, the day of the operation.'

'Yes,' said Edward.

'We were looking for an available cab when he stopped walking, opened his bag and took the finger out. We were standing beside a ditch, not far from the edge of the Heath. He had wrapped the finger in a scrap of cloth, I don't know if you noticed, and I had wondered at the time what he would do with it. But I never imagined that he would simply find somewhere convenient and throw it away. He smiled at me, and I was shocked. "Something for the rats," he said. He was about to shake the cloth over the ditch, but I took it from him.' He paused. 'It lacked respect,' he said. He smiled wryly. 'And then I had the finger in my hand and didn't know what to do with it, other than protect it. Does that make sense to you? And so I wrapped it in my handkerchief and put it in my pocket, and there it stayed until this morning, where it saved our lives. Ironically, as things have turned out, when you think that I could not tolerate the idea of its being eaten by rats.' He sighed. 'And so your dear wife, bless her loving heart, has also made her sacrifice for the good of you all.'

Without speaking, Edward continued to walk, followed by Daniel. It was only when they had reached the gate and Edward was about to open it, that he spoke.

'You love her, Daniel.'

Daniel nodded. 'I believe I do,' he said.

They stayed in the garden until it became too cold, taking it in turns to cradle the sleeping child. Twice, he seemed to be on the point of waking, and twice he relapsed once again into a numbness that Edward had begun to think of as death in life. Marisol was silent for the most part although, following the second spasm of movement, she said that there seemed to be something fighting within him, some battle that had to be completed. 'I think the other child is resisting,' she said. 'I think he does not want to leave his home in Tommaso.' She looked at Edward, her eyes moist but her expression no longer cold, as it had been before, and he was grateful for that. 'Do you think I am mad?'

'Nothing we say or do can be madder than the truth of all this,' he said. 'The truth itself is mad.'

She stood up. 'The sun has gone,' she said. 'It is time we went inside.' It was obvious that she had no desire to return to the house and Edward shared her reluctance. Entering the house felt like surrender, he thought. He eased himself up from his chair, stiff after having been seated for so long, and shifted the dead weight of Tommaso across his shoulder.

He was turning towards the house when she called his name.

'Look,' she said. He walked across to where she stood, beside one of the orange trees in its terracotta pot. He thought of the day the trees had arrived, how happy she had been. 'Look here,' she said.

He looked at where she was pointing, at the base of the narrow trunk, and saw a fresh shoot emerging from a crack in the bark. 'I was certain they were dead,' she said, marvelling. 'But look, Edward, here is another one.' She was right. The orange tree, which he had thought unsalvageable, was returning to life. She took his hand, squeezed it. 'Perhaps there is hope,' she said, reaching up and stroking Tommaso's cheek with her other hand.

'There is always hope,' he said.

Chapter Twenty-three

They spent that night with Tommaso between them on their bed. Neither of them had eaten, and neither of them slept. Over and over again, Marisol hummed her favourite *ninnananna*, the tune of which Edward knew by heart, until he hesitantly suggested that lullabies might have the opposite effect to that desired. They shared a smile, the only smile of the night. When morning came, Concetta arrived with coffee, which was gratefully received, and boiled eggs, which were turned down. She returned with a bowl of warm water, took off the night clothes Tommaso was wearing, and sponged the child down while his parents watched for signs of waking, but there was no change. He is so beautiful, Edward thought, as she dressed him in fresh clothes, and the vision of his other child came back to him, the skin and bones of him, the terrible naked fragility, even in death.

Tommaso was quiet most of the time, his breathing level, his limbs relaxed, so that he seemed a normal child. But then he would have a spasm; his arms and legs would jerk up and then retract as though his body were trying to close itself into a ball, his eyes would dart around behind their lids, and his parents would pin him down until the spasm had passed. They did not talk after these attacks. Edward was too scared to put into words what he was thinking, and he supposed that Marisol felt the same fear. It was only after the last, and worst, attack that they finally spoke. It came just after sunrise. Tommaso began to cough, as though he were choking on something. Edward picked him up and slapped his back while the damp and sweating body of his son twisted in paroxysms, gasping for air. He seemed to be on the point of suffocation when, with a final heave of his chest and throat, he expelled a stinking knot the size of a golf ball, a tangle of putrid stems and leaves.

'Concetta must have given him one of her potions,' said Marisol, furious. 'I shall never forgive her.'

'Don't blame Concetta,' said Edward.

'What do you mean?'

'Don't blame Concetta,' he repeated and this time Marisol was silent.

With infinite slowness the morning passed. They spoke to Tommaso, in English and Italian, they stroked his hands, which were warm and soft, and Marisol kissed him on his cheeks and forehead, brushing his hair back and cradling his face in her hands. Nothing woke him, and yet he seemed so calm, as though all it would take for him to open his eyes was the slightest noise, the slightest touch. George and Rosaria offered more than once to watch over him for them, and were sent away with gratitude but determination. Edward saw them standing in the corridor outside the nursery, their heads so close together they seemed to be kissing. He remembered the way George had held Tommaso the previous afternoon, the loving quality of it, and the eyes of Rosaria as they watched him care for the child, utterly absorbed. They are in love, he thought, and for a moment was relieved of his own burden. An unusually pale and silent Concetta brought them lunch on a tray, but neither of them could force themselves to eat. Soon after, Daniel arrived and was admitted to the bedroom. He sat there, but hardly spoke; his presence was comfort enough. At one point, Edward remembered something his friend had said the previous day, before he had known about Tommaso, something about good news. He asked him now what he had meant.

'George has said nothing?' Daniel said.

'About what?'

'About his plans to make Rosaria his wife.'

Marisol smiled, her first smile of the day.

'You knew about this?' said Edward.

'Not exactly, but I am not surprised,' said Marisol. 'She confessed to me some days ago that she expected him to make a proposal.'

'That is indeed good news,' said Edward. So I was right, he thought. 'I congratulate them with all my heart,' he said, although his heart was elsewhere.

'We must organise a wedding for them,' said Marisol. 'As soon as this is over. It will be a moment for all of us to start again.' She paused. 'As soon as this ordeal is over.' Her voice broke as she spoke these last words. Edward embraced her, and told her to be brave, to hold firm, to remember the hope they had shared the previous evening, in the garden, when they had seen the fresh shoots on the tree; but to no avail. She began to weep, deep racking sobs that shook her body. He held her tight, but the trembling would not be stilled. And then it happened.

'Don't cry, Mamma. Please don't cry.'

Tommaso lifted his head from the pillow and glanced around his parents' bedroom as if to establish where he was, then sat up and reached out a hand to touch Marisol, who gave a cry of joy and horror combined, so great was her shock. Edward stepped forward, laughing out loud in astonished relief, and scooped the child up, but Tommaso wriggled and stretched out both arms towards his mother, who was hysterical with delight, wanting to be taken, to be held and hugged, by her.

'Mamma,' he said. 'Do hold me now. I'm all alone.'

*

Three months later, George and Edward were waiting together before the altar at St Joseph's. The church was filled with flowers, orange blossom scented the air. The commonest flowers, the sweetest scent, thought Edward. The two men looked at each other and then at the guests, settling into their places with an air of festive expectation. On Rosaria's side there were few people: the household, acquaintances Rosaria had made during her Sunday visits to mass, some friends of Edward and his wife, with Daniel chief among them; Rosaria had insisted that they be invited. My mistress's friends are our friends, she had said when Edward demurred. George's family, on the other hand – his parents and an assortment of uncles, aunts and cousins – were out in force and occupied a good four rows. They were talking among themselves, calling out from pew to pew, intrigued to find themselves here, so far from their own part of the city, curious to see the bride. The only members of George's family to have met Rosaria before the wedding day were his mother, firmly seated in the front row beside her husband, her face almost wholly concealed by a hat the size of a small cartwheel, and his sister, Prudence, who had helped Rosaria prepare for the wedding and would be accompanying her to the altar, along with Marisol. It had been decided that Marisol would give the bride away, and that Edward would be best man. Tommaso, in a new sailor-style dress, was seated beside Concetta in the front row, his boots sticking out in front of him, and so far had behaved perfectly. The idea that he might be involved in the ceremony had been mooted, but rejected. He was still too young to be trusted, Marisol decided, and Edward concurred. The priest had initially been reluctant to celebrate the wedding, his memories of Tommaso's aborted christening still fresh, the scar on his hand still visible. But Edward had made a persuasive contribution to the church funds and all was resolved. Now, as the organist began to play the 'Wedding March', the priest's face lit up.

'Am I allowed to look?' said George.

The priest nodded. Edward and George turned together to see the bride enter the church, accompanied by Marisol, with Prudence a few steps behind them, holding the train of Rosaria's dress, all three women in white, with Rosaria the most splendid. She was holding a nosegay of orange blossom, which she passed to Marisol. Standing beside George, she lifted her veil and looked at him, then lowered her eyes, but with a smile on her lips that belied the demureness of the gesture. Edward heard her whisper some words in Italian, which made George smile as well. He took her hand in his. Together, they turned to the priest.

A series of cabs took everyone back to the house. Tables had been set up in the orangery and were covered with hams, pies and various other savoury dishes. Tea and coffee urns were placed on each table. The cakes, a central three-tiered affair with a smaller cake at each side, one for the bride and one for the groom, had a table to themselves. The trees had been moved to make room and stood like sentinels along the back wall. They were in full bloom; the scent of blossom was everywhere around them. Edward breathed it in and was suddenly aware that Marisol's eyes were on him as he did so. He wondered for a moment what thought had crossed her mind. She had Tommaso beside her, holding on to her skirt and begging for whatever she had in her hand. She was talking to George's mother, an amused smile on her face. Edward was about to rescue her, but she shook her head briefly and he understood that there was no need. He had never seen her so radiant; he had been wrong to doubt her. He looked around the orangery, a great calmness filling him. When he saw that everyone was well, he walked across to the corner where Daniel and another man stood.

'It is good to see you, Bell,' he said. 'I am glad you were able to come.'

'It is good to be here,' said Bell. 'You have done your man proud. Few valets have been treated with such largesse.'

'He is worth all this and more. He is a man of great courage and of great loyalty. Many of us might not be here at all without his efforts on our behalf.'

'I imagine that would include me,' said Bell, with a wry smile. He had put on weight since Edward last saw him, and was dressed and groomed with the elegance that had once been habitual to him.

'It certainly does.' Edward looked around. 'I see you no longer have your nurse with you.'

'That was below the belt,' said Daniel, reprovingly. 'I thought better of you.'

'I take no offence,' said Bell. 'I deserve that, and more.' He paused, before continuing. 'I have never apologised to you, Edward, if I may call you Edward. You have saved my life and I am only too aware, as I once was not, of how little I deserve it. I realise now how close I came to destroying yours. I was jealous, I think; your happiness made me so. I have only recently begun to understand that the happiness of others, even more than my own, untrustworthy as it was, was always a source of torment to me.'

'Enough,' said Edward. He held out his hand. 'Let us shake on it, and have done with it. Let Daniel here be our witness.'

'You have done well,' said Poynter, joining them. 'What a delightfully unorthodox event this is. I am so glad that you invited me. I have so few chances to extend my circle beyond the artificial limits imposed on it. The groom's sister, Prudence, is an unalloyed joy. I should hate to think of her blushing unseen and wasting her sweetness, as the poet once put it. And to think that, without your valet's marriage to his delightful signorina, I might never have had the opportunity to take tea on an equal footing with a market tradesman.'

'So you have met George's father,' said Edward.

'A most instructive conversation,' said Poynter. He linked his hands and gazed around the orangery with a satisfied air, as though looking for someone else who might entertain him, then unlaced his fingers and took Edward's elbow. 'I wonder if I might talk to you alone for a few moments.'

Edward threw an amused glance at Daniel and let himself be led away. When they were at a suitable distance, Poynter leant forward and, in a low voice, said that he had seen Rickman.

'He is a free man again?'

'I think he will never be free,' said Poynter. 'But yes, he is no longer a convict. He was released some weeks ago. I saw him quite by chance as I was walking to my bank. He was in an alehouse, a rather disreputable place, I must say. I felt someone's eyes on me and turned to see who it was and I saw him scurry off, clearly hoping to avoid me. I might have respected his wishes but I have never looked upon him with quite the opprobrium he has generally met, and I was, may God forgive me, curious. And so I followed him and finally managed to corner him in an even lower alehouse than the one before. He was trembling at first, with fear or shame I imagine, or a mixture of both. I persuaded him that he need have no fear of me, and that his shame had been washed away by his suffering. I think and hope that he believed me.'

'Why are you telling me this?'

'Because he spoke of you. You were the only visitor he had, do you know that? I must admit that I felt somewhat abashed when he told me. Like most men, I feel nothing but distaste for the Greek vice, but perhaps I judged him too harshly. Socrates shared it, and I might have remembered that.' He shook his head, as if to clear his thoughts. 'Anyway, he asked me to deliver a message to you if I saw you. He told me to tell you that he had lied to you.'

'Lied to me?'

'I believe you asked him about the story he told us that memorable evening, about his experiences with the spirit world in Africa?'

'Yes,' said Edward. 'The *obambo*.'

'Precisely. And he dismissed the story as a fairy tale, if I'm not mistaken?'

'Yes.'

'He asked me to apologise to you for having been so deceitful. The place in which he was held expected, indeed demanded, a certain – how shall I put it? – orthodoxy in terms of faith. Any deviation from the straight and narrow led to punishment of the most brutal sort, as Rickman knew only too well.'

'You're telling me that his story was true?'

'Worse than that. He told me to tell you that once you had made the acquaintance of an *obambo* you would never be free of it. He was convinced that the creature had followed him to London and had engineered his arrest. He told me that he had seen it in the prison itself, that it entered his cell at night. He had become its living home, he said. I think the poor fellow has been utterly unhinged by his misfortune.'

'You say he is still in London?'

Poynter shook his head. 'I fear not, although, for his sake, it is just as well that he has left the city. His life would not be easy here.'

'Where is he? Do you know?'

'He talked about Dieppe, and Taormina. He claims to have friends there who will give him refuge. I imagine they share his tastes.' He paused. A look of concern crossed his face. 'But, my dear boy, what on earth is wrong? You have lost all your colour.'

'No, no,' said Edward hurriedly. 'I'm just a little tired.' He looked around. 'I think I may be neglecting my other guests. You must excuse me.'

Edward told no one about this conversation, and did all he could to dismiss it from his mind. Rickman, after all, was a Uranian and

236

a fraud; his word meant nothing. His only confidant might have been Daniel, but he was engaged with some of George's cousins, who had never before had the chance to speak to an American and were keen to ask him about the opportunities the country offered. Edward listened to their conversation for a while, without speaking, until Marisol called for silence and asked the newly-weds to cut the largest of the cakes. George brought Edward one of the first slices to be cut.

'Here you are, sir,' he said.

'I think today of all days you can treat me as an equal,' said Edward with a smile, taking the cake. 'I have never thought of you as anything else.'

'You have been too good to me,' said George, the effort it took him not to add 'sir' painfully visible. 'Today is further proof of that.'

'Has Rosaria suffered from the absence of her family?'

'I think so, but she has had the mistress and they are like sisters, and Concetta has also become a friend, in her way.' He smiled. 'And now she has my family to deal with. She need never feel alone.' The two men glanced across the orangery and saw Rosaria surrounded by George's aunts, all of whom were admiring her dress. 'Look at them,' said George, with a laugh. 'All of them talking nineteen to the dozen. I think perhaps I should rescue her.'

'Yes, do that,' said Edward. 'Be with your wife.' He squeezed his arm. 'And I shall be with mine.'

Marisol was sitting outside the orangery, sunlit, a shawl around her shoulders to protect her from the first cool air of autumn. Tommaso was sitting on her lap, facing her, while she pulled faces to make him laugh. She sang to him, a nonsense song, until he began to giggle. She tickled him, and started again. 'Little Bo Peep has lost her sheep,' she sang, and he became hysterical. When she saw Edward approaching, she smiled.

'Your English songs are very foolish,' she said. 'No wonder he laughs so much.'

'It is wonderful to see the two of you together. It feeds my heart.'

'Today has been a good day for the heart,' said Marisol. 'Ouch!' she said, as Tommaso reached up and grabbed at her hair.

'Here,' said Edward, moving behind her. 'Let me take off your hat. Our work today is done. I think we can be allowed to relax a little.' He lifted the hat from her head and laid it on the table. When Tommaso reached up a second time, she raised her hands and removed the pins that held her hair in place. 'Mamma,' Tommaso said, delighted, lifting his mother's hair and letting it fall, gently tugging until it covered her face. She blew and her breath lifted it, and Tommaso shrieked with laughter. She shook her head and made a growling sound, and he clapped his hands with glee. Edward, still behind her, looked down and saw that a petal of orange blossom had somehow lodged itself in the hair of her crown, a tiny fragment of white against the black. He plucked it out, then leant forward and pressed his lips against her scalp.

'Enough,' he said.

Acknowledgments

I'd like to thank my first readers, friends and family, for their precious quibbles, corrections and contributions to this story. I'd like to thank my dear friend and agent, Isobel Dixon, and all those at Blake Friedmann who have supported me for all these years. What would I do without you? I'd like to thank the wonderful team at Gallic for their attention, enthusiasm and commitment to my work, whatever direction it may take. Finally, I'd like to thank Giuseppe, who gets to hear everything first.